JOURNEY STAR

Novels by John Michael Greer

The Weird of Hali:

I – Innsmouth

II – Kingsport

III – Chorazin

IV – Dreamlands

V – Providence

VI – Red Hook

VII – Arkham

Others:

The Fires of Shalsha

Star's Reach

Twilight's Last Gleaming

Retrotopia

The Shoggoth Concerto

The Nyogtha Variations

A Voyage to Hyperborea

The Seal of Yueh Lao

Journey Star

The Witch of Criswell

The Book of Haatan

The Hall of Homeless Gods

JOURNEY STAR

John Michael Greer

SPHINX

Published in 2024 by
Sphinx Books
London

Copyright © 2021, 2024 by John Michael Greer

British Library Cataloguing in Publication Data

A C.I.P. for this book is available from the British Library

ISBN-13: 978-1-91595-213-4

Typeset by Medlar Publishing Solutions Pvt Ltd, India

www.aeonbooks.co.uk/sphinx

THE SIX LAWS

One: No hierarchy of superiors demanding obedience from inferiors, nor any organization claiming the right to interfere in the affairs of communities except in defense of the six laws here established, shall exist on Eridan. Deliberate violation of this law shall be punished by death.

Two: No permanent community of more than ten thousand persons, nor any community located less than ten kilometers from any other community, shall exist on Eridan. Deliberate violation of this law shall be punished by death.

Three: No act or threat of violence by members of one community against members or property of any other community, except in defense of the six laws here established, shall occur on Eridan. Deliberate violation of this law shall be punished by death.

Four: No weapon of mass destruction, nor any armed or armored vehicle, nor any weapon having an effective range of more than one kilometer, shall exist on Eridan. Deliberate violation of this law shall be punished by death.

Five: No contact with machines or remains of machines made by or under the former Planetary Directorate, beyond that required to repel or destroy them, shall occur on Eridan. Deliberate violation of this law shall be punished by death.

Six: No action that causes significant damage to planetary or regional ecologies shall occur on Eridan. Deliberate violation of this law shall be punished by death.

journey star

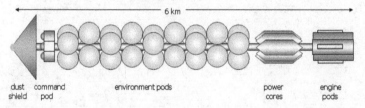

6 km

dust shield   command pod   environment pods   power cores   engine pods

CHAPTER 1

THE LAST OF THE PEOPLE

1

The wind blew cold that night. Asha watched the little fire and wondered if she would ever feel warm again.

Spring had begun already, or so she knew from the lore Grandmother had taught her. The stars said as much, wheeling overhead in bright patterns Asha had long since learned to read. Still, the message they sent had so far failed to talk the winter back to its home in the far barrens north of Pillar-of-Sky. Food plants were scarce in the hills, and the frozen ground clutched what there was in a miser's grip that made digging sticks dull and muscles ache. As for meat, she could no longer count the hands of days since the hunters came back with that. One after another, season after season, too many of them had gone hunting and never come back at all.

A stick broke with a puff of sparks, and half rolled away from the flame. Asha prodded it back into the middle of the fire with another that was still too wet to burn. Tending the fire still made her uncomfortable. That was work for women in their birthing years, not for a child of only two hands and three fingers of winters, but all Asha's hearth-mothers were gone now, gone with the others. Sometimes Asha could see their faces in the flames.

Whisper in the brush behind her warned of movement. She got to her feet, turned, clutching at the hooked knife at her side. Firelight showed familiar presences, though: Shrey, oldest of her hearth-brothers, coming out of the darkness with one of the band's two remaining guns in his hands. Two more figures followed, lean as he was, and dressed like him in winter garments of barkcloth and tanned skin. Dust grayed their black hair, one concealment of many. Their faces were taut, wary.

"Good hunting?" The question had to be asked, though Asha feared the answer.

"Not for us," said Shrey. A gesture to the south: "The Silent follow us."

Asha's hand flew to her mouth. Then: "Many?"

"Hands and hands of them," said Turl, next oldest after Shrey and the best hunter in the band. His handsome face wore a scowl. Shrey glanced at him and went on: "Their jewelfly-things are with them. We saw their camp from far off. I do not think they felt our presence, but we must be under trees by dawn or they will trap us."

"Grandmother cannot walk," Asha said.

They turned to the last member of the band. Huddled in barkcloth blankets, the old woman sat motionless by the fire, staring at nothing in particular. Shrey went to her, squatted down. "Grandmother?"

The old woman did not answer or move. Gently, Shrey took her chin in one hand, lifted it. Crusted eyes looked past him unseeing, and a line of spittle fell from one side of her mouth.

"Soon," he said, releasing her and rising to his feet. "But we have no time now. I will carry her. It is the Way."

He handed the gun to Turl, and then lifted the old woman like a blanket bundle and slung her over his shoulders. The others, Turl and young Garn, gathered up the band's few bundles. Asha collected what was left of the dry firewood and the one iron pot they had left. Then, trying not to think of the cold wind, she scooped up an armload of snow and dumped it on the little fire, followed it with a second. Darkness closed in suddenly, blotting out everything but dark shapes around her and pale stars high above.

They left the camp in single file. Turl took Shrey's usual place in the lead, and his gun stayed in his hands. The Silent knew the land as well as the People did, and could match or surpass a band's pace even when their jewelfly-things did not carry them with the winds. Underestimating them was an easy way to die.

As she followed the dark ungainly shape that was Shrey and Grandmother, Asha tried to remember everything she knew about the Silent. The People once made songs about them: hunting-songs full of old wisdom for trapping them, gathering-songs about times when the Silent were fewer and could be hunted and slain by a determined band: no one sang them now. All she could remember were murmured words among her hearth-mothers, a few memories of distant shapes in black moving across the plains, and one memory of a jewelfly-thing soaring through the sky with a noise like thunder, as she hid from it beneath trees.

The thoughts blurred into a waking dream woven out of memories, and though she knew she should keep watch for signs of the Silent in the night, she could not keep herself from fleeing into remembered warmth. She had been with her first hearth-family back then, dwelling in a land further south, far from the vast purple barrens Asha had known and learned to love in later days. The summers blazed with heat there, so that the People went unclothed more often than not, and the fires they lit in camp could burn brightly without alerting hostile eyes. The band had numbered four full hands and two fingers then, not the mere single hand that was left of her second hearth-family. Other bands dwelt within a few days' walk, too, so that now and again two or three bands would come together to feast and gamble, plan hunts too large and daring for a single band's hunters alone, and share out meat in abundance.

A single memory flared into brightness like lit tinder in the dark: Grandmother, her eyes still bright then, telling a story of her own girlhood, when the People filled the land as thick as arrowgrass. That was before the Time of the Machines, she said, and would not explain what that meant. Asha asked one of her hearth-mothers about it later on, to be silenced with a look and a gesture. No one ever mentioned it in her hearing again. She tried to turn the dream elsewhere, but it shredded in her mind like barkcloth worn too long, and she was again trudging over the thin snow, following Shrey and Grandmother through the bitter night.

By the time the first gray light showed in the east they were among blue-leaved trees, in a wood huddled in among the flanks of a rugged hill. Shrey found a sheltered hollow inside the wood, safe from sight, and set Grandmother down, then took one of the guns and went to watch for pursuit while Turl and Garn made two lodges from fallen branches and Asha found stones to ring a fire. Heaped with blue masses of fallen summer leaves, the lodges promised warmth as well as concealment, and the little fire Asha kindled warmed pieces of redroot in water for soup: a poor meal, or so she would have said in winters past, but welcome as meat after the long night.

Shrey came back as Sun lit the hill's crest above the camp. "The Silent did not follow," he said. "We are safe for a time." He took his share of the soup in a wooden cup with a murmured word of thanks, sat crosslegged on the violet-gray meadowmoss with the others. When he had finished, he asked, "Did Grandmother eat?"

"I placed meat to her lips, but she would not take it," Asha told him. She had done nothing of the kind, and all three of her hearth-brothers knew it, but the words were the Way.

"Ah." The syllable hung in the air. Asha waited, knowing what would come next.

"You know what it is she carries with her," Shrey said finally. "Another must carry it for her—for the People—now that she cannot."

"This I know." Asha's voice was toneless.

"Herbs must be given to her, and then what she carries will pass to its new bearer." He reached inside his winter garments, pulled out a packet of folded bark. "These are the herbs. I gathered them three hands of days ago."

Asha looked up at him for a long moment. "Now?"

His silence answered her. She rose, went over to Grandmother, knelt and threw her arms around the old woman, remembering bright eyes and kind voice and struggling not to weep. Tears came later, when Sun was gone and could no longer see them; that was the Way.

After a time she released Grandmother and stood up. "What must I do?"

"Chew these," Shrey said, giving her the packet of herbs. "Spit them into her mouth. What she bears will pass from her mouth to yours. The passing is not easy, they said."

Asha nodded. Three winters back, after hunger had taken her two older hearth-sisters, she had heard the same words from Grandmother, and knew what she must do. She put the herbs into her mouth and chewed them, tasting the bitter burning tang of them, and then knelt and joined her lips to Grandmother's, spitting the juice into the old woman's mouth.

A long moment passed, and then something softer than a tongue pushed out between Grandmother's lips. Asha forced herself to open her mouth wide. The thing pressed into her, choking her, and then slid down her throat. A sudden stabbing pain made her clutch her belly, and she would have cried out if the thing was not still filling her mouth. Things churned somewhere below her stomach. Her hands, as they held her belly, felt rippling movement.

Finally the last of the thing slid down her throat, clearing her mouth. Gasping and retching, Asha fell over onto her side and lay there.

Shrey came and stood over her. "They said you will know when you can eat or drink again," he said. "They did not say whether you can sing, but there are no others who can."

Asha looked up at him, half-comprehending. After a time, she struggled up to a sitting position. The sick choking feeling that had filled her was fading. She drew in a deep breath, felt the pain down at the top of her belly, but a flicker of knowledge—from where, she could not guess—told her that the wound there was healing already. "I can sing," she said.

On hands and knees, not trusting her legs to carry her, she moved a short distance away from Grandmother as Shrey stood behind the old woman, knife in hand. Closing her eyes, she began to sing, drawing out each syllable as Grandmother had taught her:

> "When we came to this world across the spaces of the sky,
> Great was our sorrow, but greater was our need.
> When we fled the places of dying and took refuge in
>   the forest,
> Strong was our dread, but stronger was our life.
> When we became the People, when we embraced the Way,
> We learned the lesson of the sharing of meat:
> What comes from the People must return to the People,
> For our need is great, but our life is strong."

She let the death-song's last word stretch out into silence, and then opened her eyes. By then the three men had already stripped Grandmother's body and were cutting off what little meat she still had on her. Her skin would have to be buried, for that could only be worked in a settled camp, and most of her organs likewise; only the meat that could be eaten that day, or dried over the fire for days to come, would find its proper use. Asha whispered an apology to the old woman's ghost, knowing that the waste would have distressed her.

She tried to stand up, but her legs would not support her, and the camp briefly went dark around her. Shrey noticed, wiped his hands on the meadowmoss, and came to her. "They said you will need sleep, and warmth. Be it so." He gathered her up, carried her to one of the two lodges, put her inside and left. A moment later he was back with some of Grandmother's barkcloth blankets, and laid them over her.

Asha thought to protest, for there was work to do, but somehow the words never quite took shape. Instead, something like the knowledge of the healing wound in her surfaced in her mind, and it called for sleep. The awareness hung there like smoke for a moment, and then sleep took her, sudden as a knife.

2

When Asha blinked awake again, Sun was looking beneath the trees from the western sky, setting blue winter-leaves aglow. She could smell the warm sweetish scent of cooking meat, thought about asking some from Shrey, who had harvest-right over it.

She knew at once that it was not yet time. The knowledge was clear, and silent. She rubbed her eyes, pulled herself half out of the lodge, sat up. She felt no different, and wondered at that. After a moment, she got up and went over to the fire, where Garn cooked meat while Shrey warmed his hands. Both of them sensed the movement and glanced her way. "It is well?" Shrey asked her.

"It is well," she told him.

He stood. "Can you walk? There is a thing you should see."

Asha considered that, nodded. "I can walk."

Shrey turned without another word, took one of the guns in his hand, and started uphill, toward the blue slopes rising above them. She followed, matching his pace as best she could.

After a short time they passed Turl, who kept watch over the camp from a hiding place among rocks just above it, and greeted them with a silent gesture. After a longer one, the trees began to thin out, and the route Shrey took began to weave along the curves in the slope, staying out of Sun's beams. Asha knew what that meant; the Silent must have followed, and the band would spend the night walking again. She whispered a word of thanks to Grandmother's ghost for the sleep. It would make the journey easier.

The crest of the hill came closer, and closer still, but at the last moment Shrey veered to one side and led her to a sheltered place where low trees huddled against the rock. Once Asha had caught her breath, he pointed back the way they had come: "Look."

She looked. The hillside fell away, the upper slopes spotted with trees, the lower slopes wrapped with them, as though with an azure blanket. Further out, the plains began, violet-gray moss reaching southwards to the edge of sight. Distant clouds caught orange light. High up in the southern sky, a point of brilliant light, *Journey Star* shone down.

A little past the beginning of the plains, two of the Silent jewelfly-things crouched on the moss, looking up at her with glittering eyes.

She nodded, but Shrey was already turning, pointing off the other way, to the north. She turned as well, looked down the other side of the hill, where the trees were sparser and the snow lay thick. More plains swept away beyond it into the distance, white with unbroken snow, and three more jewelfly-things crouched there, waiting.

Before she could speak he had turned again, pointing west. That way the hill tumbled down to join a low ridge spotted with trees, and that led to other hills, and then to mountains in the middle distance. From the ridge, not far off, a thin line of smoke rose into the clear sky.

"The Silent make camp there," he said, but Asha knew it already. No fire of the People would be allowed to mark the place of their camp in such a manner.

"Our path ends here," Shrey went on. "Even if we slipped past them in the night, the plains offer no shelter, and that way—" He motioned to the east. "That way is another death for us, worse than the one they bring. Fireflowers grow there, many of them."

Asha gave him a horrified look, ducked her head, acknowledging the baleful omen.

"So," he went on. "Turl and Garn have seen also, and we will await them here."

Asha drew in a ragged breath, forced herself calm, and ducked her head again.

"There is a thing you must know," he said then. His voice was thick with emotion. Asha turned and stared at him, for nothing was less like the Shrey she knew. "It is not our path alone that ends here. Do you recall the winter the Silent took Borth?"

Asha nodded. Borth had been the last of her hearth-fathers.

"It has been six winters. Since then, between each winter and the next, I have marked the old places where bands mark their passing. After the first winter, there were two hands of marks alongside mine. After the second, one hand and two fingers, and after each winter, fewer still. After the winter before this one, none but mine, and ever more of the Silent in the land." He took her shoulders in his hands, forced her to look at him. "We are the last. The People end here. The Way ends here."

"No!" The cry burst out from her.

"It is so."

Asha broke from his grasp and turned away from him, toward the east, where Sun's light blazed on distant peaks. She could feel Shrey's presence behind her. "See the tallest mountain," he said. "The broken one."

She blinked back tears and looked. Sun's rays made it easy to see where half the mountain had broken and slid into ruin.

"That is Pillar-of-Sky. Do you know what happened to it? Eight hands of winters ago a band of Others came there. They seized the old hidden place within, where only our eldest once went. They made—machines." He spat the word. "Many of the

People died after that. We could not kill the machines, but they killed us."

"The Time of the Machines," Asha ventured.

"Yes. There came a winter, four hands of winters ago, when the machines went away and did not return. When the winter ended, we saw that Pillar-of-Sky was broken, and all who went there to see it became sick and died. It was afterward that fire-flowers grew there, thick as meadowmoss. From that time on, the Silent pressed us hard, and we were too few to stop them as we did before the Others came.

"Borth told me a thing, in the winter before the Silent took him. He said that the Way is a cord, and the peg that held the cord in place was Pillar-of-Sky. While the peg stood, the cord held and the People held to it. But now the peg is broken." In a whisper: "The cord is lost, and the People cannot find the Way. That was what he told me."

A long silence came and went. Wind hissed through the branches around them, and the light on the white jagged peak in the distance began to turn golden.

"What of the thing I carry?" Asha asked then.

"I do not know. For six winters it would not speak to us, or Grandmother would not tell us what it said. Will it speak to you now?"

Asha stared at him, then turned her attention within. She could sense, faintly, a presence behind her eyes, watching. *Will you speak to me?* she thought at it. *Will you tell us what we must do, now that the People are at their end?*

The only response she got was a sense of silence and cold.

"It will not answer," she told Shrey. He considered that, and bowed his head.

In the silence that followed, the distant rattle of gunfire came up the slope.

Shrey whirled, raising the gun he held, but the fight was far off, hidden by trees. They heard the deep *whump* of Turl's gun, and then the sharp rattle of Silent gunfire, half a dozen shots at least; a long moment of silence; Turl's gun again, a single Silent reply, and then another silence that nothing broke.

"They will follow our tracks in the snow," Shrey said then, his voice flat. He gestured for her to hide. She hugged him tight, then backed into the shelter of the trees and found a gap between roots where gunfire would be less likely to reach her. Broken black eggshells from the previous spring, remains of ground-scuttler's or jewelfly's hatching, scattered as she brushed them aside and knelt on the ground. The death-song was in her mind, singing itself with a voice that was as much Grandmother's as hers.

Time stretched out wide as the wind as Asha knelt there, wondering when the Silent would find them and how they would kill her. Then Shrey straightened and fired down the slope. Three shots answered, but he had already thrown himself back among the rocks, and quickly reloaded his gun. He moved to another place, straightened and fired again.

Before he could lower himself behind the shelter of the rocks, two bullets tore through him. He staggered, dropped the gun, and landed on his back across from Asha, spilling blood.

A few heartbeats later a figure in black garments leapt up into the gap Shrey had filled a moment before, and leveled a gun at Asha. It was a woman, Asha saw, tall and silver-haired, with a scar across one temple. Meeting the Silent's eyes, Asha drew in a breath and began the death-song, certain that she would die singing it.

Two more of the Silent climbed over the rocks into the sheltered place as Asha sang. They were younger than the silver-haired one, and they sheathed their guns once they saw Asha and Shrey's body. Nor did the silver-haired one shoot her. Asha finished the song for Shrey, and could think of nothing else to do but begin it again, for Turl.

She finished the song for Turl, and began it again for Garn. By then she was shaking, her face wet, her voice scarcely able to force out the words. Even as she sang it, she knew it was a poor song, and doubly poor for the one who would have become her mate had he lived, but it was the only death-song his ghost would get and she made herself finish it.

The last long syllable spun away into the wind's whisper. The Silent had not killed her. Blinking back tears, Asha noticed that none of them still had a gun drawn.

"Child," said the silver-haired one, "you must come with us." The words were strangely formed, but hearing the voice of a Silent was stranger still. They never spoke, so the old songs said, except in some soundless tongue the People could not hear or follow.

"You must come with us," the Silent repeated, then came to Asha, took her by one arm and drew her gently but implacably to her feet. The thought of struggling came to Asha's mind as though from a great distance, and faded out. It was as though she stood in some other place, watching three black figures and a child in ragged gray barkcloth on a faraway hill.

The Silent led her out of the sheltered place, into the last orange rays of Sun. One of the others who had gone before glanced back toward her, and drew in a sudden sharp breath. A glance toward the silver-haired one, a glance toward the other: something passed between them that was like speech, Asha guessed, and the silver-haired one faced her, lifted her chin to look into her eyes and consider something there. Asha knew, or guessed she knew, what the Silent saw, but the knowledge was too distant to matter.

The silver-haired one nodded, then, and led Asha downslope to the south. Ahead, bright in the gathering dusk, swinging slowly eastward against the turning of the sun and stars, *Journey Star* glittered.

3

On the plains where the jewelfly-things crouched, the Silent had tents, purple-gray to blend with the moss. They took her into one of them, motioned for her to sit. Something round and bright hung from the central pole, putting light like Sun's into the tent. Asha wondered about that, but the wondering spun away into the emptiness that was in her, and she closed her eyes and waited.

Things clattered and rattled not far away, and a hot savory scent reached her and reminded her of the emptiness of her belly. She blinked and looked up to find one of the Silent before her, stocky and gray-haired. He put a tray down in front of her. On it was a cup of water, a bowl of something too thick to be soup, and two pale blue slices of something else, large as her palms and softer than roots. "This is for you," he said.

She stared at the tray, at him, then thought at the presence inside her: *May I?*

A silent sense of permission rose out of it.

Still she hesitated. Even among warring bands, sharing food or a blanket invoked the hearth-peace that not even blood-guilt could break. That was the Way. Shrey's words came back to her then, telling her that the Way was ending, but she forced them out of her thoughts.

The Silent considered her for a moment, then crossed the tent, got something else and brought it back. "You're cold," he said then. "Here." Cloth rustled, and a blanket settled over her shoulders, thicker and softer than the ones the People made. She could not make herself throw off its warmth, not after so many cold days. It would be the hearth-peace, then.

Slowly, she began to eat, and the Silent went away. The food was as strange to taste as to look at, the too-thick-to-be-soup full of unfamiliar flavors that tumbled and quarreled among themselves, the sliced blue thing rich like meat, but softer and with yet another flavor she did not know. There was much of it, too, as much as she had eaten in a whole day for a hand of winters and more. She considered leaving some aside for the next day, but that was for elders to decide, not for her. She ate, sipped the water, felt the warm heaviness of the food settle in her belly.

After a time, the tent flap opened and the silver-haired one came in. A glance toward Asha, a flicker of the wordless Silent speech to the man, and then she went to the far side of the tent and knelt at a box made of metal with odd things on its top. As Asha watched, she put something on her ears, moved other things on the top of the box, and then lifted a thing like a stick to her mouth and began to talk to it.

"Dammal Shelter, please respond. Dammal Shelter. This is Carla Dubrenden sen Halka at Camp Nine." Silence followed and then she spoke again: "Yes." Another silence, longer. "Yes, we tracked them to the hills west of New Shalsha and caught them there." Another, brief. "One. A girl, maybe ten years old, horribly malnourished. She's here in the radio tent, with a platter of food." Then: "More than that. Positive light trace." A pause. "Yes." Another. "Yes. There was an old woman with the band. They must have killed her for meat this morning."

A long silence went by. Asha began to wonder if the things over the Silent's ears were talking to her. "I think so," said the silver-haired one finally. "I'd like to take her to Mirien Shelter, to Tamar Alhaden. I don't know anyone else half so qualified." Another silence, and then Asha was sure the things were talking, for the Silent's face changed as though hearing sorrowful news. "No, I hadn't heard," she said then in a different voice. "How soon?" A brief pause, then: "Thank you for telling me. *Halka na.*"

The Silent put down the stick, did something else to the top of the box, and took whatever it was off her ears. Rising, she shook her head, sent a glance full of not-speaking to the young man, and then walked slowly toward the flap of the tent.

Asha watched her. Maybe it was the food, which had stretched her belly almost to the point of pain, or maybe the Silent's speech with the box had done the thing, but the emptiness in her was not so wide as it had been, and one question above all demanded a voice. She waited until the silver-haired woman was near her, and asked, "Why do you not kill me?"

The words seemed to startle the Silent. She looked down at Asha, then said, "We kill only when we have to."

Asha had not expected an answer at all, much less that one. She considered it, then ducked her head in acknowledgment, huddled down further into the warmth of the blanket. The Silent waited for a time, then nodded once herself and left the tent.

The man did not leave, and a little later a hand and two fingers of the Silent came in through the tent flap. Most of them glanced Asha's way at least once, but their attention was elsewhere; they wanted food from the clattering things, and rest; their movements and stances made her think of hunters back from some journey or raid. They ate of the same strange food she had been given, and some sat and talked together in low voices or the Silent not-speaking while others wrapped themselves in blankets and went to sleep. One who did not talk or sleep took a place by the tent flap. Asha had given thought to fleeing from the tent, though there was nowhere for her to go, but the guard's presence told her that the Silent knew to expect that. After a time, she pulled her own blanket around her and let the warmth of it carry her into sleep.

She woke once, somewhere in the dark hours, out of a dream of Shrey's death, and lay there shaking and weeping in as much silence as she could manage until sleep took her again; woke again with gray light stealing under the tent flap and most of the Silent gone from the tent. The same man who had given her food the night before saw her wake, and brought her another tray of food. Before she could find some way through her shame to speak of her more immediate need, he not-spoke to another Silent, a woman, who took her out of the tent to a place where she could empty herself, and then brought her back. Despite bitter cold, the Silent were busy outside, carrying their gear into two jewelfly-things while another one landed with a sound like thunder not far away.

Back in the tent she ate the food the Silent gave her, tried not to think of the questions she could not answer and the memories she did not want to face. By the time she was finished with the food, one question had pushed the others aside and pressed at the edges of her self-control. Not long after that, the tent flap opened and the silver-haired one came into the tent.

"What will you do with me?" Asha asked her.

The silver-haired one turned toward her. There was some grief upon her, Asha saw that at once. After a moment, the Silent came and sat down on the floor in front of her. "Now? We'll take you to the south. Some of our people need to see you. Then we'll take you to others of your people who live further south, who don't hunt."

Others of your people: the words shouted themselves in her mind. She stared round-eyed at the Silent. Slowly, though, realization dawned. "These others—they have left the Way."

"They live a different way," said the Silent.

"How can they live without the Way?"

That got a slight smile. "When you meet them, you can ask that."

The thought of meeting any of the People ever again swept aside the last of Asha's self-control. She burst into tears and took the older woman's hands in hers. "You will take me to them? You must take me to them."

"We leave for the south this morning," said the Silent.

Asha drew in a ragged breath. "I am ready to walk."

That got another smile. "You won't need to walk. The—" She used a word that Asha had never heard before. "—will take us there."

Asha nodded, wondering what the Silent meant, then guessed, and her eyes went round again. "The—things that look like jewelflies."

"Yes."

The thought terrified her, but fear was not the Way. She drew in another unsteady breath and nodded again. "I will go."

The Silent wasted no more time in breaking camp than a band of the People would have done. By the time Sun had cleared Pillar-of-Sky to the east, the tents and everything in them had been loaded into the jewelfly-things. Asha stood uncertainly as the Silent went about their work. The hearth-peace bound her to share the labors of the band that had taken her in, but none of the Silent asked anything of her and none of the things she knew how to do seemed to need doing.

Finally, when all that remained on the meadowmoss were the jewelfly-things, the Silent, and Asha, the silver-haired one came and led her to one of the great metal shapes. It had a door in its side, like the doors of the winter-lodges she recalled from her first memories, but that was the only thing familiar about it. She tensed against fear as the Silent led her up into the thing, went where she was guided, settled into a metal shape for which she had no name, something that held her sitting above the floor and gave her a surface to rest her back against. The silver-haired Silent sat next to her, showed her how to fasten a cloth strap like a belt over her lap.

The door slammed shut, pulled by one of the Silent. A moment later a roar filled the air around Asha, and a few moments after that, the floor lurched and tilted as the jewelfly-thing rose up into the air. Asha, terrified, cried out and grabbed the sides of the nameless thing beneath her. In response, the Silent placed a hand on her shoulder, steadying her.

Asha struggled with her fear, mastered it with an effort, then considered the hand. The Way was ending, Shrey had said, but the Way was all she knew, and the Way was clear. If another band of the People had killed Shrey and the others and taken her with them, as Shrey and the others had done with her first hearth-family all those winters ago, once she accepted the hearth-peace from them, she would be of their band. Their hearth-fathers and hearth-mothers would be hers, their blood-right and blood-guilt hers, and her meat would be theirs to share out once she could no longer eat what was pressed to her lips.

These are not of the People, she told herself. They are the Silent, the enemy—but they spared me and gave me the hearth-peace.

She thought about Grandmother, about Shrey and Turl and Garn, about the hearth-fathers and hearth-mothers she had known, before hunger, sickness, or the Silent took them away and left their ghosts to make the long journey across the sky to the World That Is Gone. It was the Way to mourn them and remember them, so Grandmother taught her, but not to bury her heart with their bones.

She considered the hand again, there on her shoulder, steadying and comforting: the gesture of a hearth-mother to her hearth-child. After a long moment, hating herself a little for the act but unable to stop, she reached up with her own hand, rested it atop the Silent's, accepting the comfort. Asha could feel the Silent's gaze upon her, but her heart was too full and too troubled to meet that glance; she bowed her head and looked at nothing, left her hand where it was.

4

How long the jewelfly-thing flew south upon the winds, Asha could only guess. There was something else near her for which she had no name, a piece of the thing's side that was hard like metal but clear like still water. Through it she could see the land streaked with snow, as though she stood high up on a hillside looking down. Sun streamed across the violet plains, made the snow bright, flared like fire in streams and meltwater ponds, but the country was unfamiliar to her and the jewelfly-thing changed its angle of flight from time to time, so tracking the movement of shadows across the landscape was more than she could do. She waited with the patience of the People.

Now and then, looking out through the clear-as-water thing beside her, Asha could see great round shapes on the land, low and gray, with things like trees rising up from them and great branches atop those that turned in the wind. Dwelling-places of the Others, she guessed; she had never seen one, but old songs told of them, recalled days long gone when the hunters of the People walked within sight of them and gathered meat as they would. The Time of the Machines had ended those days: that, and the Silent. She shivered.

Finally another of the gray dwelling-things came into sight and the jewelfly-thing flew in a great arc around it. There was something like a door or a winter-lodge's smokehole in the roof of the thing, and it opened as the jewelfly-thing slowed and neared it. Then the jewelfly-thing descended. Asha closed her eyes and seized the side of the thing beneath her with her free hand. Her other hand remained where it was, atop the Silent's.

A final jolt, and all movement stopped. Asha opened her eyes. The others in the jewelfly-thing got to their feet and busied themselves with the things they'd loaded into it. One flung the door open, letting in a great rush of noise. The silver-haired Silent did not move. She looked at Asha, who met the glance, and slowly lifted her hand off the Silent's, freeing it. The silver-haired one nodded, as though that settled something, then showed her how to unfasten the band across her lap, got up, and gestured for Asha to follow.

Outside was a room so large that hands and hands of whole winter-lodges could have been put inside it. Overhead, the great doors were sliding shut. Two or three hands of Others moved unhurriedly from one unknown task to another. The thunder-noise faded as Asha and the Silent crossed the flat smooth floor. Two of the Others were waiting by a door that led out of the room, one a man dressed in gray and brown. The other, a woman old enough to have gray in her hair, wore long flowing clothing colored like rainbows, and something about her reminded Asha of the Silent: like, and not like.

"Child," said the silver-haired Silent, as they reached the Others. Asha looked up at her. "You'll go with this one for now." The Silent indicated the woman in the rainbow clothing. "She'll see to your needs, give you medicine if you need it. You're to do as she tells you."

Asha ducked her head solemnly, as though to a hearth-mother, and the silver-haired one went past the Others and through the door.

"Come with me, child," said the woman in the rainbow-colored clothing. To the other: "My thanks, Bren. I don't think you'll be necessary." He nodded and went to join some of the Others around the jewelfly-thing, and Asha and the woman went through the door. On the other side was a passage, with passages and doors leading off it.

"My name is Emeli," the woman said, as they started down the passage. "You needn't tell me yours."

It was a surprising courtesy, the sort of thing Asha would have expected from a member of a friendly band among the People. After a moment, she remembered her manners, drew in a breath and said, "I thank you. Mine is Asha."

"Asha," Emeli repeated, the way one of the People would have done. Smiling at Asha's surprise: "Hands of hands of the People have been through this place, and we've learned a little of the Way."

Asha took that in. "Are they near?"

"The People who came here? No, they live in the forests of the south, where it's warm even in winter."

"I want to go there," Asha said simply.

"When the proper time comes," Emeli answered, so like Grandmother that the memory made Asha look away, eyes watering. "There is much to do first." They came to a door; Emeli opened it, spilling light into the passage, and motioned Asha through.

It felt like much of a day later, and might well have been, when Asha drew in an uneven breath and looked at herself in the flat clear thing Emeli called "mirror." She had given up her ragged and much-patched clothing and been washed from head to foot in hot water and something called "soap" that foamed like starleaf-sap; new clothing, warm and whole, had been given her; she had been taken to another room, where someone called "doctor"—so many new words!—examined her, placed a metal thing on her chest and a thing like bark-cloth around her arm, drew a little of her blood, and said some things to Emeli that Asha didn't understand at all.

The room with the person called "doctor" had another room next to it, with an open door between them. There was a pallet in it, and blankets, and an old man with white hair sitting on a cushion and looking at something in his lap. He was of the Silent, Asha was sure of it, though his black clothing was loose and soft, not the tough garments worn by the Silent she knew. She watched him as much as she could without rudeness, for she had never seen anyone with hair so white or a face so creased with years. There was sickness in his face, and something else for which she had no name. She found herself wondering if he saw the same room she did. He said nothing and did not look at her, and after a time she made herself look away.

Afterwards she and Emeli went to yet another room, up the things called "stairs," and ate together, sharing strange food that was not meat but satisfied the same hunger that meat did. After that, Emeli combed her hair, as a hearth-mother would her hearth-daughter's, deftly teasing out the tangles while Asha sat on the floor mat before her and let herself enjoy the warmth and the feeling, almost forgotten until the day before, of a full belly.

Then, the thing called "mirror."

She had seen her own image in water or polished metal before, but never so clearly, and never like this, not with the soft garments of the Others on her and her black hair and pale skin washed cleaner than river-water and starleaf-sap ever made them. It was as though her own hands and head had somehow been put onto one of the Others.

Then she shifted her head, and light reflected inside her eyes, a brief yellow gleam.

I am Asha, she told herself. I bear that which I bear.

The thought seemed frail, set against the solidity of the dwelling-place, of the Others and the Silent. She clutched it to herself, hoped it would be strong enough.

5

"So it's finally over," said the plump old woman in the rainbow-colored robe.

"As far as we know, yes." Carla Dubrenden accepted a bowl of pale bluish liquid, inhaled the steam, sipped. "This is splendid, Tamar. Hill country?"

The old woman beamed. "No, Mirien Shelter has its own tebbe groves now. As good as the hill country blends, by all accounts."

"I won't argue," said Carla, and sipped again.

The room around them could have been in any of the thousands of Shelters scattered over the settled part of Eridan: a cubical space with a handwoven rug on the floor, cushions for seating, bookshelves on two of the walls, a kitchen-unit set into the floor in one corner. Two narrow windows pierced a third wall, letting in the fading glow of an early spring afternoon and glimpses of a courtyard outside. Books, periodicals, and assorted clutter lay in not-quite-random piles toward the room's edges, having been moved hurriedly on Carla's arrival. Gray concrete walls and pale wood flooring made an unobtrusive background to all this.

"There may be a few stragglers left," Carla said, after another sip. "The command circle at Dammal has teams searching all through the northern barrens for traces of them. Still, I'll be surprised if they find anyone. We'd have caught this last band years ago if they'd stayed with the others out north of Wind Gap."

"Ah." Tamar sipped her tebbe. "That name's an anchor for memories."

Carla smiled, said nothing.

"You're wondering," said Tamar, "whether I'm about to tell you yet again about the hours I spent as a girl listening to messages from Abbesan about the fight against the outrunners beyond Wind Gap." She smiled too. "I know, Carla. I'm old, and becoming repetitive."

Carla allowed a chuckle, but didn't dispute the point. After a moment, Tamar said, "At least you were able to save one of them—the girl you brought back."

"Possibly," Carla said. "Once the initial shock wears off, she may withdraw, or become violent or suicidal. All of those happen often enough." Glancing up: "And for good reason, of course. It's a brutal job we've been engaged in, Tamar."

The old woman nodded. "Still, I look forward to seeing her. There have been so many rumors, so much speculation about the Indwellers. The symbionts, if that's what they are. "

"I wasn't sure how soon you'd wish to begin."

"Any time that's convenient. It's that or sit here worrying about Stefan."

A silence came and went. The lines of sun on the floor shifted.

"Is it as bad as the message said?" Carla asked.

"Worse, probably. You know how long he's had the cancer, and at this point it's very far advanced. It may be just a matter of days."

Carla regarded her tebbe for a long moment. "I'm sorry, Tamar. That's got to be bitter for you, all things considered."

"Quite the contrary," the old woman said at once. "I had the chance to spend twenty years with him, when I'd given up all hope of that." Then, in a quieter voice: "Though I won't pretend that it will be easy."

Another silence slipped past. "What are you thinking?" Carla asked.

A sudden smile. "You can't tell?"

"Your mind's better trained than that."

"I hope so," said Tamar. "What was I thinking? That it's been a very long road from Istal Shelter. It embarrasses me sometimes to remember the silly young woman I was in those days, before the battle-drone came."

"I remember," Carla said, with a smile of her own. "But I don't think you were any sillier than Stefan was, or I."

"Thank you. That's some reassurance."

They both laughed, and Tamar busied herself with the tebbe pot. "Stefan's in the medical center on the third level down," she said. "You'll want to visit him tomorrow afternoon—he's usually awake then. He'll be delighted to see you."

"I'll be glad to see him," Carla answered.

Tamar glanced up at her, catching the unspoken thought. "He's still quite lucid," she said. "Almost alarmingly so. That's partly an effect of some of the work we've done together, pushing toward the edges of the visionary state. That, and—"

"Stefan."

"Exactly." She filled both their bowls with tebbe.

6

Night stood black outside the windows by the time Carla reached the rooms Mirien Shelter set aside for Halka use, just off the Shelter's core facilities. In the stillness, the hiss of static from the radio room whispered off the concrete, audible until she came into the big square common room and closed the door behind her. Three electric lamps in handblown glass globes hung from the ceiling. Pale wood of the floor had lines of darker wood set into it, tracing out the triangle within the circle, the Halka seal.

A weariness that was more than physical pressed against her, harder than it should, and her head ached: a warning, that, though not one she needed. It had been a long day, what with breaking camp, the helicopter flight, the visit with Tamar, and then a long session on the radio with the command circle at Dammal Shelter, passing on the immediate news and letting them know that her written judgment would be on its way soon. Word would already be spreading over the radio net, letting every Shelter on Eridan know that the long nightmare of the outrunners might be over at last. Once that was confirmed, there would be celebrations like nothing Eridan had seen since the end of the War twenty years back. At the moment, to her, all that felt abstract, meaningless.

She was most of the way across the common room to the sleeping room she'd been assigned before she noticed that the door was open and a light was on. Startled, she went to the door, and found herself facing the outrunner girl they'd brought back from Camp Nine that morning. The Shelter folk had given the child a sleeping robe, blankets, and a mat, but the girl was sitting on the floor as though she'd been waiting patiently for hours and would have waited for hours more. Her thin solemn face turned up toward Carla as the sen Halka entered.

"Child," said Carla, "didn't they offer you a room of your own?"

"I asked them to bring me here," she said. Then, looking down: "Do you wish me to go to another place?"

"No," said Carla. "No, you may stay if you wish." She sat down, took off her boots.

The girl's face brightened, then took on a troubled look. "I was rude earlier," she said. "I am sorry for that. My name is Asha."

"Mine is Carla."

"Carla," the girl repeated, as though that settled something. She look at Carla for a moment, and then said, "You are sad."

Carla considered her, and nodded. "Yes. A very old friend of mine is dying."

"I am sad for you," said Asha after a moment.

"Child," said Carla, "you have much more to grieve than I do."

Asha gave her a startled look. All at once she took one of Carla's hands in both of hers and pressed it against her forehead: a sign of respect, Carla recalled after a moment. She stayed bent over the hand for a time until Carla raised her chin with her other hand. "Asha," she said, "you should sleep."

"Will you sleep?"

"Not yet. I have work to do first."

"May I help?"

"Not tonight." Carla considered her again, and allowed a smile. "Tomorrow, yes. I'll need to ask you questions—" What was the outrunner phrase? "—hands and hands of them, and write down the answers. Tonight, though, you should sleep."

The girl nodded. "Then I will sleep." She unfolded her blankets, spread them over the sleeping mat, and settled herself under them with a little sigh.

Carla watched her for a moment, then changed into her own sleep robe and pulled over a low wooden writing table from one wall. A drawer underneath it provided paper and a pen; she paused, organizing her thoughts, and then began to write her judgment on the hunt for the last free band of outrunners on Eridan.

7

Asha knelt on the floor and ducked her head in the way proper for a girl greeting an elder of a friendly band. The old woman seated in front of her, her robes colored like rainbows, nodded once in response, as an elder would, the familiar motion at once comforting and bitter with memories. She was round of body, though, in a way few of the People had ever been, and like Emeli, she had something about her that was like the Silent and not like them at the same time: the look of one who sees more than others. "Child," she said, "do you know why Carla brought you here?"

Asha kept her gaze on the floor, said nothing. The old woman laughed a quiet laugh. "Child," she said then, "I know what you're carrying. You needn't tell me anything about that if you don't wish to, but I know. We all do."

That brought Asha's gaze up sharply. The old woman was watching her. Asha looked away after a moment, made uncomfortable by the old woman's eyes. They reminded her of pools in a river, full of deeps and currents in which the unwary might too easily slip and drown.

The room was small and full of things she didn't recognize, and the places she could see through—windows, Asha reminded herself, recalling the word—let Sun look in, splashing clear yellow morning light in bars across it all. She could feel Carla's presence behind and to one side, still warm air, drumbeat-sound of one of the jewelfly-things in the distance, unfamiliar murmurs moving through the floor beneath her. She tried to pay attention to all those things, and not look at the old woman in front of her, and finally failed.

"For those who carry an Indweller," the old woman asked, "what is the Way?"

It was not a question Asha had expected, and she stared at the old woman for a moment with mouth open before catching herself and looking down. "I do not know," she admitted. "My hearth-mothers knew while they lived, and my grandmother, but they never taught me."

"Was it the Way for an old woman to carry it?"

Asha considered that. "I do not know. It was Grandmother's to carry since the time I became her hearth-child."

She could feel Carla's gaze on her then. "Before then," said the old woman, "you knew others. Did any of them carry an Indweller?"

The question stirred old memories: shouting, cries, dim shapes struggling, the harsh voice of a gun, all of it too close to the surface after the events of the day before. Asha clenched her eyes shut, tried to will the memories away, but they would not go. "No," she said in a toneless whisper. "No."

Carla's hand settled lightly on her shoulder, comforting. That hearth-mother's gesture undid the last of Asha's self-control. She crumpled forward, burying her face in her hands, weeping and shaking.

How long it was before the tears stopped, she was never sure afterwards. When they were done, Asha raised her face from her hands but would not look up. Shame tensed her shoulders: that she had wept before elders, that she had wept in the sight of Sun.

"Child," the old woman said again. Her voice sounded weary and sad, and Asha, startled, looked up at her then with red wet eyes. "You have seen too many terrible things. So many of the People have. Not all of those things were done by the People. You and I both know that."

Asha ducked her head, the motion barely visible.

The old woman motioned past her, at Carla. "Carla killed one of your hearth-brothers. You know that too."

Asha ducked her head again, a little more firmly.

"Do you know why?"

This time, the question left her baffled. The Silent hunted the People, just as the People hunted for meat; that was simply the way things were, the way they had always been. "No," she said in the same toneless whisper.

"To end the Way," the old woman told her. "To stop the killing of people for meat."

That startled Asha more than anything else the old woman had said. "How can you live without meat?"

The old woman allowed a smile. "You've learned new words since you came here yesterday, haven't you?" she asked.

"Here's another: protein. It's the thing in meat that you can't get from plant foods. If you don't get it, you starve."

Asha pondered that.

"We have other ways of making protein. We don't need to get it from meat. The food you've eaten with us has protein in it." The old woman considered her again. "We tried to teach the People how to make protein, but they would not leave the Way."

Asha bowed her head, trying to make her thoughts fit around the old woman's words. They were truth, she knew that: the food the Silent and the Others ate was not meat, but made her feel satisfied the way meat did. And that meant—

She wrenched her thoughts away. One thing had to be spoken, she knew. "The thing I carry," she said, her voice unsteady. "It will not speak to me."

The old woman took that in. "Did it speak to your grandmother?"

"When I was young. Not for a hand and a finger of winters."

"Will it speak now?"

For answer Asha turned her attention inwards, to the presence of the other. "It is—like this," she said, and briefly pressed her eyes and ears shut with her hands. "It does not answer."

"Do you know why?"

She looked up at the old woman again, and tears filled her eyes. "It will not tell me."

Carla's hand touched her shoulder again, comforting. This time Asha managed to blink back her tears and did not shame herself by weeping. She settled her shoulder back against the hand, letting herself sense the strength behind it.

"Child," the old woman said, "I'm sorry. I don't mean to cause you more pain. We'll talk again another time. If the thing you're carrying starts speaking to you, will you tell Carla?"

"I will," Asha said.

"Thank you."

Asha ducked her head in farewell, got to her feet. Carla was already standing. Asha took one of the Silent's hands in her own, went with her to the door.

When it slid open, though, two people waited outside. One was a brown-haired woman in black garments like a Silent's, but long and heavy, falling to the floor as though she never needed to run. The other was a man with black hair and a lean haggard face, in clothing of a color Asha had rarely seen, the color that belonged to the World That Is Gone. The name of it rose in her memory only after a moment: *green*.

Carla turned back into the room at once. "Tamar, it's Amery and Jerre." The old woman gave a delighted cry and rose awkwardly to her feet.

"We got here maybe a quarter hour ago," the man said. "The helicopter up from Zara found a tailwind somewhere."

Asha glanced from face to face, and then turned to Carla. "Should I go to the Halka place?" *Halka* was another new word for her, the name that the Silent used for themselves and the Others—the Shelter folk, she reminded herself—used for them. The word still felt awkward on her tongue.

"Yes," Carla said. "Tell Marc that he'll need to sign for another room. If you need anything, child, let him know."

"I will do that," Asha said. She ducked her head in farewell to Carla, then, tentatively, to the two strangers, before slipping past them into the corridor outside. As she walked away, she could sense their eyes following her. The watchfulness of the Silent was in them, and something else, something for which she had no name.

8

"Carla," said Stefan Jatanni. "It's good to see you again."

"I'm glad I could make it in time," Carla replied. He nodded calmly in response, as she expected, acknowledging the reference to his impending death. That was the Halka way, but she knew there was more to it than that. She'd known Stefan since childhood, recalled the sharp-edged clarity he'd had even as a boy.

The room off the Shelter medical center was small and bare, four meters on a side, with bedding rolled up neatly out of the way and a scattering of cushions for seating. Two small windows let in golden afternoon sun to blend with the glow of an electric lamp. A neat line of books stood against one wall. The old man who sat near them, though his once-muscular frame had become gaunt and frail, seemed to fill the space in a way Carla couldn't quite define.

"So tell me," she said then. When his expression posed the obvious question: "Everything, of course. It's been, what? Two years now."

"There isn't much to tell," he said. "Ever since the cancer showed up I've stayed here with Tamar, but you know that already. We did a fair amount of work on the borders of the visionary condition while I was still well enough. And you? Chasing outrunners in the northern barrens, or so I've heard."

"I ran out of battle-drones to hunt," she said blandly, and he laughed. It was a faint tired laugh, not like him at all, and she had to struggle to keep from wincing.

"But you caught something this time," he said. "Something you brought back with you."

"Tamar's told you?"

A shake of his head denied it. "I didn't read it in subtle awareness, either."

She took that in. "Stefan," she said, "what are you seeing?"

It was not a casual question. Memories stirred, twenty years old: a judgment circle, with Stefan sitting among them in *ten ielindat*, the Halka posture-of-awareness, describing the vision that had come crashing into his mind a few days before. On that vision, the survival of humanity on Eridan had ultimately depended.

His glance and slight smile told her that he'd caught the image. "Nothing so dramatic as that. A year ago, maybe more, I began having glimpses of—" A gesture indicated uncertainty. "Movement. Something moving far away. Over time a few more details came through: faint sounds, like a voice whispering at a great distance. A sense of waiting. A sense of danger, and of possibility. That was all."

"Did you submit those to a judgment circle?"

"Of course. They declared them undecidable and sent a judgment south to Zara."

Carla nodded. Another memory twenty years old showed itself briefly: the judgment circle at Talin Shelter that had forever changed the way the Halka order handled its visionaries.

"But that was all I had until four days ago. On that day I had those same images surge up again, and an image of you came with them. Along with that was a certainty that you were about to bring something of very high importance here to Mirien."

"Four days ago," said Carla. "What time?"

"Just after sunset here." His glance told her once again that he had anticipated her thoughts. "Two hours before the radio room here received your message."

"When we finished the fight the last outrunner band. Do you want to know what I brought back with me?" Stefan motioned, inviting, and she went on. "A girl, the only survivor of the band. She has one of the Indwellers in her."

He nodded, as though that didn't surprise him. "I wish I could see her."

"I can send for her now if you like."

A shake of his head gave his answer. "Thank you, but no. I don't have the time."

He turned away from Carla, to the books along the wall: a mercy of sorts, as it gave Carla the moment she needed to silence her reaction. His movements were uneven and slow, and Carla could feel the last embers of his strength waning. "But there's another thing," he said. He extracted a packet of folded papers from between two books, handed it to her. "This is to be opened after I'm gone—not before. It concerns the future of the Halka order."

"Visionary material?"

His face communicated nothing, and Carla nodded after a moment and pocketed the papers. "Should I be the one who opens it?"

That earned her another of his slight smiles. "Of course. It had to be either you or Amery, and I don't expect to see her again."

"She's here," Carla told him, and was gratified to see a flicker of surprise. "She and Jerre both got here this morning. As soon as I leave, if you're feeling well enough, they'll come in."

"I'll manage," Stefan said.

Heightened senses told her how little time he had left, and she got to her feet. "I'll let them know." She turned toward the door.

"Carla."

She glanced back at him, saw a familiar smile on his face.

"You've been a very good friend to me, all these years. Thank you."

Words failed her, and the silent innerspeech of the Halka offered nothing better. She nodded, acknowledging, knowing that he would understand.

A moment later she was in the corridor. Amery and Jerre sat on the floor just outside, but stood at once as she came into sight. Amery spoke in the silent innerspeech of the Halka: *Now?*

Do not delay, Carla told them both, waited until they were past, and fled.

Tessat-ni-Halka shol ielindat, the way of the Halka is clarity of awareness: those were the words, familiar to every member of the Halka order, that circled through her mind as she made her way to her quarters. They offered only a frail bulwark against her own emotions, the feelings she'd analyzed and accepted decades back, when she'd first known for certain that she loved Stefan and that he could never love her. Someday it would matter to her immensely that she had been able to say goodbye to him, that his last words to her had been full of gratitude for her friendship. She knew herself well enough to be certain of that. At the moment, though, none of it meant anything. The whole of her life just then tasted of dust and ashes, of failed dreams and might-have-beens.

The corridors between the medical center and the Halka quarters were all but deserted, which was one source of comfort, and the common room in the Halka quarters was empty, which was another. The thought of further solitude appealed to her; she crossed to her sleeping room, and only after she'd opened the door did she remember that Asha was waiting inside.

The girl lay curled up under a blanket, but as Carla stopped in the doorway she blinked awake and sat up. A brief silence came and went, and then Asha said, "You are very sad."

Carla considered her, and then came the rest of the way into the room and closed the door, knowing there was nothing else she could do. She sat, pulled off her boots, and only then said, "The friend I told you about will die today."

Asha pondered that. "You are not beside your friend."

"He has other friends. I left him so they could talk with him."

The girl took one of Carla's hands in both of hers, pressed it to her forehead. When she looked up again, she held onto the hand. "I would speak," she said in a very low voice, and when Carla nodded again: "You are kind to me as a hearth-mother is kind. I know you do not follow the Way. I know I have left the Way. I know the Way has ended. But I would be kind to you as a hearth-child is kind."

Carla took that in. Subtle awareness, the double-edged gift of the Halka, showed her the girl's feelings as though they were spread out on the floor: grief, terror, uncertainty, loneliness, a frantic grateful clinging to the one source of comfort she'd found, and something else, a stirring of affection so tentative Carla hesitated to name it at all. She could see her own thoughts and feelings just as clearly, noted how often the hand she'd placed on Asha's shoulder had been guided by something other than purely pragmatic concerns. "I don't know the Way," she admitted then. "What sort of kindness do you mean?"

Asha's thin solemn face regarded hers. "I would stay with you and help you in whatever way you ask. I would keep watch when there is danger and share my warmth when nights are cold. I would weep when you weep and laugh when you laugh. When you are old I would share m—share *protein* with you." She stumbled a little over the unfamiliar word. "When you die I would sing the death-song so your ghost can cross the spaces of the sky to the World That Is Gone. And now I would do whatever gives you comfort."

"The Halka also have a Way," Carla said after a moment. "When certain things happen I must go and fight, and you'll have to stay behind and wait for me." Asha ducked her head, acknowledging. "But—" A sudden thought surfaced. "What about the others of the People, the ones who've left the Way and live in the south?"

"I do not know them," said Asha. "I know you."

She looked at the girl for another moment. All the reasons why it would be wiser to evade the issue came to mind, neatly organized, but none of them mattered enough. "Where the Halka way doesn't forbid it, I'd be grateful for your kindness."

Asha's face lit up. Tentatively, she moved closer and slipped her arms around Carla's waist. Carla put an arm around her shoulders, and the girl nestled her face against Carla's side, let out a long ragged breath, another.

Time passed. Carla let herself sink into the silence that filled the sleeping room, found herself taking unexpected comfort from the thin arms that circled her. It was easier to attend to that than to brood over Stefan or her own knotted feelings.

Then she felt the faint shift she expected, echoing through the innermind, the subtle realm of unities that linked mind to mind and gave Halka and Halvedna alike their powers. She closed her eyes and bowed her head. Another interval of time passed, unmeasured, and then she sensed patterns of movement. Long before those condensed into the sound of footsteps approaching the Halka common room, she knew who it was and what news she brought. She pressed Asha's shoulder, a signal she hoped the girl would understand.

Asha looked up, ducked her head, let go of Carla and sat a short distance away, silent and patient. Carla heard the footfalls slow outside the door, said, "Please come in."

It was Amery, of course, her face pale and composed, just as Carla had known it would be. "Stefan?" Carla asked.

Amery nodded, let subtle awareness communicate everything that had to be said.

"Thank you," said Carla, and Amery nodded again and closed the door.

CHAPTER 2

THE PLACE OF WHISPERS

1

Asha had wondered, since Carla had first mentioned her dying friend, how those who did not follow the Way dealt with their dead. She had not expected to learn the answer so quickly, or in such detail. The day after the friend's death, though, she submitted meekly to the ministrations of a hairbrush in her hearth-mother's hand, made sure her clothes were as they should be, and followed Carla down a stair into the deep places of Mirien Shelter, walking one pace behind her, silent and attentive.

They were not alone. A slow patient line of people descended the stair and another climbed back up again, some of those in both lines Halka, others Shelter folk. Hands of hands of people had already been down the stair, or so Asha gathered from the talk she heard, and hands of hands more would follow, for Carla's friend had been honored among Halka and Shelter folk alike for his deeds. The two who descended just ahead of Carla, the ones she'd met in the room where the old woman had spoken of the Indweller—they were Halka, Asha was sure of it, though the man still wore green clothing and the woman wore her heavy black robes, not the close-fitting black garments Carla wore, the clothing the People had feared as the mark of the Silent. She considered herself, dressed like Shelter folk in a purple outer robe and a yellow inner robe, with soft shoes that whispered on the stair, and wondered why she didn't feel out of place.

After they had descended a hand and two fingers of levels, they left the stair, went down a short bare corridor, went through a door into a small and equally bare room. There on a low table covered in black barkcloth, an old man in black robes lay face up: eyes closed, hands folded over his chest, wrinkled face bloodless and still. She knew the face at once, for it was the old man she'd seen next to the room with the person called "doctor."

Two sen Halka knelt on the bare floor facing the old man, one by his head and one by his feet, motionless as he was but alert like hunters ready for prey. Asha considered them, guessed that they sat so to honor him, but noticed the guns at their hips—the short lethal guns of the Silent, quicker to fire than the long rifles of the People—and felt uneasy.

Others were in the room already, and so Asha was not surprised when her hearth-mother led her to one side and sat on the floor to wait. Asha sat also in the same manner, kneeling on both knees and then sitting back on her heels. It was a Halka way of sitting, and it had pleased her to learn it, so that she could do as Carla did.

Low murmurs of speech whispered off the bare gray walls of the room as the others went forward to the body and did something there that Asha could not quite make out. She waited for a time, to be sure that speech was permitted, and then turned to Carla and said in a low voice, "I would speak."

Carla glanced at her, nodded.

"Did he hunt the People while he lived?"

That fielded her a look Asha couldn't interpret. "Yes, more than once."

Asha ducked her head, acknowledging. "Then I should sing the death-song for him." In answer to her raised eyebrow:

"We treated the Si—the Halka so, when they died at the hands of the People. My hearth-fathers said that because they were brave, they were worthy to walk across the spaces of the sky to the World That Is Gone."

Carla took that in, glanced at the man in green and the woman in black robes. Asha could almost see the silent not-speech pass between them. Finally Carla turned back to her. "When I signal you," she said, "please sing for him. He would have been honored."

Asha ducked her head again. One at a time, the others finished whatever it was that they did, and left the room. Carla rose to her feet, and so did Asha. The man in green and the woman in black had already stood, and the man in green went to the silent shape on the table, paused for a time, and then bent, took something from a bowl on the floor, and scattered it over the old man. He backed away, and the woman in the heavy black robes did the same things.

Then it was Carla's turn, and Asha followed her, standing back respectfully while her hearth-mother stood grieving and then scattered whatever it was over the body. Finally Carla stepped back. Asha approached the old man, pondered the haggard lines of his face, and then turned to the bowl on the floor.

Her hand jerked back when she realized what was in it: feathery white windflowers of a kind she knew at once: fireflowers, the most baleful of all omens. To disturb the ground where those grew, or even to spend too much time in such a place, was to welcome sickness and death. That the Halka dared bring such an omen inside their dwellings astounded her, and that they scattered it over their dead—that spoke of a fearlessness so great that she did not wonder that the People had fallen and the Way shattered before it. She stared at the flowers for a moment, glanced at the body to see many more of them lying there, and then made herself pick up a few of them and scatter them as well. Then she glanced at Carla, received the expected nod.

She backed away from the baleful flowers, knelt on the floor facing the old man, closed her eyes and began to sing, her voice low and mournful, drawing out the syllables as Grandmother had taught her and the Way required:

"When we came to this world across the spaces of the sky,
Great was our sorrow, but greater was our need.
When we fled the places of dying and took refuge in
the forest,
Strong was our dread, but stronger was our life.
When we became the People, when we embraced the Way,
We learned the lesson of the sharing of meat:
What comes from the People must return to the People,
For our need is great, but our life is strong."

She opened her eyes then and got to her feet. When she turned around, the man in green and the woman in black robes were staring at her. So were others who had just come through the door. One of those was Tamar, the old round woman in the rainbow-colored robes.

Uncertain, Asha glanced at them, then crossed the floor to stand beside her hearth-mother, who took her hand in silence and led her out of the room.

2

"That was just possibly the eeriest thing I've ever heard," Amery Lundra said.

"The outrunner death-song?" asked Carla. When the younger woman nodded: "I won't argue. I've heard it many times now—every time we were able to get members of a band to surrender, someone sang it for their dead—and it still gives me chills."

The two of them sat in one of the stark little rooms in Mirien Shelter's Halka quarters: the one Amery and Jerre had been assigned, two doors from the one where Asha curled up asleep while Carla was busy. Jerre had gone elsewhere—the Shelter hallow room, Carla guessed, to mourn in solitude, and guessed also he'd be there for hours yet.

"It wasn't just the song itself," Amery said then. "It reminded me that all along we've treated the outrunners merely as a threat. They were also a people—a people we've destroyed."

"I know," said Carla.

Amery went on as though she hadn't heard. "There was a word for that in some of the languages of Earth. Did you know that? The word was 'genocide.'" She stumbled slightly over the unfamiliar syllables.

"I know," Carla said again. "Can you think of anything else the Halka could have done?"

Amery glanced up at her, then looked down again, defeated. "No," she admitted. "Not when the only alternative was to let hundreds of Shelter folk every year be killed for meat. And there's the Third Law."

"'No act or threat of violence,'" Carla quoted, "'by members of one community against members or property of any other community, except in defense of the six laws here established, shall occur on Eridan.' We could hardly have expected the Shelter folk to keep that law if we let the outrunners violate it."

"Of course not." With a bleak expression: "All things considered, I'd rather that we'd only had battle-drones to fight." She drew in a breath. "But you wanted to show me the papers Stefan gave you."

Carla nodded, extracted them from her pocket. An adhesive disk of the kind used to seal letters held the packet shut. Carla tore that open with a quick movement and handed the sheaf of papers to Amery, who took them, unfolded them, took in the beginning of the top page and then glanced at Carla. "Have you read these?"

A flicker of innerspeech answered in the negative, and Amery kept reading, setting aside one page after another. Once she'd finished, she handed the papers without a word to Carla, who read the first lines and blinked in astonishment:

THE CONVENTION OF ZARA
A supplementary judgment in dissent

Amery glanced at her, then away. "Keep reading."

Carla skimmed over the first two sections, required by tradition but irrelevant here: the first explaining how Stefan had become involved in the case, the second recounting the events under judgment. Being born on Eridan was enough explanation of the first, since the laws and procedures enacted by the Convention of Zara two hundred twenty years back remained in force, and now that the outrunners were gone there was no inhabited corner of the planet where they did not hold. As for the second, every human action on Eridan in the three centuries since the arrival of *Journey Star* could have been included, though Stefan had been mercifully brief. Most of his narrative centered on the War and the final struggle with the outrunners in the twenty years afterward. It was the next to last section that mattered, Carla knew, and she slowed as she reached it, let subtle awareness pick up what it could from the handwriting and the choice of words as her conscious mind processed their overt message:

Since the signing of the Convention the Halka have had two primary tasks: to defend Shelter folk from battle-drones and outrunners, and to enforce the Six Laws. The Halka have always considered the second of these tasks more important than the first. Shelter folk have rarely shared this view. From their perspective we Halka exist principally to defend them, and it is only a slight exaggeration to say that they have submitted to the Six Laws because that was the price of the protection we offer. More precisely, it was part of the price, for Shelter folk also feed, clothe, house, and provide trade credit for the Halka in exchange for that protection. We have no power to force the Shelter folk to do this. For two centuries they did so voluntarily, because the alternative was to be left to deal with battle-drones and outrunners themselves.

The War twenty years ago ended the threat from battle-drones. The defeat of the last bands in the northern barrens will end the threat from the outrunners. As time passes and memories fade, the Shelter folk will no longer be willing to carry indefinitely the burdens we place on them. Nor can we expect a steady stream of Shelter folk prepared to take baya and enter our order, as in the past—I trust I need remind no one how many of us took that step after our own encounters with battle-drones, outrunners, or the bitter consequences of their actions, and I trust most sen Halka have also noted the decline in the number of candidates for baya since the War. Once the outrunners are no more, that decline will accelerate.

The Halka order must therefore be ready to pay the price of its victory—a price that will mean either the end of the order or its transformation into something wholly different. In one way or another, the defense of the Six Laws will pass to other hands in the years ahead. That, too, the Halka order must be ready for.

Carla glanced up at Amery, then turned to the last section of the judgment, where she expected to find precise and carefully worded proposals for the future of the Halka. What she found instead was a single sentence:

The Halka order should take no action in response to these concerns.

Astonished, she shook her head, set the papers down on the floor, and said, "Do you have any idea what to make of this?"

"None whatsoever," said Amery. "There's been some very tentative discussion at Zara about what the future of the order might be, once the outrunners were gone. Nobody has gone so far as drafting a written judgment. I don't think anyone dared."

"Stefan didn't want this read until he was gone," said Carla. "I'll also remind you that he didn't specifically ask me to send this out for him." Amery gave her a querying look, and she went on. "I will, of course. Whether he's right or not, I think the order needs to consider this. But I know it's going to provoke a storm." With a little helpless gesture: "Especially given that final section. I wonder what he meant by it."

"I have no idea," said Amery. "If you like, though, I'll put my name on it too."

"Please," Carla said. With a smile: "I recall another supplementary judgment in dissent you signed along with me."

"It's a habit," said Amery with an answering smile. She turned toward the low writing table up against one wall, got an adhesive disk and a pen from a drawer under it, and handed both to Carla, who signed her name on the bottom of the last page and handed the document back to Amery. A second signature followed. Once that was done, Carla sealed the packet of papers shut again, and on one side of the packet wrote in block letters:

> **Carla Dubrenden s. H.,**
> **Amery Lundra s. H.,**
> **Mirien 2114**

She glanced up at Amery then. "Who's at Kerriol these days?"

"Jorj Tallan. He's been running the message center there since they brought him back from the far side of Wind Gap."

Carla nodded, wrote:

> **Jorj Tallan s. H.,**
> **Kerriol 1108**
> **judgment—open distribution**
> **STANDARD CODING**

As she wrote, of all the memories that might have surfaced, what came to mind was something she'd said to Asha the day

Stefan died. The Halka have a Way, she'd said, and missed the irony that the phrasing implied. Now that irony stood before her, inescapable. When the Halka put an end to the outrunners' Way, had they done the same to their own Way without knowing it? The question hung in the silent air as she finished addressing the judgment, handed the pen back to Amery.

3

"The doctor says I'm doing well," said Asha.

"The doctor is right." Tamar picked up a hand-sized device of glass and polished metal, pressed the button on one side with her thumb, held it close to the back of Asha's head and then moved it slowly down the spine.

Naked to the waist, Asha sat in the middle of Tamar's study, with Carla a watchful presence not far away. The cushion Tamar had readied for her sat neglected to one side, for the girl had picked up the habit of sitting on her heels in *ten ielindat* as the Halka did, and would sit no other way. The marks of malnutrition had begun to fade from her body, though Tamar guessed she would always be small, her growth hindered by insufficient protein. The device in Tamar's hand buzzed and tingled. The old woman cleared her thoughts and opened herself to the innermind, waiting for the trace she knew she would find.

There—something that was not Asha, along one side of the spinal cord. A motion of the induction probe found a parallel presence on the other side. It reacted to the probe like nerve tissue, produced echoes of sensation and motion that Tamar could read. She traced both lines down to the bottom of Asha's ribcage, felt the signal fade below that. When she brought the probe in front of Asha's belly, she caught a muted presence: the bulk of the Indweller was in the upper abdominal cavity, between spine and stomach, well sheltered.

She set the probe aside, picked up one with a deeper focus, held it close to the hollow under Asha's ribcage, and pressed the button that activated it. The innermind brought her the reaction—sudden, and just as suddenly stifled—but it didn't take Halvedna training to hear Asha's sudden indrawn breath.

"What is it?" she asked the girl.

"It cried out."

"The Indweller?"

"Yes." Eyes lowered. "It spoke no words, but it cried out."

"That's something." She put down the probe. "Thank you, Asha. You may put your robes back on. I hope you aren't chilled."

"No." The girl ducked her head, managed a shy little smile. "It's very warm here."

She dressed quickly, tied her robes shut, turned to Carla, who said, "Wait for me in the Halka quarters. I'll be there in a little while." Asha ducked her head again, got up, and made off, fumbling only a little with the door.

"She really is doing well," Tamar said then.

"Maybe too well." Carla's expression betrayed worry. "I've never seen or heard of a case of an outrunner child adapting so easily to Shelter life."

"You've mentioned some difficulties."

A gesture dismissed them. "Night terrors, sudden tears, depressed moods, the sort of thing I'd expect to see in any child after a sudden shock. She hasn't just been through a sudden shock. She's been taken out of a nomadic tribal culture and brought into a world of—" Another gesture indicated the Shelter around them. "Helicopters, wind turbines, vat-grown protein, literacy. All the other outrunner children I've heard of, after a week or two in a Shelter, were huddled, confused, desperate to get back to open country and a life that made sense to them. Asha's shown no signs of any of that."

"I'm fairly sure the symbiont is responsible," said Tamar. She put the probes away in a cabinet on one wall, turned back toward Carla. "Tebbe?"

"Please." After a moment: "The Indweller? How?"

Tamar went to the kitchen-unit set into the floor, knelt by it, got water heating. "I don't know if you followed the debates about the Indwellers." Carla shook her head, and Tamar went on. "There were two theories. One was that they were a non-human life form that had somehow adapted itself to parasitize human hosts."

That earned her a puzzled look. "None of the native life forms should be able to do that—the biochemistry's too different."

"I know. There was some discussion of the possibility that they were no more native to Eridan than we are—that some species from elsewhere reached this world before we did. But—" She shrugged. "Now we know better. The symbiont in Asha is made of human nerve tissue, or something that responds to induction probing exactly like human nerve tissue." The water boiled, and Tamar poured it into a pot with a spout, added violet-colored tebbe leaves. "If I had to guess, genetically engineered human nervous tissue."

Silence hovered in the little room as the tebbe steeped. "So," Carla said, "a creation of the Directorate."

"Maybe." Tamar got out two bowls. "We have no records at all of what might have been done aboard *Journey Star* on the voyage here, and very little about what happened in the first sixteen years after planetfall, before the coup. Still, more likely than not, you're correct." Tebbe splashed into the bowls, fragrant. She glanced at Carla. "For Asha's sake, I hope the symbiont doesn't count as banned technology."

A quick shake of the head answered her. "That was settled by legalists a century and a half ago. The Fifth Law specifies machines. Life forms don't count as machines even if they were modified." She took a bowl from Tamar, sipped at it, sighed with relief. "But you were going to tell me how it might be helping Asha."

"True. I'm old, Carla, and I ramble." She sipped tebbe. "It appears to be able to produce the whole range of brain chemicals—those that heighten stress, those that relieve it. Asha's nervous system reacts as though she's got a steady flow of stress-relieving chemicals going into her bloodstream. Those aren't coming from her body, and the Indweller is the most likely source." She took another sip. "It's conscious, by the way."

"The Indweller?"

"Yes. The last tests I did confirmed that. It's awake, and aware of anything Asha sees or hears. It also doesn't want anyone to know that. It has something like mindtraining, some way of shielding its thoughts from me, and there's something else—some other influence that has shaped its mind in a way that I can't identify at all." A final sip emptied the bowl. She reached for the tebbe pot and motioned with it to Carla, who finished hers and set it down to be refilled.

"Speaking of shielded thoughts," Tamar said then, "you didn't mention that your head is aching. I'd gladly have made tebbe earlier."

Carla gave her an amused look. "I shouldn't be surprised that you'd catch that. Still, it's nothing new."

"Do you get them often? Carla, you should see a doctor. At our age that can be a sign of something serious."

Carla looked away and said nothing. Another, deeper silence filled the room, stayed for a while. "I wish you'd told me," Tamar said finally.

"Not when you had Stefan to worry about, and then to mourn." Carla's glance met hers squarely. "Tamar, something like two-thirds of the people who fought in the battle of Mirien got one kind of cancer or another. With so many drones blowing up and spraying radioactive isotopes all over the battlefield, it's a wonder we didn't all die of it years ago. In my case—" She touched the scar at her temple. "A slow-growing brain tumor, starting where I was wounded, as you might expect. I was diagnosed eight years ago, and I could have at least as many years left to live."

Tamar regarded her. "Which is why you were hunting out-runners at an age when most sen Halka are doing things quite a bit less active."

"Of course. The final stages won't be pleasant, and an out-runner's bullet would have been quick." She shrugged. "And the thought that I could help put an end to both the things we've fought all these years had a certain appeal."

"You're still thinking of Istal Shelter."

"I like to think that someday, people on Eridan will be able to go about their lives without having to worry that something will lunge out of the forest and kill them."

Tamar nodded slowly, and reached again for the tebbe pot.

4

The next day Carla was on her way to the Halka quarters when a young man in the radio room spotted her, stepped out into the corridor as she passed, and said, "Sen Halka? There's a message from the command circle at Dammal Shelter."

She turned. The man was barely old enough to remember the War, she guessed, and faced her with the awe tempered by familiarity that so many Shelter folk directed toward the Halka of late. "Thank you. For me?"

"For Jerre Amadan and all sen Halka."

Carla tensed. A general message like that could mean serious trouble. She followed him into the radio room, where static growled from loudspeakers on the wall and bulky trans-mitters and receivers kept Mirien Shelter connected to the rest of Eridan. The message log lay open by the main receiver, but the message had been copied out in full on two sheets of paper, and the young man handed those to Carla. She read them, first with a puzzled look and then with astonishment, and glanced up. "This is remarkable. May I take these to the Halka quarters?"

"Of course, sen Halka."

She thanked him and left. A short hallway led from the radio room and the other core facilities of the Shelter to the Halka quarters. Carla wasted no time covering the distance. By the time she got to the common room three people were waiting for her, having sensed her movements already: Jerre, Amery, and a young sen Halka from the hill country, Tomas Gerdan, who had stopped there on the way south from the hunt for the last outrunners.

"You'll all want to read this," said Carla, raising the sheets of paper. "It's from Dammal. Jerre, they want a reply from you as soon as possible."

He took that in. "Banned tech?"

"That's what they're not sure of." She gave him the message.

Jerre read them, dark eyes darting back and forth. Carla didn't need subtle awareness to gauge when he reached the improbable part of the message; the sudden widening of his eyes told her that. He finished reading the message, handed it without a word to Amery, then said to Carla, "You know the Dammal command circle and I don't."

Carla gave him a wry look. "Meaning you want to know if they're likely to jump to a conclusion without evidence. I'd be less surprised if they suddenly sprouted leaves. Tena Corren's the senior member; you may not remember her but I know Amery does."

Amery finished with the papers, handed them to Tomas. "I certainly do. If Tena says she's found something from before the Directorate, I'd take it seriously. Still—"

"I know," said Carla.

Tomas reached the improbable passage then, and did a double-take. Looking up: "I didn't think anyone even got that far north before Shalsha."

"The Colonial government mapped the whole planet," Jerre said, "and they did a basic ecological and geological survey. That much is in the records at Zara. Beyond that, I don't think anybody knows." He turned. "They'll get their reply right away."

"If they need a legalist," Amery said with a smile, "you might tell Tena that at least one is available."

That got a little choked laugh from Jerre. "I'll let her know." He set off for the radio room. Amery watched him go, turned to the others.

"It'll be interesting to hear what turns up," Tomas said, handed Carla the papers, and went back into his room. Carla glanced at Amery, then at the two sentences of the message that mattered most. The first was halfway down the first page: *When we cleared the rubble and the outrunner offerings we found doors marked with the emblem of the Colonial government, with no sign that Directorate personnel tried to remove or deface it in their usual way.* The second was the last few lines on that page: *The facility seems to be in working order, but no one here has the technical background to figure out its purpose or to be sure of its date. We need to know that in order to determine whether it should be destroyed or not.*

"Tomas is right," Carla said then, and handed Amery the message. "I'll want to hear all about what Jerre finds." She began to turn away.

"Do you have any commitments just now?" Amery asked.

Startled, Carla glanced back at her. "No," she said, "except for Asha. Why?"

"I'd like you to come with us." Meeting her questioning look: "You know the northern barrens and the outrunners better than I ever will—maybe better than anyone else among the Halka these days. If this facility was as important to the outrunners as Tena thinks, you might be able to help them identify it." Then: "Asha might be able to help us, too. She obviously knows quite a lot of outrunner tradition."

There was more to it than that, of course. Subtle awareness let Carla read clearly enough the unspoken part of the request, the desire to spend a little more time with an old friend before the inevitable happened. Had Amery talked to Tamar? It seemed likely.

"I'll want to talk to Asha," Carla said. "As far as she's concerned I'm her hearth-mother and she's my hearth-child, and that puts some responsibilities on me." She paused. "But if it's not a problem for her, of course I'll come."

5

The helicopter hangar was as big as Asha remembered, but less unsettling. She followed her hearth-mother, keeping pace as best she could with a blanket roll tucked under one arm and a pack of unfamiliar shape slung from the other shoulder. They had found her new clothes fit for traveling—inner and outer robes that only went to her knees, loose trousers, good sturdy shoes, a coat for cold weather—and given her a share of the other gear. Delighted by the honor implied by that giving, she did her best to stifle the uneasiness that the looming shape of the helicopter roused in her. Overhead, the great doors slid slowly open, revealing pale sky.

A quick glance back over her shoulder showed the other two who would be traveling with them. She'd been properly introduced to them the day before, though she had known them for more than two hands of days already, knew also that they were mated and had children of their own. The woman who wore heavy robes of Halka black was named Amery, and she was a keeper of lore for the Halka, one others asked when they wished to know their Way better. The man who always dressed in the color of the World That Is Gone was named Jerre, and what he was remained a mystery to Asha. There were things about him that no one mentioned in her hearing, and the lean haggard lines of his face whispered to her of griefs and solitudes. She watched him when she could and wondered, for there was something about him that reminded her a little of the People. It felt, she decided, as though he was not-Shelter folk and not-Halka in something like the same way she was.

Carla took her by the hand and helped her climb up into the helicopter, and she smiled up at her hearth-mother and followed her to the seats. Though she hadn't been in a helicopter since that first flight south to Mirien, she remembered how to fasten the strap of cloth across her lap. Carla sat next to her, and the other two sat in seats behind theirs. The door slid shut. The helicopter made its rumbling noise and shook itself as though waking up.

Asha took hold of the arm of her seat with one hand, bracing herself, but left the other hand free. She glanced at Carla, who met the glance, read it in the Halka manner, and placed one of her hands on Asha's shoulder, just as she had on that first flight. Asha beamed, set her hand atop Carla's, and drew in an unsteady breath, waiting for the sudden upward lurch.

It came, and Asha did not cry out. Pleased at her own boldness, she looked out the window as the helicopter rose through the hangar doors, turned, mounted higher into the air, until the six things like trees with turning branches were below and the land spread out in blues and purples as far as she could see. Here and there she could see the tree-things of other Shelters in the distance, the turning branches spinning slowly in the wind.

Time passed. The helicopter sped on, though it did not feel to Asha as though it was moving. Instead, the land seemed to rush past like water, flowing out of the distance ahead, spilling into the distance behind. If she raised her eyes and looked forward, past the one called "pilot" whose hands told the helicopter where to go, she could see through the window there. That was where she first saw the blue shapes in the distance, at first a low presence at sky's edge, then rising higher and higher until she recognized them as mountains, great soaring white-tipped peaks tall as Pillar-of-Sky, a line of them like hunters walking one after another from far in the north to far in the south. Her breath caught, and she wondered whether even the helicopter could fly high enough to rise up over those tall jagged crests.

The helicopter flew on, the mountains came closer, and just past the shoulder of the one called "pilot" she saw a gap between two of the peaks, lower than any other space between the great blue masses ahead. That stirred old memories: she had learned songs about such a place, where the mountains bent low so that the winds and the People could pass over them. Few sang those songs even when Asha was young, because there had been fights between the People and the Silent near the place where the mountains bent, fights the People had lost. Then when she was a hand of winters old, the last few who sang them stopped, because another fight had been lost there by the People, and the Silent were streaming northward in ever greater numbers. It was the following spring that her hearth-father Borth led the band west and north into places none of them had been before, trying to escape the Silent and find meat to hunt. That was when they had come to the land of vast purple distances, violet-gray plains, and huddled blue thickets that framed most of Asha's memories.

The People are no more, she told herself. The Way is no more. I am hearth-child to one of the Silent—to one of the Halka. I accepted the hearth-peace from them. The thoughts seemed frail, set against so many bitter memories, but after a time the memories somehow mattered less, and she looked out the window again.

By then the helicopter was at the mouth of the gap between mountains. Stark walls of gray rock rose up on both sides. Between them, just when the land stopped rising and began to fall once more, toward a broad sweep of plain edged in the distance with silver, the tree-things of a Shelter rose up into the wind. Around it, from rock wall to rock wall, every tree had been taken away, leaving a great open sweep of violet-gray meadowmoss with no hiding places at all. A single glance told Asha the story: the Shelter kept watch there to stop the People from passing through the gap.

The helicopter slowed, circled the Shelter, sank down in the space in between the tree-things with their moving branches. A door in the Shelter roof opened. Asha pressed her hand against the hand on her shoulder, and took hers away; Carla glanced at her with the Halka-look that saw so much, patted the shoulder and released it. Asha beamed at her.

Moments later the helicopter had settled on the bare flat floor of the hangar: a hangar much larger than the one at Mirien Shelter, Asha saw when she jumped down from the doorway, her blanket roll and pack burdening her again. Two hands of helicopters sat on the great sweep of the floor already, some of them much bigger than any Asha had seen, and space remained for as many more. She stared at the vastness of it, then hurried after her hearth-mother, who was crossing the hangar toward a group of waiting sen Halka. She caught up to Carla, then fell back a pace, set pack and blanket roll down, waited respectfully with hands folded and head bowed while her hearth-mother spoke words of greeting to one of the Halka, a woman with graying black hair and a scarred face, and then to the others.

By then Jerre and Amery had come up as well. The woman with the scarred face greeted Amery with a smile and every sign of delight, but turned to Jerre with a hesitation Asha could taste. "Sen Amadan," she said to him.

Jerre regarded her, and then said, "Sen Halka."

How the familiar title could be a challenge on his lips, Asha did not know, but so it was. The woman with the scarred face nodded once, as though conceding.

"And this is Asha," Carla said then, and motioned her forward with a fractional movement of her head. Asha approached the woman with the scarred face and the other Halka, ducked her head in greeting as Carla said, "My hearth-child, as the outrunners would say."

"Asha," said the woman with the scarred face, as though she was a member of another band of the People. "My name is Tena.

Be welcome to Dammal Shelter. We've seen quite a few of the People here, of course."

Asha glanced up at her face, suddenly wary, but the eyes that met hers had no threat in them. She ducked her head again, acknowledging. Behind them, the helicopter that had brought them from Mirien Shelter roared and rose upward, beginning the flight back.

6

Asha expected the Halka quarters at Dammal Shelter to be like those at Mirien. Instead, she found an entire floor given over to the Halka, with a common room the size of the helicopter hangar at Mirien Shelter and hands of hands of rooms to sleep in, so many that she had to make an effort to remember the way to the one she and Carla would share. Most of them stood empty, though she guessed they had once all been full. As soon as her blanket roll and pack sat there next to Carla's, she followed another sen Halka, a woman named Shar, who was short and lean and made sudden sharp movements like a jewelfly. They went back up the stair to another room, a pleasant sunny space where a middle-aged man in robes of a familiar rainbow pattern welcomed her, spoke with her, and shared a meal with her.

His name was Bran, and he was Halvedna: another new word for Asha, the word for those who wore the rainbow-colored robes and who saw hidden things in something like and not like the way the Halka did. She liked speaking to him, for he asked questions as an elder of the People would, about her health and how well she slept and what she had learned. He seemed pleased by her answers, too, and that gave her the confidence to ask a few polite questions of her own. She listened with wide eyes as he described growing up far to the south where it never snowed even in winter, joining the Halvedna, and walking all the way north to Wind Gap after something called the War, when Halka and Shelter Folk came there to build Dammal Shelter.

When he had finished, she gathered up even more of her courage and said, "When I met the sen Halka called Tena she said that many of the People had been seen here."

"Indeed they have," Bran told her, smiling. "You've heard of the People who've left the Way, and gone to live in the forests of the south? Most of them stayed here for a while before the Halka took them south. I spoke with most of them, and especially with the children. That was why Carla asked me to see you. She wanted me to make sure you were well."

"My hearth-mother is very kind to me," Asha said, looking down.

"Yes, she is," said Bran. "But there's another thing as well, of course. We know what you're carrying, and I know a little more about the Indwellers than most."

She glanced up at him then. "Have you seen another who bears one?"

"No," Bran admitted. "As far as anyone knows, yours is the only one that survived. I was able to talk to some of the People who had spoken to one. That's all."

"Do you know how to make this one speak to me?"

She knew how he would answer before he spoke. "I wish I did."

They talked a little more, and then he sent for someone to take her back down to the Halka quarters. When she found her way back through the empty spaces to the little room where her gear and Carla's sat side by side, her hearth-mother was nowhere near, so she knelt, sat back on her heels, and turned her attention toward the thing inside her.

I think you are awake as I am, she thought at it. *I think you see what I see and hear what I hear. I think you are not so much like this as you were.* She clenched her eyes shut and covered her ears with her palms, just for a moment. *Will you not speak to me? My hearth-mother Carla is kind to me, and she will be kind to you.*

The Halvedna are kind to me, and they will be kind to you. A sudden thought struck her and made her smile. *We share our meals and sleep under one blanket. It is not fitting that we should be strangers.*

Was that a hint of wavering in the silence that confronted her? She could not be sure. If it happened at all, though, it lasted only an instant, and afterward the silence remained, cold and hard as ice in the deep places of winter.

7

The next morning they boarded another helicopter, a big one full of cargo, for the flight out to the facility the message had described. Carla went to the hangar early, an old habit of hers. Asha trotted along behind her, bright and lively as a flame in a world gone gray and cold. While they waited for the helicopter to finish taking on cargo and for the other passengers to arrive, she asked Asha about her talk with Bran Jemison the day before. She'd spoken with the sen Halvedna afterward, and nodded to herself as he'd told her some things about Asha she already knew and a good many things she didn't, but it pleased her to listen to the girl's voice and hear her comments, by turns naïve and unexpectedly shrewd, on Bran and Dammal Shelter.

Eight other sen Halka who were flying with them on errands of their own came one at a time and joined the two of them on one side of the hangar, close to the helicopter. Then, as time grew short, Jerre and Amery came through the doors at the hangar's far end and crossed the oil-stained concrete floor. As they did, one of the Shelter folk who had been busy fueling the helicopter saw them and stiffened, standing for a moment pale and motionless as though he'd seen a ghost walking. A moment later he finished some task, spoke briefly to the other Shelter folk, and crossed to where Carla and the other sen Halka stood. Every movement he made yelled of hope and dread to Carla's perceptions, and she guessed, long before it became clear from his route, that he meant to speak to Jerre.

He stopped a short distance away: a young man, Carla realized, probably still in school though old enough to do Shelter work. Once Jerre glanced at him he came a little closer and said, "Sen Amadan." Jerre nodded, and he went on. "My name is Tallis Dumaren. I know about your project, and I—I want to help if I can."

Carla could read the quick flicker of subtle awareness as Jerre sized him up. "You're finished with your schooling?"

"In two months, sen Amadan. I've studied engineering. I do Shelter work on pumps, engines—anything mechanical. I've wanted to work on your rockets since I was little."

A moment passed, and Jerre nodded again. "The project can always use someone who knows how to handle machinery. When you're done with school, come to Zara. We'll find work for you to do."

The young man's face lit up. "Thank—thank you, sen Amadan. Thank you. I promise you won't regret it." He backed away, then turned and hurried back to the fuel hoses.

By then the helicopter was loaded with cargo and ready for boarding, and Carla made sure Asha was ready and then started across the concrete floor. Once everyone was settled in the passenger space, she turned toward Jerre and asked, "How often does that happen?"

Jerre allowed a little dry laugh. "Almost every time I leave Zara and go to another Shelter. It's nothing like it was right after the War—back then, wherever I went I'd have ten or fifteen or twenty people come to offer their help with the project, when we didn't yet have a place to work or any trade credit for the raw materials. I had to tell most of them to talk to me again in two or three years—and two and three years later, most of them wrote to me or came to Zara once we'd established our College there."

Carla nodded, remembering the excited rumors and the enthusiasm that had echoed from one end of Eridan to the other in the years after the War. Just then Asha said, "I would speak." When Carla nodded her permission: "What is a 'project'?"

Jerre answered. "That's the work that I do, Asha. I build rockets." It required no subtle awareness to tell that she didn't know the word. "Machines that fly straight up through the air into the sky. If everything goes well, in another ten years or so, one of my rockets will carry two people up to *Journey Star*."

Asha's eyes went round, and both her hands went to her mouth. Before she could say anything further, though, the helicopter engine growled to life and made conversation impossible. She sat back in her seat and glanced up at her hearth-mother. When Carla put her hand on the girl's shoulder, she placed her own thin hand atop it.

The helicopter lurched into motion, but Asha showed no sign of distress. She had a window beside her again, by Carla's arrangement—the sen Halka had noticed on their previous flights how avidly the girl had watched the land slip past—and stared through the glass as the helicopter rose above Dammal Shelter and headed east through Wind Gap.

Carla looked with her, for the scenery was worth watching. The trees were different, not so tall as the merias and thildas that made up most of the forests further west, but more brightly colored: she saw winter leaves the pale blue of the sky, and newly budded summer leaves the vivid red of blood. Off in the distance a band of silver marked a long narrow gulf of the sea, and a faint blue edge beyond it the long rocky peninsula, not yet named, where those first surveys in the brief interval before the Directorate had found lavish mineral resources. Someday, she thought, someday there will be Shelters all along the shores of the nameless sound and Shelters up and down the length of the great peninsula, the longest on Eridan—

She glanced at Asha, then, as uncomfortable memories intruded. And all the while, she thought, whether they know it or not, they will be watched by the ghosts of the outrunners, the people we destroyed so that future could happen.

The helicopter turned northward in a great arc, flew onward. After a time, to her surprise, Carla caught sight of bare soil, excavations, the first gray concrete walls of a future Shelter. A quarter hour later she spotted another, further away. Recollection stirred after a moment, sluggishly: the command circle at Dammal had laid plans to encourage settlement beyond Wind Gap as quickly as possible once the outrunners were gone, to make sure that no one would ever again have the chance to take up the Way. That made every reasonable kind of sense, but somehow it left Eridan feeling diminished.

Words she'd spoken to Tamar came suddenly to mind: "I like to think that someday, people on Eridan will be able to go about their lives without having to worry that something will lunge out of the forest and kill them." That day had arrived already, she'd known or half-known that when she'd said the words. Seeing ground being broken for Shelters, in country where Shelter folk had once only come as meat, confirmed it as nothing else could have done. Why did that make her feel like grieving?

Time passed and the helicopter flew on. Another Shelter in the first stages of construction came into sight, vanished in the distance to the south. Then the helicopter slowed and turned. Yet another cleared area came into sight, with purple-gray tents close around it and the first trenches for retaining walls gaping open to the sky. That was their destination, Carla guessed even before the helicopter started to descend.

The bustle of landing drove troubling thoughts from her mind, but soon enough she and Asha had their gear stowed in one of the tents. With Amery and Jerre behind them they followed a tall burly sen Halka across the camp to the larger tent that served temporarily as a Halka common room and communications center. There they spoke briefly with the Speaker of the command circle there, Shennan Ameral, a tough black-haired woman half Carla's age who asked a few pro forma questions, described what little they'd been able to learn from the ritual offerings the outrunners had left at the site, and all the while treated Jerre with a polite wariness

Carla knew too well. Maybe a half hour later, with an escort of two sen Halka to guide them, they left the camp and headed east toward the lower slopes of the mountains.

Though the forest around them as they walked was no different from the one she'd seen from the air, the walk lightened Carla's mood rather than depressing it. Subtle perceptions she'd spent most of a lifetime honing brought in every detail of her surroundings, spoke of jewelflies and ground-scuttlers, wind in the fading winter-leaves of the trees, bone-white fungoids crawling blindly across the forest floor. She could sense with perfect clarity, as she'd sensed when they returned to Camp Nine with Asha, that the north country was free of outrunners all the way across the barrens to the distant northern coast, unvisited by humans since the Directorate's time. This once, that reflection didn't trouble her. She followed the guides through the forest, one part of her mind watching Asha, another alert to her surroundings, the rest simply taking pleasure in a spring day in the forests of Eridan.

8

The facility was maybe three kilometers away from the camp, under what looked at first like a hill. Only a second, closer look revealed the hill as a concrete bunker, covered with soil and overgrown with trees: a bunker of a kind Carla had only read about before that moment. The Colonial government had built those to shelter critical installations, the books said, back when human settlement on Eridan was new and no one knew yet what the planet might throw at them. An excavation on one side had uncovered a doorway, gaping open into blackness.

The moment the doorway came into sight, Asha's breath caught. Carla turned toward her. "What is it?"

"There were stories," said Asha. "Among the People. A hill that is empty inside, like a cooking pot turned with its bottom up, on the side of the mountains that faces the sunrise.

Only the elders went there. My hearth-mothers and hearth-fathers called it the Place of Whispers."

"That's a good name for it," said one of the sen Halka who guided them. "You'll see why in a few minutes."

"Did they tell you anything else about it?" Amery asked the girl.

She ducked her head. "No. Such things were not for children to know."

Three small tents stood near the doorway, and a scattering of sen Halka kept unobtrusive watch: until and unless a judgment circle ruled that the facility didn't fall under the Fifth Law, access to any such place was subject to strict rules. A flicker of innerspeech between Amery and one of the guards sorted out any questions about their right to be there. Another guard went into a tent and came out with two electric lanterns. Those clicked on, spilled pale yellow light over the raw scar of the excavation and the crannied gray concrete that lined the doorway. A second flicker of innerspeech, and Carla turned. "Asha, it's important that you not touch anything inside." The girl ducked her head again, acknowledging.

Single file, they went into the bunker. The electric lamps cast distorted shadows on the concrete passage, illuminated the heavy blast doors at its end. Each of those latter had an emblem on it, cut out of metal and welded onto the door: an image of Eridan as seen from space, with both continents visible, surrounded by a wreath of oddly shaped leaves that didn't look like they belonged to any plant on Eridan. "Bright Earth," Amery said aloud, and Carla's silent reaction was similar: the seal of the Colonial government was something she had never seen before outside of old books.

One of the sen Halka who guided them did something with the blast doors, and they pivoted smoothly outward, still perfectly balanced after three centuries. The moment they swung open Carla heard a low sibilant whisper from the darkness beyond. An instant later she realized the space beyond the doors wasn't entirely dark. Tiny points of light of a dozen different colors flickered and danced within.

They filed into the space. The electric lamps showed a rectangular room some ten meters across and five deep, the walls lined with panels of unknown function in which thousands of lights blinked on and off. The ceiling above, vaulted, had indistinct dark shapes hanging from it. The sibilant whisper seemed to come from all sides at once. It was not random noise, Carla realized that at once: patterns shaped it, faint but detectable, and at regular intervals something like a rushing or rustling seemed to pulse through it.

She walked a short distance into the room, stopped. Asha, keeping her promise, hung back and folded her arms, tucking each hand into the other sleeve. Meanwhile Jerre examined several of the panels and then turned. "I need a formal legal opinion," he said.

"Go on," said Amery.

"In my assessment, the most effective way to find out if this facility is subject to the Fifth Law is to see if the machines respond to command language. I need to know whether that's permissible in the present case."

"Under current case law," Amery said, "any mode of contact with Directorate machinery not explicitly forbidden by the Six Laws is permissible if used solely to identify, repel, or destroy that machinery. Command language isn't excluded from that."

He nodded, spoke to the other sen Halka in the inner-speech: *Will you serve as witnesses that the question was asked and answered?*

Of course, Carla replied, and caught the parallel responses from the others.

Jerre turned to the nearest panel, paused, and then said aloud, "*Thra num byel chon, ang dal. Sei, brin, thon.*"

Nothing happened. Asha gave Carla a glance, baffled and uneasy.

"*Cho va sye mrem, sri dal. Thil, mra, thon.*"

Silence followed. Carla glanced at Asha, noted the girl's puzzlement and the presence of the other mind in her, suddenly alert and intent. She pondered that for a time, then turned her attention again to the machineries that surrounded them.

"*Dau thra khil srai, bye dal. Aesh, mhai, thon.*" Another silence passed, and then he said: "Activate voice input. Override code three, nine, three, two, Ouroboros."

"Acknowledged." The voice came from speakers in the ceiling: a woman's voice, Carla would have said, except that no human throat had shaped those syllables, and no trace of emotion or consciousness showed in it.

"Pause," said Jerre, and turned to face the others. "This is a Colonial facility. The Directorate invented command language to make sure no one but its personnel could use advanced technology. Before then computers and robotics responded to ordinary language, the way this facility just has." He turned back to the panel. "Resume. List available options."

"Override code insufficient," the voice replied.

"List security level," Jerre said then.

"Override code insufficient," the voice said again.

"List facility requirements."

"None." No emotion showed in the voice, but the word still seemed freighted with a finality Carla could sense.

Jerre paused for another moment, nodded, and then said, "Acknowleged. Suspend override code. Suspend voice input."

"Acknowledged," the voice responded. The lights continued to flicker, and the sibilant whisper went on without a break.

9

"I'm not surprised there's no record of the facility," Jerre said. He sat among sen Halka, his green garments an anomaly in a circle otherwise unrelieved black. "The override code I used was restricted to the highest levels of the old Colonial government—I have no idea how the Bredin Shelter network learned of it. If that code wasn't enough to get the computer to give me a listing of what the facility can do, or even tell me its security level, it must have been one of the most closely held secrets the Colonial government had."

"Secret enough that the Directorate never learned of it?" Shennan Ameral said.

"That's my best guess," said Jerre.

"And the purpose of the facility?"

A quick eloquent shrug answered her. "I wasn't able to determine that."

They sat inside the tent that served the Halka as a common room: ten of them in all, half the sen Halka in the camp just then. Carla and Amery sat next to each other near the door, Jerre a short distance away. From outside, muffled sounds told of another trench being cleared so a concrete retaining wall could be poured. Carla had glanced down into the trench as she'd walked past, Asha at her heels: burly men stripped to the waist and women almost as lightly clad labored with shovels and picks, strained on ropes to haul buckets of soil and rocks to the surface.

"We'll begin our deliberations," Shennan said then. "Sen Amadan, is it possible for you to join the circle briefly?"

"Of course. I do still remember how."

That fielded him a wary look. "Doubtless." She glanced to one side, the other; innerspeech settled the details. Carla, who had joined judgment circles more often than anyone else in the tent, waited for the flicker of subtle awareness that cued her, used three deep breaths and a murmured phrase to trigger the first level of trance, then moved down into the second level, where thoughts flowed easily from mind to mind. The circle groupmind, the controlled collective hallucination that kept personalities out of the way of the circle's deliberations, assessed her as it would any other unfamiliar sen Halka, admitted her to rapport. It did the same with Amery just as quickly, but with Jerre it paused: the presence of mindtraining that was

not of the Halka, maybe, or the knowledge of a judgment forever hanging over him? Carla could not tell. She waited as the
groupmind considered, and then opened itself to him.

Jerre Amadan. Shennan's innerspeech came through the
groupmind. *Show us what you saw at the facility, and explain the
basis for your assessment.*

Of course. Images and echoes flowed through the groupmind to the others: the dancing lights and whispering sounds,
the legal opinion he'd requested and received, the three
sequences of command language he'd used without effect,
the translations of the sequences, and then the words that had
awakened a response from the machines. All the while, Carla
could feel the minds of the other sen Halka focused on Jerre,
less interested in what he said than in the movements of mind
and will beneath his words, anything that would betray dishonesty or secret intentions. When he finished, without haste,
the groupmind released him, and the others turned their
attention to Amery. *The legal advice you gave*, Shennan said.
*I was unaware that command language could be used under any
circumstances at all.*

*If you have a copy of the current Summary here, I would be happy
to show you the key decisions*, Amery sent back. Filtered through
the groupmind, the words shed their cargoes of emotion, but
Carla could sense Amery's irritation. *If you want a more detailed
analysis you would need to consult volume eighteen, sections eleven
and forty-eight of the General Code. For obvious reasons, I've spent
most of the last twenty years studying the decisions and regulations
concerning banned technology.*

Shennan paused, then sent, *I don't question your competence as
a legalist. I simply expressed surprise.* Amery acknowledged that
with a wry flicker of thought, and Shennan and the groupmind
both turned to Carla. *You know sen Amadan*, the Speaker said.

Carla could not suppress a smile. *In a manner of speaking.
I witnessed his reception into Halka training, I was one of his three
examiners before baya, and I was present when the judgment circle*

at Talin Shelter ruled his case undecidable. His sponsor in the Halka order was one of my closest friends. I have visited him and his family eight times since the War. How much do you and the circle want to know about him?

I want your considered opinion as to his loyalties.

It was not the question she had expected. *To certain ideals, absolute,* she sent after a pause. *To the Halka order, firm, but qualified by those ideals. If he believed it was necessary to violate our laws and traditions he would do so, and then turn himself over to a judgment circle to be shot. He's done that once already, as I'm sure you know.* Then: *More generally? I would trust him with my life—and I would trust his assessment of technology just as far.*

Shennan acknowledged that. *So noted. We face a momentous decision, however.*

May I offer a suggestion? Amery responded at once. *You're correct that the facility you've found may be a matter of great legal importance. For that reason it might be best to call a judgment circle of senior legalists to decide its fate.*

Do you intend to be part of that circle?

No. I have other responsibilities, and potential personal conflicts as well. Nor will I recommend legalists for the circle. A general call by way of the message network might be an appropriate way to handle the matter.

Even through the groupmind, Carla could feel the sudden sense of relief as it moved around the circle. *That advice seems prudent,* Shennan sent. *Thank you.* A moment of silence as the other members of the circle gave their opinion, and Shennan went on: *I will prepare a request. Perhaps the two of you can see that it goes out once you leave.*

Carla and Amery agreed to that, and Shennan broke rapport. The others followed, unraveling the circle for the moment. As Carla blinked out of trance, Shennan turned to Jerre and said, "Thank you for your assistance."

"Of course. Would it be appropriate to ask about the decision?"

"We've decided to hand the matter over to a proper judgment circle of legalists."

Jerre nodded, as though it was the obvious thing to do. "I'd submit a judgment if that was an option. Since it isn't, perhaps you'll tell the legalists that I'd be happy to submit a written account of my observations if that would be useful to them."

"I'll inform them of that," she replied.

Carla, feeling more than usually irritable, unfolded herself from *ten ielindat* and got to her feet. Pain spiked in her head, a familiar companion; a quick motion of awareness dulled the sensation but could not remove it. She managed the briefest of courtesies to the members of the circle, left the tent, and walked across the camp as quickly as she could, trying not to notice the harsh irregular noises of picks and shovels in the nearby trench.

Asha was sitting comfortably at the door of the tent when she got there. The girl had a little stack of arrowgrass leaves—Carla dimly recalled her picking them as they walked back from the facility—and was plaiting them into a pouch of the sort the outrunners used for fire-making gear. The moment she saw Carla, though, she set the half-finished pouch aside, and said, "Hearth-mother, you are not well, I think."

"No," Carla admitted. "I have a headache."

Asha took that in, went into the tent, and settled again by the head of one of the sleeping mats. "I know a way to help. Lie with your head here." She patted her lap.

Startled, Carla considered the request and decided to humor the girl. Once she'd shed boots and jacket, she lay on the mat and rested her head on Asha's thin knees. "Like this?"

"Yes." The girl's fingertips pressed against Carla's scalp, hard, and begin to trace little circles. Pain spiked and then unexpectedly began to fade. The fingertips shifted, and the same thing happened again.

"Thank you," Carla said after it happened a third time. "That's very good."

"I am glad." Asha's face, serious and intent, hovered over Carla's. "Was it walking that made your head hurt?"

"Not at all." She let out a ragged sigh as Asha's fingers unknotted more tensions. "No, I felt better when we were walking than I've felt in months. Years, maybe."

"Did you walk more then?"

Memories stirred. "All the Halka did. When I was younger, there were battle-drones—machines that killed people. We fought them, and we never knew where one would show itself, so we walked from Shelter to Shelter all over Eridan. Then twenty years ago the War came, and at the end of it all the battle-drones were destroyed."

"Twenty," Asha said; she had begun to learn number-names. "Four hands?" When Carla agreed: "The People called that the Time of the Machines. Hands of hands of hands died and none of the People could do anything to stop the machines."

"They almost did that to us," said Carla, closing her eyes as Asha's fingers worked on her forehead. "It was a very close thing."

A silence filled the tent, broken only by the muffled distant sounds of the laborers in the trench. Asha's fingers kept moving, seeking out knots of tension and unraveling them. "When we walked just now," Asha said then, "it was like the end of winter when I was young, when we left the winter-lodge and went unclothed and ran and sang in the sunlight. The people at Mirien Shelter are kind, but when most of them look at me I know they are thinking—" She fumbled over the words: "Outrunner girl. I wish we could walk from Shelter to Shelter the way you did before the—the War. The Way is no more, I know that, and I would not return to it even if that was not so, but I miss being small under the great empty space of the sky."

Carla considered that, and finally said, "Maybe we can do that."

The circling fingers faltered. "Tell me how," Asha pleaded.

"I'm old," said Carla. "Old enough that I could have stopped fighting years ago." Words she'd spoken to Tamar whispered in her mind; she silenced them with an effort. "And now there's no one left to fight. It used to be rare for sen Halka to live to my age, but when they did, most of them went south where there were few dangers—and they walked."

Asha closed her eyes, bent, pressed her forehead against Carla's, and Carla could feel tears trickling down.

The idea hovered, tempting. Of all the ways I could spend what time I have left, Carla thought, is there a better one? None came to mind. "Let's do that," said Carla then. "We'll have to fly back to Dammal Shelter first, and I'll have to write a judgment and make arrangements, but once that's done we can start walking, and see how far we get before the rains come."

Asha kissed her forehead. "You are so kind to me," she whispered. Then she sat up, her face tear-streaked, mouth bent in a little fragile smile, and started rubbing Carla's scalp again.

CHAPTER 3

A VOICE IN DARKNESS

1

They left Dammal Shelter early on a blustery day, when clouds hid the mountains to either side of Wind Gap and sharp chill gusts came down from time to time to remind them that glaciers still kept company with winter on the high crags. Asha was so excited she practically danced as they left the Shelter's main westward entrance and followed the trail west across the great bare sweep of meadowmoss.

For her part, Carla felt not excitement but a sense of peace. She'd written a preliminary judgment on the facility, sweating over every phrase until her last official act as a sen Halka was exactly what it should be, and left it in the letter-basket in the Dammal Shelter radio room to be distributed to the Halka message net. News was waiting for her when she got to the radio room, for the last Halka patrols across the northern barrens had returned, reporting no trace of surviving outrunners. Though the command circle at Dammal Shelter would remain active for the time being, and plenty of sen Halka would keep patrolling the northern edge of settlement for years to come, word had already spread south, and celebrations had begun: feasting, dancing, fireworks. Carla was glad that the response at Dammal was quieter, a matter of relief shot through with habitual wariness, so that Asha didn't have to face crowds rejoicing because the People were gone and the Way ended forever.

That evening, once Asha was asleep, she'd stayed up late with Amery reminiscing about Stefan, the War, all the many things they'd both seen and known in an era they both knew would soon fade into memory. The next day she'd written up the letter of intent that placed Asha definitively in her charge, since an outrunner child couldn't be allowed to roam free, not until a judgment circle freed her from Halka guardianship. Once that went out to the message net in the usual way, the two of them spent a last night in the mostly empty Halka quarters, and then washed, dressed, ate, shouldered packs and blanket rolls, and climbed the stair to Dammal Shelter's surface level and the doors to a wider world.

The trail west across the open ground was bare earth well packed: no surprises there, for thousands of sen Halka and tens of thousands of others had come that way since the building of Dammal Shelter just after the War. A little over two kilometers from the Shelter, the cleared area ended and the trail began zigzagging down a steep slope thick with trees. Carla recalled the last time she'd climbed that stretch of trail, one of a group of fifty sen Halka on their way to the fighting in the north, a heavy pack full of ammunition and grenades burdening her. Trail and trees were unaltered, or so they seemed just then, but she had changed and so had Eridan.

That first day's walk brought them just over ten kilometers to Amath Shelter, and another walk of equal length the next day took them to Varra Shelter, where Wind Gap began widening out to westward, opening onto the upland plains between the mountains and the eastern end of the Kaya Hills. By then they'd already begun to settle into a rhythm of travel: rise and leave early, set an unhurried pace, reach the next Shelter toward afternoon, and stay there until the next morning. So far north, most Shelters had at least one or two sen Halka in the Halka quarters: most of them grizzled veterans who had chosen places to settle down in old age, now and then someone younger drifting back south now that the fighting was over. She knew some of them, and most of the others knew of her, if only because she'd been part of the command circle at Mirien Shelter during the War. It made for some friendly conversations and some awkward ones, but she was used to that.

The Shelter folk were always helpful, and not only because Carla wore Halka black. She quickly got used to the way that Shelter radio staff sent word ahead that an old sen Halka and a young girl were on their way, and noted with amusement how often the Shelter folk assumed that Asha was her granddaughter. Well, what of it? she thought one evening, as she and Asha settled down to sleep in Halka quarters otherwise empty, after a long pleasant walk through open forest and a quiet evening talking about little things that didn't matter. If Stefan had fallen in love with her instead of Tamar, and they'd had children, one of their grandchildren might be Asha's age. The thought amused her, but it also brought a certain sense of completeness, as though the complexities of a troubled life had finally come out right at last.

So the journey unfolded. Three times, where there were long gaps between Shelters, she and Asha camped out under the stars. Carla marveled at the way that Asha could coax a little smokeless fire into producing enough heat to boil water; the two of them gathered edible fungoids and newly budded summer leaves to add to the travel food they'd brought with them; they slept curled up together and when morning came, stripped, bathed, and splashed each other in a nearby stream, laughing, while the sun dried dew off their blankets. Not so very long before, Carla knew well, an old woman and a girl could not have risked traveling alone in the north, much less sleeping out at night, for outrunners still found their way south too often, and before the War the risk of stray battle-drones was all too real.

Eridan was becoming a different world, and now and again the changes she saw unfolding around her left her speechless in amazement. We did that, we Halka, she thought one morning as she and Asha toweled off beside a stream and pulled clothing back on. We defeated the Directorate, we defeated the battle-drones they left behind, and we defeated the outrunners, so the people of Eridan can live their lives in peace. The thought glowed in her, a sunset glory to light the end of an era.

Weeks passed. By the time the two of them reached Mirien Shelter, Carla was tired enough that she needed a week of rest before going on, and that gave her the chance to spend hours talking with Tamar for what she knew would probably be the last time. When she and Asha left again she felt stronger, and the days that followed were as beautiful as a spring on Eridan could be, bright sun from a luminous blue sky, summer-leaves unfolding in a chorus of purples and blues, white windflowers slowly uncoiling and fluttering in the breeze above gray-violet meadowmoss, jewelflies and ground-scuttlers hatching from angular black eggs tucked in among fallen leaves and going to their differing destinies, and Asha's delighted gaze taking it all in, reminding Carla of her own youth.

Of course there were troubling notes now and then. The headaches came more and more insistently, and neither Asha's massaging fingers nor such medicines as the Shelter doctors gave Carla could do much more than blunt the pain. Other neurological symptoms began to show themselves, faint at first. She'd waited for them for eight years and knew the message they brought with them.

Then there was Stefan's final judgment, with its unsettling implications and its baffling last sentence. Most of the sen Halka she met in the Shelters where she and Asha stayed said nothing about it, but now and then one who'd read it and recognized her name asked her what she thought of it and what the future of the Halka order might be. To the latter question she could offer no answers at all. If the order followed Stefan's advice and did nothing about the change in the world, the consequences he'd traced out were inevitable: she could see that clearly enough, a shape in the innermind nearly close enough to touch. Yet the traditions and regulations that surrounded the Halka and shaped their actions forbade any other course: she could see that just as clearly. More than once she stayed up late talking with another sen Halka, trying to find some option that might keep the Halka order intact so that it could defend the Six Laws for centuries to come, and every time the discussion ended without result.

Now and then, too, Asha ended up huddled and miserable for a day or two, sometimes because of memories or bad dreams, sometimes for other reasons. She learned to avoid the children of the Shelter folk, for the moment they realized she was an outrunner child—and they always did, there was always some mistake that betrayed her—they went silent and backed away from her, and no words of hers or anyone else's could make them do otherwise.

All those were things she understood and expected. Another troubling note was less easy to interpret, however, and it began as a faint sound she caught in the Shelter radio rooms.

She heard it first at Mirien Shelter, one morning just before dawn when she'd gone to the radio room to see what the message net had to say: an old habit, she told herself, useless now but hard to break. The news was ordinary enough. The legalists who'd gone to the installation north of Dammal Shelter had sent to Zara for information on a historical question, and requested the written account Jerre had offered them: no surprises there. A respected legalist at a North Country shelter had penned a response to Stefan's final judgment and sent it out through the message net; Carla considered reading it, decided against it when the pain in her head spiked in response. A quarrel between two hill country Shelters had been settled by another circle of legalists, and a young woman who'd stolen valuables from a Shelter in the south and fled with them had been caught at another Shelter fifty kilometers away, and she and the valuables were being taken back by the Shelter folk themselves, to face whatever penalty her home Shelter might set. She finished reading the message logs, turned to leave the radio room.

Then she looked up sharply, listening to the static that came over the loudspeakers.

Exactly what she was hearing, she could not tell at first: a faint modulation of the static, something that seemed to recur at intervals. She stood there, focused subtle awareness on the sound, frowned when she perceived nothing meaningful. After a while, she went to the radio operator and said, "Do you notice anything different about the static?"

He glanced up at her, startled: nearly as old as she was, with a thin rim of gray hair around a bald scalp, eyeglasses perched on a great beak of a nose, tired eyes. Moments passed as he listened. "Yes," he said after a moment. "And it's not the first time we've had odd static in the last year or so. But I couldn't tell you what it is, sen Halka."

They both listened for a while, but whatever it was faded out, leaving the ordinary steady crackle. The operator shrugged, and Carla thanked him and went back to the Halka quarters.

Thereafter, as she and Asha resumed their journey south, she made a point of listening to the static in the radio rooms of each Shelter they passed. More often than not she heard nothing, and it took some time for her to work out that there were only two times of day when whatever it was could be heard, a short period around sunrise and another around sunset. That made no immediate sense, and it took even longer for her to realize that whatever it was, it was getting faintly louder as the weeks passed. Carla pondered that, and one evening wrote a letter about it to Jerre Amadan and sent it ahead to Zara.

2

The route she and Asha took south from Mirien Shelter led them along the foothills of the mountains. That was deliberate, for Carla felt her own mortality come closer as they walked,

and the thought that Asha might find a home among the resettled outrunners after she was gone was much on her mind.

One evening, weeks south of Mirien, she decided to talk to
Asha about that, and was startled to find the girl calm about
the prospect. "I know you are old," she said, ducking her head,
"and I will live long after I sing the death-song for you. If you
think it best that I go to live with the People in the south after
you are gone, I will do it."

"You should meet them, at least," said Carla. "We're not far
from where they are."

"Then I will meet them." She took Carla's hand in both of
hers. "But I will not go to live with them until you are gone."

"I wouldn't ask you to," said Carla. Asha's face lit up, and
she flung her arms around Carla, who put her own arms
around the girl and patted her shoulders.

Two days later they came to Ibril Shelter and found more
than a dozen sen Halka staying in the Halka quarters. "There's
a band of resettled outrunners in the foothills just east of here,"
one of them told Carla as they sat in the common room late that
evening, after Asha had gone to sleep, when cold stars glittered
outside the windows. "Almost a hundred of them, and another
band of fifty or so twenty kilometers further south."

"Have you had any trouble with them?" Carla asked.

A brisk shake of the head answered her. "They follow
something they call the New Way—all the resettled outrunners do that now. They live out in the open in barkcloth tents,
harvest meria bark, medicinal plants, anything the Shelters
want from the upland forests, and trade that for protein
and whatever else they need. They don't have guns—they
understand that we can't allow that—and the Shelter folk
are starting to get used to having them around. We make sure
that everyone feels safe and nobody gets cheated, and the
Halvedna have people with them. Mostly hermits up from
Andarre—the outrunners say that the hermits are the only
people they've met in the south who live in a way that makes
any sense to them."

That seemed promising, and Carla told Asha about it the next morning. The girl listened in perfect silence, her eyes round. When Carla finished, she ducked her head and said, "When should I meet them?"

"I need to rest for a day or two before we go on," Carla said. That was half true and half a decision of convenience, but Asha ducked her head at once and said, "Then you will rest and I will go meet them tomorrow."

In the morning, accordingly, she washed and dressed for travel, and went with a young sen Halka named Marden Dall— one of the few young sen Halka Asha had ever seen—who had been among the resettled outrunners a few days before and knew the way to their camp. They talked as they set out north of east through a forest of tall unfamiliar trees, passing through pools of shade and shafts of sun slanting down through the canopy of spreading blue summer leaves. Marden knew more about the resettled outrunners and their New Way than Carla had passed on, and he also had questions of his own, about Carla and the old man named Stefan that Asha had seen so briefly. "I had an uncle," he said. "His name was Toren Dall, and he died fighting battle-drones north of settled country the spring before the War. He knew Stefan Jatanni." He said the last words, Asha thought, the way someone might say *He defeated a hundred enemies* or *He went to Journey Star*, as though some greatness clung to the memory.

"I saw sen Jatanni once before he died," she said after another silence. "And I sang the death-song for him. Sen Dubrenden—" She knew by then to call her hearth-mother that around sen Halka or Shelter folk. "—said I should do that."

"I'm glad to hear that," Marden told her. "I think he would have felt honored."

That cheered her, and so did his words as they crossed a deep fast-flowing river on a wooden bridge and came to the mouth of a valley, where a creek flowed down to join the river. Marden pointed up it, toward where Asha could see distant shapes too angular and brightly colored to be trees. "Their camp's right up there. I'll come back an hour or so before sunset and wait for you here. We've brought others to them before; they'll want to talk with you, have you work with them for a while, so they can get to know you a little. They might take you to one of the hermits who lives near here."

Asha thanked him, ducked her head in farewell, and went up the valley toward the shapes: tents, she'd realized at first glance, hands and hands of them, dyed in the bright colors that the People had not dared to use in plain sight for many hands of lives. As she walked toward them, she could spot meria trees that had been stripped of their outer bark for barkcloth, neat little patches of bare earth where something had been dug out with digging sticks, and plenty of young edible fungoids, bone-white dots the size of her fingernails, but very few large enough to be worth harvesting and eating: signs of habitation she'd learned in earliest childhood, the marks that showed that a band of the People was somewhere close by. She'd had to fear those signs back then, for reasons she still tried not to think about too often, but those fears had become empty when the Way ended.

She came close enough that she could see people in among the tents, and watched them until she was sure that they saw her. Then she sat down on the meadowmoss not far from the creek, bowed her head, and waited. It was their choice to approach her or not: that had been the Way, and whether it was the New Way or not, it was the only Way she knew.

She did not have long to wait. An old man and two younger women approached her, stood a short distance away. With her head bowed, she could see them only to the waist. "Who are you, child?" the old man asked, his voice just as it should be, cautious but not unfriendly. "Where are you from?"

"My name is Asha," she responded without raising her head. "I lived with my hearth-brothers in the hills west of Pillar-of-Sky until winter's end. You need not tell me your names."

One of the women murmured to the other, and though Asha could not make out the words, the voice sounded pleased. "How did you come here?" the old man asked.

"One of the Silent brought me."

"The Halka," he corrected her.

"The Halka." She hazarded a fragile smile. "They gave me the hearth-peace, and one of them brought me south to—" She had to struggle briefly to remember the name. "To Ibril Shelter. She told me of the People who live here, of the New Way, and another sen Halka, Marden Dall, walked with me here this morning."

"We know Marden Dall," said the old man. One of the women, the one who had murmured, spoke then: "Asha, my name is Kiran."

"Kiran," the girl repeated.

"Did you come here wishing to dwell with us?"

It was more, much more, than Asha had hoped. "I have a task to finish," she said, trying to keep her voice calm. "The sen Halka who brought me south is old and ill, and I help her as a hearth-child should. But when she leaves to walk across the sky to the World That Is Gone, maybe there will be a place for me."

"Maybe there will," said Kiran, her voice kindly. "Come with us now. You should meet others and see something of the New Way."

"I welcome that," said Asha, beaming. She stood up and raised her head.

The welcoming look on Kiran's face lasted only for an instant, replaced by horror. The other woman backed away, equally aghast. The old man stepped forward, took her chin in an ungentle hand, tipped her face upwards. "You have an Indweller," he said in a voice grown suddenly harsh.

"It does not speak to me," Asha said.

The old man let go of her, shook his hand as though to fling something unclean from it. "You have heard of the New Way," he said in the same harsh voice. "It is like a tree with many branches. One of those branches is that things like the one you have inside you must never again come among us. We know their counsels and their lies and we refuse them. Go." His voice shook. "We will not kill you because of our vow, but never will any who follow the New Way offer you the hearth-peace. Go and do not come back!" One long finger jabbed down the valley the way she had come.

She stared up at him a moment longer, appalled and hurt, and then ducked her head, knowing that she had no other choice. "I will go," she said. "If I had known I would not have come. I am sorry." They stood facing her, unyielding, and she turned and started back down the valley toward the bridge.

3

Tears streamed down her face by the time she came to the bridge, and for once it did not matter to her that she wept in the sight of Sun. It would be many hours, she knew, before Marden Dall came back for her. She could find her way back to Ibril Shelter herself, she knew that too, but the thought of making that solitary journey and then explaining to Marden and Carla why the People had turned her away—all at once, that felt too bitter to bear. She slowed as she reached the middle of the bridge, went to the rail, watched the water as it streamed past, cold and deep and swift. It would be so much easier, she thought, to climb over the rail and fall, and let the river take her and her sorrow with it all the way to the ocean.

Please do not, said a voice inside her, a voice she was certain was not her own.

Baffled, she stood there, and then realized what it had to be. *You.* She sent the thought deep into herself, where the Indweller was.

Yes.

You! Pain and grief kindled suddenly into fury. *You would not speak to my hearth-fathers or my hearth-mothers or my hearth-brothers, and you let them go to their deaths. You would not speak to sen*

Alhaden. You would not speak to me. Why do you speak to me now? Is it only to save your own life that you speak? She could sense it watching her in silence, and fury flared again. *When my hearth-mother Carla is gone I will take a knife and drive it through you. My life will be worthless then, for no one anywhere will welcome me, and if I have nothing else then, at least I will know that I kill you as I kill myself—*

Just then a wicked thought occurred to her, so wicked she would have never have let herself think it if not for her sorrow and her rage. *No, I will not wait,* she said to the Indweller. *I know the herb that will force you out of me. I will chew it and swallow the juices, and I will spew you out onto bare ground, and I will watch you twist and shrivel like an edible fungoid on a hot rock, and I will laugh. I will laugh and be glad as you die.*

The Indweller regarded her, and in the silence she began to taste a bitterness and a grief greater than her own. *There were times,* it said, *many of them, when I would have begged for either of those, the knife or the bare dry ground. Nor do I deserve better. Yet I will ask you not to do it, because there is a purpose before me now.*

I care nothing for your purpose, she told it, but the white-hot fury that had seized her was trickling away somehow.

I know. Perhaps I can offer you some gift in exchange for letting me live.

I want nothing from you.

You do not yet know what I can offer. Let us walk back to the Shelter and talk as we go. If nothing I can give you will matter enough to you, then you will need to find the herb anyway, and we both know that it does not grow beside rivers, or any place where the ground is wet.

She considered that, and after a moment nodded and went the rest of the way across the bridge. Sun was higher, but she had grown up knowing how to find her way in wild country. It took only the slightest effort to correct for the changing angle of the shadows and strike out through the forest toward Ibril Shelter.

Why would you not talk to me or to anyone else? she demanded of the Indweller.

Because I wished only to die, it said. *Once the Halka took you with them, that changed along with other things, but I do not trust the Halka, and I have the purpose I mentioned. No, I will not name it. You will know soon enough and so will every human being on Eridan.*

Asha pondered that. *Why do you not trust the Halka?*

The bitterness and grief she'd sensed earlier showed itself again. *If I answered that question and you spoke of it to Carla, as of course you would, she would shoot us both dead before you finished speaking. If she did not, another of the Halka would do it.*

I want to die, Asha told it, bursting into tears again. *The Shelter folk will not have me. The People will not have me. When my hearth-mother Carla is gone no one anywhere will offer me food or shelter or comfort. Why should I hide from Halka bullets?*

You do not want to die, it told her. *You merely want to feel the pain less than you do. I can do that for you. Shall I show you?*

She stopped walking, drew in a ragged breath. *I want nothing from you,* she told it again, but she knew the words were a lie even as she said them, and she was sure the Indweller knew the same thing.

I will show you, it said, confirming her guess. *If you walk it will take a little less time.* She considered that, started walking again toward the shelter.

In the country where she'd lived until the Halka came, up against the edges of the purple northern barrens, the spring rains sometimes came sweeping in from the west like mist, blotting out the distant hills and shrouding the nearer ones in drifting veils of gray. That was what Asha thought of as she walked, for something swept across her mind like the rain, shrouding the miseries that pressed close to her and blotting out those that were further off. The miseries remained as the hills did, she knew that, but with each step that she took it became a little easier not to think of them.

I do not want to thank you, she admitted after a time.

*Then do not thank me. Think of this as repayment for the hurt
I have caused you.*

I—I will. Then: *How do you do it?*

You do not know the words I would need to use to explain it to you.

She nodded after a moment. *There are so many things I do not
know.*

Another silence came and went. Wind hissed in the great
splayed summer-leaves far overhead, let splashes of morning
sunlight down onto the forest floor. *Then I will offer you a
thing in exchange for my life,* the Indweller said. *I will teach you
about plants.*

By then the misery was veiled so thickly that Asha managed
a little scornful sniff. *I already know about plants.*

Not the way I know about them. All at once, without any voli-
tion of hers, her attention turned to a patch of windflowers that
rose from the forest floor, feathery bone-colored shapes half
uncoiled, rising already as high as her knees. *Do you know that
plant? Can you tell me its name, where it grows, what it tells about
the soil beneath it?*

It was a plant of the south and she did not know it. Caught,
she reddened. *I cannot.*

In the moment that followed, without any other change she
could sense, something opened in her, like a door in a Shelter
swinging open to let her into a room she had never seen before.
She knew in that moment that the plant was called Calley's
windflower in the language she knew, and *Pinnifer calleyi* in
another language she did not know. She knew that it grew in
hilly country across the southern half of the northern continent,
though what a continent was she had no idea. She knew that it
grew where the soil was rich in something called calcium,
and not otherwise. She knew that it reproduced by seeds and
not by spores, though the difference between those two things
was far from clear to her. She knew a hundred other details
about it, most of them reaching away to touch other things she
did not know.

That knowledge is yours now, the Indweller said. *You will not forget it even if you chew leaves of* Galax multiloba *and spit me out onto the bare ground. Do you wish to learn about another plant? Choose any plant you like.*

Dazed, she pondered that, and then walked over to one of the great soaring trees. *This one,* she said to the Indweller. *Teach me about it.*

Another door opened inside her, and she knew that it was called daula in her language and *Daula altiora* in the other language, that it was a sporophyte whatever that meant, and a member of the family Ambifoliaceae whatever that was. Facts came crashing into her mind, many more than the Calley's windflower had brought with it, for the windflower was one of many windflowers but the daula was the peg around which countless other plants, and other living things too, traced the circles of their lives. There was so much that before it all finished settling into place, she had walked more than half the distance back to the Shelter.

Can you teach me about every plant there is?

Of course, the Indweller told her. *Not all at once, but one at a time, as I have done. You may learn one more plant today, and then tomorrow I can teach you more.* It paused. *If I do that, and teach you plants every day, will you let me live?*

She did not answer at once. Off in the distance, through gaps in the trees, she could see the soaring tree-things—wind turbines, she reminded herself, my hearth-mother calls them wind turbines—that rose above Ibril Shelter. The prospect of going there and explaining what had happened to Carla and Marden and the other sen Halka had somehow lost all its sting. More than anything else, that made her want to agree, but she temporized. *Teach me another plant,* she said to the Indweller, *and then I will choose.*

The presence in her had no lips to smile with, but she could sense amusement from it, knew that it knew she had already made her choice. *Certainly. Choose any plant you like.*

She glanced around, spotted a little plant with odd thick leaves huddled in among the roots of one of the great daulas. It looked nothing like the other plants she knew. She walked up to it and thought at the Indweller, *This one.*

Something a little like a rueful laugh flickered through the presence inside her. *Yes, it would be that one.*

A third door opened, but unexpected things waited inside it. The plant's name was *Mnemophora oswaldia* in the language she didn't know, and in her own language it had no name at all, just a taut warning that it was not to be mentioned to anyone who wasn't authorized by the Office of Restricted Projects, whatever that might be. It grew here and there in daula forests, hiding in the shadows with its own thick root tangled in among the roots of the daulas, and it spread by spores like most of the plants of Eridan, but most of what she suddenly knew about it was an incomprehensible torrent, in which words like *biochemistry* and *psychology* and *collective unconscious* tumbled around each other, joined somehow to a place called Andarre and people called hermits and then, suddenly, a single word she recognized, freighted with incomprehension and dread: Halka.

I do not understand, she said to the Indweller.

I know. Its silent voice seemed weary. *I will explain it to you as you learn more words and more things. Will you let me live?*

Yes, she said after a moment. *I—I will.*

The wind turbines of Ibril Shelter beckoned. She turned away from the strange little plant, began the final part of the walk back.

4

"Please be seated," the eldest of the sen Halka said, and motioned toward the circle. Asha ducked her head, acknowledging, and settled next to Carla, in *ten ielindat* like the others. Her soft purple Shelter robe provided the only spot of color amid gray concrete walls, pale wooden floor, and Halka black.

Carla had just a moment to give the girl a glance before the groupmind prompted her to enter into rapport with the other members of the circle. The acts that followed were smooth as river-rounded stones after so many years—the three deep breaths and the murmured phrase, the shift from first to second level of trance, the quick movements of thought that acknowledged the other sen Halka in the circle. The groupmind had been established for years—the circle at Ibril Shelter had been set up as soon as outrunners were resettled nearby, ready to serve as a command circle or a judgment circle as need required. Though neither had been necessary, the circle had stayed, partly to reassure the Shelter folk nearby and partly because there was so little else for sen Halka to do. That made things much simpler when Asha had returned that day with her astonishing news.

"Asha," the Speaker of the circle said then. "Please tell us everything you told sen Dubrenden about the Indweller earlier today."

Asha ducked her head again, and began to speak. She had to struggle with tears when she explained about the outrunners and how they had turned her away, and again when she spoke of standing on the bridge and wanting to die, but as she began to recount the conversation with the symbiont her voice grew calm, and she repeated what she'd learned about the three plants as though she was reading aloud from a book she did not understand. The similarity was strong enough that Carla had to remind herself that Asha had never learned how to read.

The things she'd learned about Calley's windflower and the daula tree were ordinary botany, Carla knew enough to guess that much, and one of the other sen Halka in the circle—a gray-haired man who'd trained and worked as a botanist in a hill country Shelter before the War, and taken baya after it—confirmed it with quick movements of awareness that the groupmind shared with the others. It was the third plant that mattered most, and here Asha's voice faltered. "I'm not supposed to repeat what I learned to anyone who is not authorized by the Office of Restricted Projects," she said, stumbling over the unfamiliar words. "Under penalty of internment in a factory camp."

That caused a ripple of shock around the circle, but the Speaker, a veteran of the War named Erec Ennasen, simply nodded. "The Office of Restricted Projects no longer exists," he said. "Its duties were taken over by the Halka more than two hundred years ago. On behalf of the Halka order I authorize you to tell this circle everything."

Relief showed visibly on Asha's face. Over the minutes that followed, as she plodded through words and concepts she clearly didn't understand, the groupmind of the circle became more and more tautly focused. "The current state of knowledge in biochemistry and psychology alike is insufficient to make any sense of the experimental results," the girl finished in a halting voice, "and anecdotal data offer little help. One theory suggests that compounds in *Mnemophora oswaldia* somehow weaken the barrier between the conscious and subconscious minds, but this would not explain some of the effects. The old hypothesis of a collective unconscious may be the only way to account for these effects.

"The difficulty before us at this point is that the potential uses of *Mnemophora oswaldia* are no longer an academic matter. The plant is central to the practices of the Andarre hermits, and the decision the Directorate made to tolerate the hermits, in order to give malcontents and the irrationally minded a harmless distraction, seems singularly unwise in retrospect. Ever since the first rising at Andarre, Security Command personnel have been confronted by insurgents who act as though they have the capacity to read their opponents' thoughts, and recent intelligence reports have tracked the rise of a movement or organization that seems to be exploiting this capacity systematically in combat—a force that apparently calls itself Halka. What they might be able to do as a result of their own research

into this plant remains one of the great unknowns we face."
Asha looked up then. "I hope you know what that means,
sen Halka."

Despite the solemnity of judgment, that got flickers of
amusement from the circle. "Some of it," said Ennasen. "Did
anything else happen after you learned that?"

"I reminded the Indweller that I promised to tell sen
Dubrenden when it talked, and what it talked about. It told
me it wished I would not, but knew that I would. I told it that
the Halka had been kind to me and would be kind to it. It did
not answer. So I came here and waited for sen Dubrenden to
come back from the doctor, and then told her everything but
what I told you about the third plant, and she sent for you and
the others."

"The Indweller has the right to speak to us if it wishes," said
Ennasen.

"It will not speak," Asha said after a moment. "It is like this
again." She placed hands over ears, clenched her eyes shut.

The Speaker nodded. "Then we will proceed to judgment."
He closed his eyes and entered rapport, and the groupmind
relayed his thoughts to Carla and the others. *While this is not
a formal judgment circle, it is our responsibility to assess this case
and forward a preliminary judgment to other sen Halka. You are all
familiar with the relevant traditions and rulings. How would you
propose dealing with this case?*

No response, Carla told it. *I cannot answer impartially.*

Please explain, the groupmind said in answer.

*I have too much affection for the girl to want any harm to come
to her. I am aware that my judgment will be distorted by that.*

Acknowledged. The groupmind paused as though relaying
that to the others. *With that taken into account, what proposal
would you offer?*

Carla, used to the habits of circle groupminds, had half
expected that response, and took a moment to recall as much
as she could about the relevant case law. *She should remain*

under close Halka supervision. She has already been taught about the Six Laws, and she should be requested to inform the Halka at once if the symbiont suggests to her that she should break any of them. She should be taken to a place where what she learns about botany can be copied down and assessed. That is what I would suggest.

Acknowledged, the groupmind repeated. A silence came and went, edged with innerspeech conversations Carla could sense but not hear. *A consensus exists,* it said then.

Present it, Emmasen instructed.

In the still center of awareness, the voice of the groupmind:

First: *The girl has done nothing contrary to any of the Six Laws, and her welfare therefore cannot be disregarded by this circle.*

Then: *What actions the symbiont may have taken in the past cannot be judged by the available evidence. Its actions during the time under assessment do not include a violation of any of the Six Laws, and past decisions have consistently ruled that life forms, even artificial ones, are not machines subject to the strictures of the Fifth Law.*

Finally: *The proposal offered by Carla Dubrenden sen Halka is the most defensible of the options available to us.*

Eleven sen Halka pondered this. *Is this the considered judgment of the circle?* Erec Ennasen asked.

The response came back promptly: *Yes.*

The Speaker broke rapport. The others did the same. "Thank you," Carla said to them.

Ennasen nodded, and turned to the girl. "Asha, have you been taught the Six Laws?"

She ducked her head. "Yes, sen Halka."

"If the Indweller asks you to break any of them, in even the slightest way, you must not do it, and you must tell sen Dubrenden or another sen Halka at once. Do you understand?"

Again the ducking motion. "Yes, sen Halka."

"Thank you. You should go now." A glance and a flicker of the innerspeech passed the same message to Carla, who responded in kind and got to her feet. Asha stood also and took her hand, and the two of them left the common room together.

They had nowhere in particular to go—it was simply a matter of courtesy among Halka for those not part of a circle to leave it to conclude its work and formulate the structure of the written judgment the Speaker would pen shortly—so Carla let habit lead her down the corridor to the radio room, close to the Halka quarters as always. Asha clung to her hand, but Carla sensed that the girl's attention was elsewhere. With the Indweller? She guessed so. She waited until Asha seemed less preoccupied, and then asked, "Talking to it?"

Asha glanced up at her. "Yes. It doesn't know what the Six Laws are. I tried to explain them, but I'm not sure I did it well. Maybe you can explain them again to me sometime."

"Of course," said Carla, smiling. "I know them tolerably well."

That earned her a luminous smile. They walked a little further, up to the door of the radio room. Golden-red light of sunset spilled out the door—the Shelter radio room had skylights, a luxury few Shelters further north had been able to risk in the old dangerous days. Carla opened her mouth to say something to the girl, but stopped, stared into the radio room.

The strangeness in the static was audible again: something faint and rhythmic moving through the familiar hiss of the loudspeakers. This time it was just enough louder than it had been to allow her to recognize it: the low rushing or rustling sound that had pulsed through the sibilant noise at the Colonial government facility north of Dammal Shelter, the building the outrunners had called the Place of Whispers.

A moment later, subtle awareness made her glance at Asha. The girl felt nothing more than a sense of perplexity, Carla could tell that, but something else looked out through her eyes and listened through her ears with cold intensity. Carla regarded the girl for another moment, then said, "Asha, does the Indweller know what that sound is?"

Asha paused for a conversation Carla could not hear. "It will not say," she said then. "I think it knows, but it will not say."

The low rhythmic pulse continued. Through the skylights in the room beyond, the red glow of sunset faded as evening deepened toward night.

5

They left Ibril Shelter the next morning, veering away from the mountains and any risk of further meetings with resettled outdwellers. The weather remained mostly clear, though high streamers of cloud spread now and again across the sky, first heralds of the rains to come. The forest thinned, but that meant a greater range of plants, and the Indweller kept its promise, installing knowledge of botany in Asha's mind: three or four plants each day to begin with, working up from there to a dozen or more, and to cascades of more abstract knowledge as well. Each evening Carla had her repeat some of what she'd learned during the day, and listened as much to to the growing richness of the girl's vocabulary and the increased complexity of her sentences as to any details of botany. So far south, Shelters stood as close together as the Second Law allowed, so there were no more nights out under the stars, but some of the days were as luminous in Carla's mind as those in the first weeks of the southward journey.

There would not be many more such days. Carla could tell that easily enough, from her own flagging strength, the neurological symptoms that grew harder to ignore, the worsening headaches. When they left Ibril Shelter she'd hoped to be able to take Asha all the way south to Zara, but long before clouds started thickening toward the rains, she was certain she would not get that far. Her plans contracted to the immediate necessities: go as far south as she could with Asha before the rains set in or her health failed, meet the inevitable there, arrange for Asha to go with another sen Halka the rest of the way to Zara, and send a letter to Jerre and Amery asking them to take care of the girl.

With that decision made, it became easier for Carla to settle into the rhythm of their travel, set aside her memories of the years behind her and her thoughts about the days ahead, let the pace they took from Shelter to Shelter depend on her own condition, and enjoy the spring weather: beams of sunlight splashing down through the thinning forest, windflowers uncoiling to spread featherlike before the breeze, broad patches of meadowmoss soft and springy beneath her boots, ground-scuttlers scurrying out of their path and jewelflies darting here and there beneath the trees.

That lasted for eight bright days. Toward evening of the eighth day, as the sun sank toward the broad flat sweep of the plains to westward, the two of them crossed the bare space where a protective ring of metal had once warded off battle-drones, reached the main entrance to yet another Shelter, went through familiar routines before settling into the Halka quarters for the night. Another sen Halka was there, the people at the door told Carla, and she was startled to find a familiar face in the Halka common room: Tomas Gerdan, who'd come through Mirien Shelter while she'd been there and read along with her the message from Dammal Shelter.

That was pleasant, and so was the casual conversation they made over the evening meal, in which Asha joined tentatively. Later, though, when Asha was already asleep and the two of them sipped a final bowl of tebbe each before settling down for the night, Tomas gave her an uncertain glance. "May I ask a question?"

"Of course." A flicker of innerspeech let him know that the words meant what they said.

"Thank you." He paused, gathered his thoughts. "I've read Stefan Jatanni's final judgment, and I have no idea what to make of it."

That earned him a little weary laugh from Carla. "I don't know anyone who does. If everything goes well I'll be in Zara in another two months or so, and I plan on asking the legalists there what they think of it."

A silence surrounded them for a time, freighted with issues that still mattered more to Carla than she liked to admit to herself. "You were part of the command circle at Mirien during the War, weren't you?" When Carla nodded: "When I was in training, my sponsor taught me that the Mirien circle overturned more than one Halka tradition during the fighting." She nodded again, and he went on. "I wonder if the order needs to do something similar."

Carla considered that. "What are you thinking?"

"I don't know. I haven't gotten that far yet." He met her gaze squarely. "If Stefan Jatanni is right we won't be able to uphold the Six Laws for long. The First Law allows us to interfere in the affairs of communities in defense of the Six Laws. Maybe we need to take that in a broader sense now."

"The Convention of Zara," she said, "explicitly forbids the Halka from doing anything of the kind, and the Six Laws don't override the rest of the Convention. We can request help but we can't require it. Even during the War that rule stayed in place."

"Then sooner or later the Convention will have no one left to defend it."

"I know." When his gaze didn't waver: "Tell me this. Would you seriously propose taking Shelter goods at gunpoint or forcing unwilling people to take baya? That's what would be required, you know."

His gaze faltered then, and he closed his eyes. "No," he admitted. Echoes of his own ordeal under the dwimmerwine, sharp-edged in memory, surged up in his mind so forcefully that Carla had to make an effort not to read them. "Of course not. But there has to be some way the order can keep going."

He knew better. She could sense that, too, but had mercy on him. "That's why I want to see what the legalists at Zara have to say about it. Amery Lundra's there already, of course. If there's something the order can do about this, she'll find it."

Tomas gave her a relieved look. "You're right, of course. I haven't studied law beyond the basics." Considering her: "I've thought more than once about remedying that, now that the outrunners are gone. Do you know if sen Lundra is qualified to teach students yet?"

"Not as far as I know. If you want to find a legalist to teach you, though, you might stop at Kerriol. There's been a judgment circle working there for three or four years now, dealing with whatever comes over the message net, and I know some of the legalists."

His face lit up, he thanked her, and what little conversation passed between them before they went to their sleeping rooms stayed far from troubling subjects. Still, as Carla changed into her sleeping robe, settled on the mat next to Asha's, and got her blankets arranged around her, Tomas' words and the ragged emotions behind them circled in her thoughts. How many other sen Halka, she wondered, brooded that night over the bitter paradox Stefan had traced out, the inevitability with which the final triumph of the Halka would be the Halka's undoing? How many of them might consider taking the step the Convention of Zara forbade, using force to preserve the Halka, and in the process turn the Halka into a mirror of the thing it was born to destroy? Those questions kept watch in the night, unanswerable, until sleep finally took her.

6

The next morning they turned south, following the ragged line where trees on the east gave way to sweeping plains of violet meadowmoss to the west. Lacking larger plants to learn about, Asha turned her attention to the moss, borrowed the hand lens that Carla carried like every other sen Halka—one of the lesser tools of the Halka, but one with an ancient place in the order's traditions—and flopped on her belly when they stopped to rest, studying the featherlike shapes that made up half of the moss, the fungoidal threads that made up the other half. Carla watched her, sensed the silent whispering of the symbiont's voice in the girl's nervous system, used that to distract herself from questions she did not want to think about.

It was after the third such rest that she spotted a stark white shape jutting from the plains southwest of them. She recognized it at once, glanced at Asha, made a quick decision. "Do you see that?" she said, pointing.

Asha ducked her head, acknowledging. "What is it?"

"A monument." Asha didn't know the word, and it took a little while to explain the concept, but when she grasped it she said, "May I see it?"

"I think you should," said Carla. "There are four of them on Eridan, and every child goes to see one of them before they're much older than you are now." That was more than enough for Asha, and within a few minutes they were crossing the moss plains toward the white shape.

It rose up as they approached, a soaring rectangular shape of white stone as tall as the towers that held up a Shelter's wind turbines. Asha's eyes widened. Carla, who'd learned in childhood how much labor over how many years had gone into the four monuments, watched her and nodded. She recalled with sudden aching clarity an autumn day long years in the past, a group of children—herself among them—leaving an unfamiliar Shelter to walk to a different monument with the same wide eyes and the same silent uncertainty.

They came to its foot eventually and walked around to the other side, where two words were carved in huge letters high up on the stone, and a bronze sculpture group, larger than life, stood on a low pedestal thrust out from the monument. The two words were ANNUM TAL, and the sculpture portrayed a mass of sprawled corpses, gaunt and contorted. In the midst of them, a single living figure—a woman dressed in rags—rose up on one knee and reached out both arms toward the silence of the sky.

"Something happened here," said Asha, her voice low with dread.

"Yes. A very long time ago." A fragment of memory came to Carla's aid then. "The death-song talks about places of dying, about how the People fled into the forest to escape them. Do you know anything more about those?"

Asha glanced up suddenly, as though the question shocked her. "Yes. All the People knew of the places of dying. There were songs about them I learned when I was very small. In those days we were not the People yet, and the Others—the Shelter folk were not the Shelter folk and the Halka were not the Halka. That was the time of the Rulers." She said the word as though it tasted foul. "If you displeased them, or for no reason at all, they would send you to one of the places of dying to work with too little food and too little rest until you died."

"This is one of those places," said Carla. "Annum Tal, one of the factory camps of the Directorate—that's what the Rulers called themselves. Almost a million people died here." She hadn't been sure how well Asha remembered the larger number-names, but the appalled look on the girl's face answered that question at once. "This is why the Halka are the Halka. The Halka came into being to end this, and once we destroyed the Directorate, we pledged to keep anything like this from happening ever again."

Asha regarded her for a long moment, then came over to her, put her arms around Carla's waist, held her tight, and said, "Thank you." Carla returned the hug, drew in a long ragged breath, bent to kiss the top of the girl's head.

They left the site of Annum Tal a few minutes later and set out toward the wind turbines that marked the site of the nearest Shelter. All the way there, something silent and cold seemed to hover in the landscape, or maybe it hovered in Carla alone. She could not tell. As they walked, she thought about the outrunners—the People, as Asha still called them from time to time—and the chill and the silent void deepened around her.

We did to them what the Directorate did to us: that was the thought that circled through her mind over and over again as they walked. We starved the outrunners, we harried them, we drove them to their deaths or shot them dead ourselves. Was that why Stefan had written his final judgment as he had, setting out the final crisis of the Halka and then proposing that nothing should be done about it? Had he judged the Halka order, there at the last, and found it worthy of no better fate? Memory stirred, bitter: this child who clings to my hand knows that I killed her hearth-brother in front of her eyes—

The rest of the thought unfolded itself remorselessly: And the hearth-brother, if he was old enough at the time, helped kill and eat Asha's birth family, who killed and ate others, Shelter folk more likely than not among them. In a hideous moment of insight Carla could see death following on death, outrunners killing Shelter folk, Halka killing outrunners, all the way back to the time of the Directorate, to an era of battle-drones and factory camps and a dream of rekindling life on Earth that had almost ended human life on Eridan. That terrible image filled Carla's mind as they crossed the last kilometer or so to the Shelter.

Its name was Cadell Shelter—she learned that after they arrived, and wondered why she hadn't remembered it, for she'd studied maps as they made their way south. The Halka quarters were otherwise empty, but the Shelter folk had kept them clean. There Carla and Asha bathed, ate a pleasant meal with two members of the Shelter council and their families, talked about what Asha had learned about meadowmoss once they were by themselves again, and settled down to sleep while the last traces of sunset were still visible in the western sky.

By the next morning Carla knew that they would be traveling no further. Overnight the clouds had turned from a high thin overcast to billowing gray masses heavy with moisture, and by the time the two of them had washed and eaten, distant thunder rumbled through the Shelter's ventilation ducts and heat lightning flared bright and formless in the clouds. She and Asha sat in the quiet of the Halka quarters and started talking about what they would do next and where they would go, but before that conversation could get far, the first raindrops flung themselves against windows nearby. The two of them looked at each other. Another flurry of rain came down, and lightning blazed overhead. By the time the thunder rolled the rain was falling so heavily that the view out the windows was a wet blur, and fresh cool air scented with rain came in gusts through the ventilation system.

Watching the rain fall, Carla breathed a silent thank you to the unpredictable spring weather of Eridan. When she'd blinked groggily awake that morning she'd assessed her failing strength and wondered if perhaps it might be wiser to stay at Cadell Shelter. All through the rhythms of the morning she'd brooded over the same question. Was she simply tired after the long walk south, or was there more to it than that? She could not tell, and the rain made the question irrelevant.

The next morning, though she'd spent half the previous day and nearly all night sleeping, she felt no better rested, and Asha's massage did little to dull an inescapable headache. She went to talk to the Shelter medical staff early in the day and arranged for an appointment with the doctor late that afternoon, but she already knew well enough what that would reveal. That afternoon, as Asha sat staring at nothing and tried to absorb certain elements of botany that went past the names and uses of individual plants, Carla wrote the letter to Amery Lundra she'd known she would have to write, asking Amery and Jerre to find a place for Asha. Though she'd rehearsed what she wanted to say countless times on the walk south, writing the letter was a slow process, and she had only just finished when it was time for her to head down to see the doctor and face the inevitable.

She was back hours later. She and Asha ate a meal together in the companionable silence of those who have said all they need to say, and made an early night of it. It took only a few minutes for the steady rushing of rain on the window to lull Asha to sleep, but for once Carla could find no sleep in her, and Halka disciplines that should have taken care of the difficulty proved unavailing. After a time, she sat up, got her sleeping robe settled around her, and gazed out the window at the rain-washed darkness.

Minutes passed, and then a hoarse whisper spoke behind her: "Carla."

She glanced back, startled. Subtle awareness told her that there was no one in the sleeping room but her and Asha, and yet the voice hadn't sounded like Asha's at all.

"Carla." The voice spoke again, and this time subtle awareness let Carla sense Asha's lips moving in the darkness.

"Asha?" she asked, startled.

The answer came at once, in the same hoarse whisper. "No."

"You're the Indweller."

"Yes." Before Carla could respond: "You are dying."

"Yes." It was easier to say the word than she'd expected. "Yes, I am."

"There is an alternative," said the voice.

The rain drummed on the window for a long while as Carla sat there, half of her certain that she didn't know what alternative the Indweller offered her, half of her just as certain that she knew exactly what it meant. "Go on," she said at last.

CHAPTER 4

THE ROAD TO JOURNEY STAR

1

Spring stood poised on the edge of summer in a blue and
cloudless sky as Asha and Carla climbed the slope through
knee-high windflowers. They took the way slowly, for Carla
wasn't strong, and had to stop at intervals to catch her breath
and gather her strength for the next stage of the climb. Asha,
smiling, kept pace with her. The two of them said what had
little to be said and otherwise let the wind in the flowers con-
verse for them. Faded memories pointed Carla to the right
route, and they crested the low ridge at a point where the land
fell away and gave a matchless view of the broad valley below:
the valley, the rising hills beyond it, and Zara in the middle, not
quite shaped like any other Shelter on Eridan.

Something besides the wind turbines and concrete roofs of
Zara broke the sweep of meadowmoss below them, something
Carla didn't recognize at first and Asha didn't recognize at
all: a tall slim white shape that stood on a concrete pad, rising
like a small tower half a kilometer from the foot of the ridge
and a full kilometer from Zara. Little shapes that had to be
people clustered around the concrete pad, began to move away
from it.

"Bright Earth," Carla said. "I had no idea he was that far along."

"What is it?" asked Asha.

"A rocket."

Asha gave her a puzzled look, then remembered. "The thing that will go to *Journey Star*."

"Yes. I don't think this one's going there yet, but eventually, yes."

The people kept moving away, heading back behind other concrete shapes that Carla suddenly realized were shaped to ward off blasts. An instant later she caught the implication, gestured for Asha to sit down on the meadowmoss, and joined her there. To the girl's questioning look: "Unless I'm very wrong, we're about to see something astonishing."

The people got behind the sheltering concrete. A few minutes passed, and then suddenly smoke shot out from the base of the rocket, where it rested on the concrete pad. As the roar of its engine reached the watchers on the ridge, the white shape began to rise, slowly at first, atop a pillar of smoke and flame. Asha let out a cry of amazement. The rocket picked up speed and soared straight up into blue distance until neither of them could see it any more.

"Where will it go?" Asha asked.

"I have no idea, but we can find out." She started to rise, and Asha stood up at once, took her hand, and helped her to her feet. A moment of searching through blurred memories pointed Carla toward the trail that led down to Zara.

Something close to an hour passed before the trail brought them to the foot of the ridge, and meadowmoss stretched out before them to the concrete shapes and beyond. Long before they got to the pad where the rocket had been, someone left the shadow of the concrete and came hurrying over to meet them. It was no surprise to Carla when the distance closed and she recognized Amery Lundra.

"Carla!" she said when they came within speaking distance. "Welcome to Zara. We got your letters, of course. You're well?"

The old woman gestured: yes and no. "I had some rough patches on the way south but I'm still on my feet. Asha's been endlessly helpful."

"I'm glad to hear that." Amery turned to the girl. "Asha, it's good to see you again. Thank you for taking care of Carla."

Asha ducked her head, acknowledging. "My name is Asha Dubrenden now."

"I'm glad to hear that." Then, to Carla: "You're not the only welcome guest here, you know. Would you care to guess who else arrived a few days ago?" When Carla motioned for her to go on: "Tamar."

Carla blinked in evident surprise. "That astonishes me."

"It astonished everyone. I expected her to stay at Mirien for the rest of her life. Still, it's true—she's retired as a mindhealer and come to Zara to do research. We'll see her this evening." She motioned toward the concrete shelter. "Jerre's over with the radio team. He'll be delighted to see you both. Did you see the launch?"

They crossed the meadowmoss, talking about the rocket. All the while Carla considered Amery. She'd expected to find her in the heavy black robes of a Halka legalist, not in a short robe and trousers—Halka black, to be sure, but a light comfortable fabric, not the sturdy barkcloth gear the Halka traditionally wore. That hinted at other, greater changes.

Jerre Amadan was in the midst of a small crowd, crouched over a mass of complicated electronic gear. He was supervising the work of a younger man Carla was sure she had seen somewhere, but sprang up as soon as Carla and Asha came into sight and hurried over to them. "Welcome to Zara, both of you. I'm sure Amery was too polite to mention it, but we were both worried about you, Carla."

"I was worried about me. Still, here I am." Then: "Tell us about the launch. We got to see it from the ridge."

"I wish I could have been there to watch," said Jerre. "This was a test of the first stage. The rocket that's going to go to *Journey Star* will have two stages, one stage to go above the atmosphere and the other to get to *Journey Star*'s orbit, and getting the first stage in working order was one of the big hurdles. The second stage should be easier, though the capsule for the crew's going to take a lot of hard work."

A faint rhythmic sound came through the air then, almost exactly like a distant helicopter. Carla glanced around and then gave Jerre a puzzled look, for she saw nothing in the air in any direction. Jerre grinned, and a flicker of subtle awareness prompted her: *Up.* She followed the prompt, and saw a tiny dot high overhead with a faint blur around it. A minute or two passed before she was sure it was coming closer.

By then Jerre had gone back to the young man at the electronic gear. Following him, Carla saw that the young man was staring into a little glass screen with utter concentration, and both his hands gripped something that looked uncannily like the controls of a helicopter. The noise from above grew louder. Finally, as she gazed upward at the distant descending shape, Carla recognized it: the rocket she and Asha had watched from the ridge had somehow sprouted helicopter blades from its upper end, and those formed a whirling disk above it. Down it came, not quite smoothly, drifting in a direction that Carla realized would take it to the concrete pad where it began its flight. All conversations stopped; the young man at the controls did something with switches; the rocket slowed its descent just above the pad and settled down with unexpected delicacy, sitting upright almost exactly where it had been before the launch. The rotor blades slowed and sagged.

Whoops and cheers sounded from behind all of the concrete shelters. The man at the controls looked up with a tentative smile. "Very well done," Jerre said to him, and he beamed. That was when Carla finally recognized him: the young man who'd spoken to Jerre in the helicopter hangar at Dammal Shelter.

A burst of innerspeech passed between Jerre and Amery then, and Amery turned to Carla. "Can I walk the two of you to the College now? It'll take Jerre and the launch crew a couple of hours to finish up here and haul the rocket back to its shelter, and there's no need for us to wait around for them."

"You won't be needed?"

A quick shake of Amery's head denied it. "My share of the work is to make sure everything's done legally, and write a monthly report to the judgment circle." With a little laugh: "That, and talk to other legalists about Stefan's judgment. The College of Law has been debating that since it first arrived."

"That doesn't surprise me," said Carla. "What do the legalists think of it?"

"They're not happy. No one can think of a reason why he's wrong about the problems we face, and no one's been able to find an alternative to his conclusion. But we can talk more about that on the way. Shall we?" Carla nodded, agreeing, and once she'd done so, Asha ducked her head and followed them.

2

"It's fairly straightforward," said Jerre. "Here's Eridan." His hands mimed a head-sized sphere. "Here's *Journey Star*." A finger traced a circle around it, indicating the starship's equatorial orbit. Carla watched his face the whole time. Asha, fascinated, watched his hands. Around them, a room that could have been in any Shelter on Eridan offered the familiar comforts of arrowgrass mats and barkcloth cushions to sit on, tebbe from the kitchen-unit in the corner, evening light spilling golden-orange through a window. Here and there, drawings in simple black frames hung on the walls, drawn in charcoal or ink in a tense elegant style: Jerre's work, Carla had mentioned. Asha hoped she could look at them more closely someday.

"All we have to do is get a manned capsule up there," he went on. "*Journey Star* was designed and built for a five hundred year voyage, in case this system turned out not to be habitable when we got here. From everything we've been able to detect by radio, its systems are still fully functional—they've been in standby mode since Shalsha fell. So once we can get people up there, we can instruct the onboard robots to make the necessary modifications, and start getting things ready for the voyage back to Earth."

"I imagine you'll need plenty of rockets for that," said Carla.

"No, that's the beauty of it. *Journey Star* had sixteen landers, big craft that can carry fifty people from orbit to Eridan and back. Nobody's sure what happened to six of them, but the other ten are still docked to the ship—my students have spotted them through telescopes. Once we can send people up there, we can get some of the landers functioning, and as soon as that happens, the rocket can go to the museum here in Zara for children to stare at."

"As soon as that happens," Carla repeated. "When?"

Jerre's smile faded a little. "Long enough that I won't be around to see it leave for Earth. It's taken twenty years already to get engineers trained in rocketry, simpler rockets built and flown, and the first stage tested. Even if everything goes well, it'll be another ten years at least before the second stage and the capsule are ready, and once we have the landers and we can start getting ready for the voyage, another twenty years to refit the ship, train the thousands of people who will need to go, and get everything aboard for the atmospheric reengineering protocol—it would be quicker if we had more trade credit, but there are limits to what people and Shelters can afford to donate. The most I'm hoping for myself is that I have the chance to board *Journey Star* before I get too old to risk space travel."

Carla nodded, said nothing. After a moment, Asha ducked her head. "Sen Amadan, may I ask a question?" His gesture invited it, and she went on. "Why go to Earth? The World That Is Gone is—" Her hands splayed out as though grasping at subtleties, failed to catch them. "Gone."

"Do you know what happened to it?" Jerre asked her.

"The songs I learned when I was young said that the ones who lived there were very powerful and very foolish, and they fouled the air until it caught fire and burned them all." A little uncertain smile bent the corners of her mouth. "Now I know about the greenhouse effect."

Jerre sent a surprised look Carla's way, and Carla laughed. "I know. The Indweller was programmed with an astonishing amount of information about the life sciences, and it's taught all of that to Asha. Ask her anything you like about botany sometime."

"I'll start right now," said Jerre. To Asha: "You know about carbon dioxide?" She ducked her head. "Its role in the greenhouse effect, and in plant metabolism? Good. *Journey Star* uses huge tanks of blue-green algae to keep the air on board oxygenated. Imagine what would happen if you started seeding Earth's upper atmosphere with blue-green algae, to break down the excess carbon dioxide."

Asha's eyes went wide. After a moment, though, she said, "What about the water vapor?"

Unexpectedly, Jerre grinned. "I wish you were a student in one of my systems ecology classes. Yes, that was one of the big questions that had to be worked out. Certain chemicals have to be sprayed into the upper atmosphere, too, to get the water vapor to condense into droplets and start to fall as rain. For something like a hundred and twenty years it'll boil off again as steam before it reaches the ground, but the evaporation and condensation will pump heat to the upper atmosphere and radiate it into space."

Asha was still considering that when the door opened and a lean brown-haired girl of fifteen came in. "Noni sent me with the room keys," she said. "Sen Carla! It's so good to see you again." Carla beamed and held out her arms, and the girl trotted over, dropped to her knees, and gave the old woman a hug. She drew back, turned. "You must be Asha. I'm Tami. Welcome to Zara." Asha ducked her head in greeting.

"We should probably get our things settled," Carla said then.

"I can do that," said Asha at once, and went to their packs, which were sitting in a corner of the room.

Tami rose as well. "Can I help?"

Asha tried to think of some polite way to evade the request, could find none. "Please," she said. The two of them scooped up the gear and left the room.

"You met Tati and Noni up in the north country, didn't you?" Tami asked once they were outside, walking down a corridor with doors on either side. "Now you've met me, and you'll meet my brother Stefan a little later. Just don't call him Stefi. Now that he uses his whole name he sulks if somebody forgets that."

Asha tried to make sense of that, ducked her head anyway. Tami, watching her, said, "You have no idea what I'm talking about, do you?"

"No," Asha admitted, and braced herself for the inevitable rejection.

"Outrunners don't do names the same way we do, I guess," Tami said then, in the same tone as before. "With us, if you're named after someone, the way most people are, you use the short form of the name while they're alive. I was named for Tamar Alhaden—you've met her, haven't you?—and I hope I have gray hair before anyone calls me anything but Tami. And of course you know about Stefan Jatanni."

"Yes," said Asha after a moment, trying to make herself believe that this Shelter girl was somehow not behaving like every other Shelter child she'd met. "I saw him once when he was alive. It was the day I first came to Mirien Shelter."

Tami stopped at a door, unlocked it, pulled it open. The room inside was clean and pleasant, with two narrow windows in one wall, a small skylight, a framed drawing by Jerre of a strange tree that seemed to strain upward like a reaching hand. The two girls went to work at once, getting clothes and other things settled into the closets. "Noni and Tati took us north to see him three times," Tami went on, "and he came here once to do some research in the archives. He always frightened me a little—he always seemed to see more than anybody else I ever met. Noni says he was always like that. But you sang the death-song for him after he died, didn't you?"

Asha ducked her head. "It was the Way." An instant later she realized that Tami wouldn't know what that meant. "The way of the outrunners."

"I'm glad," said Tami.

"Thank you," Asha said then, and nerved herself up to the question she most wanted to ask. "Most Shelter children won't speak to an outrunner child. You will. Why?"

That earned her a wry look, a glimpse at feelings more complex than the effervescent cheerfulness Tami had displayed up to that point. "I'm not really Shelter folk," she said. "Because of who my father is."

That left Asha entirely perplexed. Guessing: "Because he makes rockets?"

Tami turned to face her, wide-eyed. "You really don't know? I thought that everyone on Eridan knew about him." Then, recovering: "I'll see if I can talk Noni into telling you the whole story sometime. Tati doesn't like to talk about it." She closed a final drawer. "Come on. If we wait too long they'll go to eat without us."

3

Over the weeks that followed, Asha settled into the rhythms of life at Zara, so different from the way she'd lived before the Halka came or the rhythms that had shaped her days and nights on the long road south with Carla. At Cadell Shelter she'd learned about Shelter work, the labor each day that everyone put in to keep the Shelter running, but Shelter work at Zara wasn't the same. She'd swept floors and washed dishes while waiting out the rains at Cadell, but her Shelter work at Zara mostly involved explaining things to one or another of the colleges. There were twelve colleges, each housed in its own part of the Shelter, each with its own scholars and students and things to study. More than one of them wanted to know things she knew, and at Zara, Tami explained to her, teaching someone something counted for Shelter work.

For two weeks, accordingly, she went to the College of History early each morning, ate a meal there at midday, and came back toward sunset, after telling a circle of scholars as many songs and stories and traditions of the People as the time allowed. Another week went to the College of Arts and Crafts, where she showed a pleasant old man with bushy white hair all she knew about making things from arrowgrass, and after that the scholars at the College of Life Sciences wanted to hear what the Indweller had taught her about plants. Sooner or later, she guessed, she would run out of things to tell scholars and go back to dishes and brooms, but for the time being it was pleasant to sit and talk instead, or remember the way Grandmother had taught her to make a basket for gathering roots and see just such a basket take shape in her hands.

Meanwhile Carla was doing something deep in the archives of Zara, the great echoing rooms full of shelves and books where everything that had ever happened on Eridan was chronicled. Tamar was doing the same thing in a different part of the archives, and neither Tami nor anyone else seemed to know what either one of them was doing. Jerre kept busy with his duties as dean of the College of Space Sciences, the smallest and youngest of the colleges at Zara, teaching classes in systems ecology and astronautics, superintending the building of the engine that would power the second stage, writing letters to thank distant Shelters for the trade credit they'd donated, training teachers who would someday train *Journey Star*'s crew. Amery watched, answered legal questions, and often went to the other side of Zara to the great dim echoing halls of the College of Law, where the legalists talked and talked about something that had to do with Stefan Jatanni. What it was, Asha did not know, and nothing she'd learned from the Indweller seemed to bear on it. She filed the question away in her mind.

She had other things to think about, though. Within a few days of her arrival, without either of them having to do anything in particular to make that happen, she and Tami Lundra had become fast friends. Tami showed her around Zara, made sure she had everything she needed, took her to the museum at the center of Zara where relics from the past waited in glass cases, sat with her talking about anything or nothing when lessons or Shelter work didn't intervene. Her brother Stefan was a more distant presence, a thin intent boy fascinated by his father's project. The other boys and girls at Zara stayed well away from them, and when the adults looked at Asha she could almost hear them thinking "outrunner child."

She did not mind. She knew, from a long solemn talk she'd had with Carla at Cadell Shelter, that once Carla was gone, Jerre and Amery would become her hearth-parents. She'd accepted that with an effort, but she knew now that when that happened she would have a hearth-sister to confide in, and a hearth-brother and hearth-parents who would not turn their backs on her. Thinking of it, she wept sometimes out of sheer relief.

She heard from Amery, one quiet afternoon, the story about Tami's father that Tami had hinted at the day they'd first met: how Jerre Amadan had been born in the hidden place under Pillar-of-Sky, a child of the Others who had come there to build machines, the folk who called themselves Bredin Shelter; how he'd been sent south to spy out the land, suffered hurt, and received healing; how he'd become a sen Halka, and then when the War came, how he'd flown a helicopter to Pillar-of-Sky to pass judgment on his own people and end the War with their deaths; how he'd come back to face the judgment of the Halka on his acts, and how the Halka had refused to judge him. She'd listened wide-eyed and then thanked Amery for telling the tale, ducking her head low.

"I have another name," Tami told her that same evening, in a low solemn voice. "It's not a name I can ever use, but I have it. It's this: Tamara Clarice Emmer. It's an Earth name—children on Earth took their father's last name, not their mother's, and Tati's an Emmer—and it's also my name in Bredin Shelter."

Asha took that in. "Do the Halka know?"

"Of course, and the Halvedna too. Noni asked a judgment circle to approve it before Tati started teaching me and Stefan the mindtraining."

"Then Stefan has another name too."

She nodded. "But it's his to share or not."

Asha understood—there had been secrets like that among the People—and she'd promised Tami not to mention her other name to anyone. That night, though it was late when she settled under her blankets and the day had been long, it took Asha a long while to get to sleep. She thought of broken Pillar-of-Sky, the little she'd learned of the Time of the Machines, the little she knew so far of the man who would be her hearth-father sometime soon, and slipped at last into unquiet dreams in which machines moved here and there in the darkness, threatening presences she could never quite see and never quite escape.

Still, there was much for her to learn. She arranged to sit in on some of the classes in systems ecology Jerre taught, and was delighted to find that what she'd learned from the Indweller gave her background enough to let her follow the lectures. Twice, to her astonishment, one of his students asked her for help with questions of botany, and thanked her profusely when she'd explained the thing he needed to know. The students in the College of Space Sciences were Shelter folk and they still seemed wary of her, but not as much as others. Something set them apart from other Shelter folk, she gathered, like the thing that set Jerre apart though not so deeply, like the thing that set her apart. That eased her mind now and then.

"Do you know how to read?" Tami asked her once. They were sitting in a courtyard between the College of Space Sciences and the College of Architecture, where an astonishing thing, a tree from Earth, spread strange green leaves like needles in the sunlight and filled the air with an alien scent, sharp and aromatic. There were fewer than forty of them in all of Eridan, Tami had said, all descended from two that survived the Insurgency in a place called Werelin, and they thrived only with constant tending. Asha liked to sit beside it and stare up past its gnarled brown trunk and green leaves at the sky, imagining the distant time when the World That Was Gone was thick with such trees.

She was doing just that when Tami asked her question, and it took a moment to pull her thoughts free. "Yes," she said. "The Indweller taught me."

Tami nodded as though that was the most ordinary thing on Eridan. "Good. I should show you the Common Library sometime soon." In response to her puzzled look: "The colleges all have their own libraries, but those are all books for scholars and students, not books to read because you want to. Those are in the Common Library."

"What kind of books?" Asha asked.

"Stories. Mostly from Earth, but not all. There are people who make new stories here on Eridan now, you know."

The thought of making a new story seemed vaguely wicked to Asha—to her, stories were things you learned from your grandparents and passed on to your grandchildren without changing so much as a word—but she ducked her head. "I'd like to see the Common Library."

"We can go there tomorrow." Wind hissed in the needles of the tree from Earth, and both of them paused to listen. "Does the Indweller talk to you often?" Tami asked then.

"No. It did for a while, when it was teaching me things, but after I learned everything it knew, it stopped saying much." She raised her head then, knowing that Tami would see the yellow flash in her eyes, and it still brought a moment of delight and amazement that the sight didn't make her friend back away.

Another silence passed, pleasant. "I wish I knew what sen Tamar and sen Carla were looking for," Tami said then; she always used the honorific with those names, and Asha wondered now and again if she should do the same thing. "Noni tells me they're not busy in the same part of the archives or even on the same floor, but they're both spending every spare hour looking for something, as though it's very important." Glancing up at Asha: "Do you have any idea what sen Carla wants to find?"

"No, none at all," said Asha. That was not even close to the truth, but Asha had promised not to speak a word about the tremendous thing Carla meant to find, and though it stung to lie to her friend she knew she had no other choice. She kept her feelings from showing on her face, and Tami nodded and spoke about something else.

4

"I wonder if you can spare some time to talk," Carla said.

Jerre looked up from a sheaf of blueprints—a glance at them showed Carla they were detailed plans for the second stage of the rocket. "I should probably say no," he admitted, "but I won't. If I keep thinking about hydraulics much longer I think I'll probably start making noises like a pump."

Carla laughed, settled in *ten ielindat* on the arrowgrass matting that covered the floor. "No doubt. I wouldn't bother you, but I've found some things in the archives that I think you should know about."

Jerre gathered up the blueprints, set them aside. "Please go on. You haven't yet told me what you were researching, you know."

"I wanted to be sure I wasn't chasing jewelflies before I said anything. Still, I gave you a hint some time ago." To his questioning glance: "The letter I sent you about the static."

"I wish I'd had the time to follow up on that." Considering her: "The letter said you thought you were hearing the same thing we heard at the facility north of Dammal."

Carla nodded. "I'm certain of it now. It's become much clearer."

"So it's getting louder," Jerre ventured.

"Or coming closer." Jerre gave her a startled glance, and she went on: "How much do you know about antenna theory?"

"A little." He was watching her now, intent, his thoughts unreadable. "Why?"

"I talked to the radio staff at Cadell Shelter, where Asha and I waited out the rains, and learned a certain amount. Depending on how you build and position an antenna, it can pick up radio waves from every direction, or just one direction, or anything in between. Shelter radios use horizontally polarized antennas, so they receive waves from every direction—" She spread her hands in a flat plane. "But not from above."

Jerre nodded slowly. "Go on."

"So the signal is reaching antennas all over this continent at sunrise and sunset. At Cadell and then again at Iubel Shelter, not far north of here, I borrowed a device called a radio direction finder—do you know about those? Good. Both of them showed the signal coming from due east at sunrise and due west at sunset."

"That implies," said Jerre slowly, "that it's coming from the direction of the sun." After a brief pause: "From space."

"Yes." Before he could respond: "Here's one more detail. I found quite a bit of information about *Journey Star* in the archives here. There was an old technology that uses radio waves to detect objects in space."

"Radar," said Jerre. "I'm familiar with it."

"Exactly. *Journey Star* and her sister starships used several forms of it. The main navigational radar had a beam that swept back and forth, like this." Her hand flexed at the wrist, right, left, right. "Think of how that would sound through a receiver."

Jerre regarded her for a long silent moment. "You're suggesting that a starship is coming toward Eridan."

"It's the only explanation I've been able to think of."

"Have you prepared a judgment?"

"As soon as I've confirmed it I plan on calling together a judgment circle, submitting the whole matter to its members, and advising them to declare the Red Sky emergency code at once. If I'm right, this is a potential emergency on a planetary scale."

"Momentous, certainly," said Jerre. "But an emergency?"

"We have no idea what their intentions are." Carla leaned forward slightly. "Perhaps they've come on some peaceful errand, but we can't assume that. They might be intending to colonize Eridan—and if they have technology more advanced than ours and no scruples about using it, they could quite conceivably do to us what we did to the outrunners."

Jerre took that in, and after a moment nodded slowly. "You suggested that you can confirm your guess," he said then. "How?"

"How much do you know about the hills just south of here?"

"Next to nothing."

"They were set aside as an ecological reserve within a decade of planetfall. That's been confirmed on Sixth Law grounds by judgment circles since then—some of the terrain's steep enough that farming or logging could cause serious erosion problems here, and a long distance downstream as well. Some records I found, though, suggest that there's more to it than that. To be specific, I think there may be another facility there like the one we saw north of Dammal. It should be only a few hours' walk into the hills."

"You're going."

"Asha and I—but I want you to come with us. You know more about the old technologies than anyone else on Eridan just now. It should be easy to find, and once we locate it and identify it we can return here, call a judgment circle, have it excavated, and compare the signal to the records in the archives. That should be evidence enough to justify Red Sky."

Another pause, and then Jerre nodded. "I'll have to discuss this with Amery—"

"Of course."

"But I'll come. How soon do you plan on leaving?"

"As soon as possible." To his querying look: "There's one further implication I don't think you've caught yet. The starship, if that's what it is, is staying in the part of the sky closest to the Sun when seen from Eridan, which keeps them from being seen at night. Why?"

Jerre's eyes widened sharply. "They're trying to hide."

"Exactly. Approach from any other part of the sky and they'd be spotted. It wouldn't even need the telescopes your College of Space Sciences has—you know as well as I do how many Shelters have telescopes and hobbyists who watch for comets and the like. So the question is why they're hiding—and some of the answers aren't things I want to think about."

5

They left early the next morning. Asha was beaming, Carla serene, Jerre mostly silent. He and the girl wore ordinary traveling clothes and carried packs with a little food and some traveling gear, while Carla put on the heavy black barkcloth gear she'd worn for so many years, complete with the gun at her hip. "Unnecessary, I know," she said to Jerre, indicating it. "But I've worn it so long I feel naked without it." Asha smiled up at her, said nothing. Jerre nodded, then asked for a moment's delay, went back inside, returned without saying what he'd done.

No trail led the way Carla meant to go, but that posed no obstacle at first. The meadowmoss swept away, a gray-violet carpet, to the hills a kilometer south. When they reached the edge of the hills Carla led the way up through daula forest, following a route so exact that Asha guessed she'd committed it to memory. Wind whispered in the canopy high above, let stray glints of sunlight angle down to the forest floor. Ground-scuttlers and jewelflies accented the stillness of the forest without breaking it. A stream they followed for most of a kilometer as it angled up into the hills, splashing over rocks or filling deep clear pools, did the same.

Hours passed, the sun climbed, and a few high clouds drifted over. The three of them stopped at intervals so that Carla could rest. A little before noon they crossed a low rise between steep tree-covered hills and picked their way slowly down the slope beyond it. At the foot of the slope a narrow band of meadow-moss filled the valley bottom, and beyond that a hill rose up, sparsely dotted with shrubs.

"Our goal?" Jerre asked Carla, indicating it.

She smiled. "I think so. You noticed the shape, of course."

Jerre allowed a little bleak laugh. "I haven't forgotten everything I learned from Stefan."

Asha glanced from one of them to the other, puzzled. Jerre glanced at her and said, "Look at the hill. Think about what it would look like if it didn't have any shrubs on it, and if the soil that's built up to the left of it wasn't there."

It took Asha a moment to realize what he meant. "The Place of Whispers," she guessed.

"Good. Yes, the shape underneath is the same." To Carla: "If we start back now we can have people with shovels here by this time tomorrow."

"I know. I'd like to take a closer look at it first, though."

"Yes, I thought you would," he said.

It was the only warning Asha had. Jerre moved suddenly, and all at once Carla's gun was in his hand and he sprang back, out of reach. As he stepped back further, his other hand moved, discarding something long and black from the gun, pulling something identical from a pocket and slamming it into place. A muffled sound warned of a round being chambered. By the time Carla had turned to face him, he had the gun in both hands, leveled at her.

"Enough," he said. "I know what's going on here, but not why. So we're going to have a conversation I'm fairly sure you don't want to have."

"Quite the contrary," said the old woman. "Though I expected to begin it myself."

By then Asha had gotten past the first moment of shock, and braced herself to do what she knew she had to do. Before she could move, though, Jerre spoke. "Asha, if you try to get between us I'll shoot her dead." He did not look at her. "I have Halka training. I know what you're thinking of doing. What you're going to do instead is take seven steps back and then sit down and put your hands in your lap."

After a frozen moment, she obeyed. Then, as she settled into *ten ielindat*, a compulsion seized her and she blurted out, "Please don't hurt them." The moment the words were out, the compulsion left her and she brought her hands to her mouth, horrified that she'd revealed one of the secrets she'd pledged to keep.

"You haven't forgotten anything you learned from Stefan," said the old woman then.

"Thank you," said Jerre. "Yes, I learned that trick from him." His gaze focused tautly on the old woman. "You can sit down also—though I'm not sure what to call you. You're the symbiont, of course. Is there any of Carla Dubrenden left in you?"

"Her memories," Carla's voice said. "I have most of those. The last of her brain function failed weeks ago. I don't suppose it matters to you that I made sure she felt no pain."

"Was that the bargain she made with you?"

"Part of it." Carla's body settled easily into *ten ielindat*. "My intention all along was to explain the whole matter once we reach our destination. Before I do that, will you satisfy my curiosity? I thought it was possible that you would figure out what happened to Carla, but it would interest me to know how you did it."

Jerre considered that, nodded. "First, you lied to me about where you learned about radar. I know every document in the archives about the subject—we had to figure out how to build radar gear to track our rocket launches. The things you told me aren't in any document in Zara. That left only one possible source.

"Second, I knew Carla Dubrenden fairly well, and I knew the flavor of her thoughts. Your mind could imitate that, but not perfectly. I also sensed that you have some kind of mindtraining that Carla never had, something a little like the training I got growing up in the Bredin Shelter network—and there's something else present in your mind, something I can't interpret at all. Those have only one possible explanation.

"Third, the moment I saw you this morning I knew that you had an empty magazine in your gun. Subtle awareness told me that it was too light to have bullets in it. Carla would never have done that—and if she did, she would have known that I would sense it. Then you went out of your way to draw attention to the fact that you'd brought your gun. Since I knew it was unloaded, it seemed most likely that you expected me to take it from you at some point. That was why I went back inside just before we left: I pocketed one of Amery's spare magazines, so I could turn the trick back on you."

"As you did." She gestured, palms up. "Ask me anything you wish. I'll leave my mind unshielded so you'll know I'm not misleading you."

Jerre paused briefly. "What would have happened if we'd gone closer to the facility?"

"Asha would have pressed a button on a device I built and gave to her. It's set up to send a signal to the facility and set off a set of emergency preparations. The way into the facility would have been open in a matter of minutes, and what's inside would leave standby mode."

"You want me to ask what's inside."

"The fate of humanity on Eridan may depend on what's inside."

Jerre said nothing, waited.

"The day we arrived you talked about the landers that came here with *Journey Star*, and you said that no one knows where six of them are. That wasn't quite accurate. Two of them were kept at Shalsha, and were destroyed by the atomic weapon. The other four had been put in emergency bunkers long before then by the Colonial government, in case something went hideously wrong and the colonists had to be evacuated at once. To the best of my knowledge all four of them are still in their bunkers, and one of those bunkers is in front of us."

Jerre said nothing, and the gun in his hands did not waver.

"An unknown starship is coming toward us," said the symbiont. "We have no way of knowing why—not yet. Our world will be completely helpless unless a few people can reach *Journey Star* before the starship goes into orbit around Eridan. That was why I brought you here. I know about considerably more than botany, and I passed on to Asha all the technical knowledge she needs for this. You know at least as much about astronautics as anyone on Eridan. The lander can get us to *Journey Star* in a matter of hours, and then we can do something about the starship if we have to."

"Legally speaking," said Jerre, "a judgment circle should rule on this first."

"We may not have time for that. If you like, once we reach *Journey Star*, you can send a launch and have a judgment circle join us in orbit."

Jerre paused again, and then nodded. "Asha," he said without looking at her, "where's the device your hearth-mother gave you?"

"In a pocket in my outer robe," the girl said in a small voice.

"Take it out and press the button."

She ducked her head, extracted a small metal box from her robe, and pushed the button on it. A moment of perfect still-ness passed. Then two sudden explosions shook the hill on the far side of the valley, sending great clouds of dust billowing up and shaking the air like spring thunder. The dust clouds drifted slowly away. Where they had been, the top of the hill was clear of trees, and a gash had been blown into the hillside, revealing a tunnel into darkness.

"It should be safe to go in immediately," said the symbiont. "Shall we?" Before Jerre could answer: "Of course Asha and I will go in front of you."

"Will you lend me your gun belt?" Jerre asked.

"Of course. It's hardly of use to me at this point." Moving slowly, she unbuckled it, took it off and tossed it so it landed on the meadowmoss in front of Jerre. He nodded, set the gun down on the moss, put on the belt, then picked up the gun and holstered it. The whole time his gaze never left her.

"Asha," Jerre said then. "You can go help your hearth-mother stand up, and I'll follow the two of you into the facility." The girl ducked her head, sprang up, and went to the old woman's side. Jerre waited while Carla's body stood, turned, and started for the hill. Then he followed at a precisely measured distance.

6

The concrete tunnel and the blast doors behind it were iden-tical to those the three of them had seen north of Dammal Shelter, complete with the seal of the old Colonial government, unmarred by Directorate hands. When the blast doors swung open, though, what they revealed could not have been more different. Instead of flickering lights and whispering sounds, sunlight slanted down through a gaping hole where the ceiling had been, lit a blunt gray-white cone twenty meters high. Stenciled on the side of the cone in faded blue, next to an open hatch at ground level, was the seal of the Colonial government and the number 11.

"Excellent," said the symbiont. "I'll confirm systems functionality once we're aboard and we can launch as soon as the lifter coils reach full charge."

"You're assuming that I'll agree to that," said Jerre.

The smile had nothing of Carla's personality in it. "Everything Carla knew about you tells me you won't turn down an opportunity like this. Once this is over, if things go well, you and your college will have *Journey Star* at your disposal."

"And if things don't go well?"

That got a wry glance over her shoulder. "Then we'll do what we have to." She started across the concrete to the hatch, Asha keeping pace close beside her. Jerre followed.

He'd studied detailed plans for *Journey Star*'s landers at Zara, so the interior didn't surprise him: the narrow ramp inside the hatch slanting steeply up to the passenger compartment, with its banks of reclined seats and its dim lighting; the ladder rising from there to the cockpit, where four more of the seats faced flat black screens. Once the three of them were in the cockpit, the symbiont said, "Strap yourselves in. It won't be long." Asha sat next to her. Jerre made sure that Asha was secure, got their packs stowed, then took the seat on the other side of the child and fastened the straps across himself, making sure that the gun remained free.

"Activate voice input," said the symbiont. "Override code eight, nine, six, eight, Kilimanjaro."

"Acknowledged," an unhuman voice responded from above them.

"Prepare for immediate launch. Our destination is *Journey Star*. Calculate and apply optimum orbital trajectory. Activate."

"Acknowledged," the voice said again. Below them, the hatch hissed and clanked shut, and an assortment of low indistinct sounds spoke of machineries waking. In front of them, the black screens lit up, showed the view above: the great round gap in the ceiling of the bunker, a blue sky dotted with clouds beyond that. Against that, numbers appeared and changed.

"We have just under five minutes," the symbiont said then.

"I have some questions," said Jerre.

"Ask them."

"When did you know about the starship?"

"As soon as I heard the radar signal at Facility Twelve."

"The Place of Whispers."

"Yes. There were originally three of those—the one north of Dammal, another near Werelin and a third on Dal Island. The latter two were destroyed after the Insurgency—the Directorate used them as communications bases, so your Fifth Law doubtless got applied to them. Facility Twelve was too far north to be of any use."

"What were they originally?"

"Listening stations meant to detect approaching starships. They monitor every radio signal that reaches Eridan from space. The whispering we all heard was the radio background of this part of the galaxy. The Colonial government thought it was just possible that another ship might be sent this way, from Earth or one of the other colonies. So did the Directorate, until the Insurgency made it a waste of time to worry about anything else."

Jerre regarded her for a time, but she stared at the screen, watching numbers change. After a moment he went on. "My other question is about the light trace—the reflection from the retina that shows an Indweller's present. Asha still has it. You don't. Why is that?"

"A simple bit of misdirection," said the symbiont. "Asha's been taking doses of an herb that produces an effect close enough that it can be mistaken for the test at a casual glance. As for me, I simply grafted my visual nerves into Carla's, rather than putting my own retinal layer into her eyes. That's irreversible, by the way, and so are some of the other things I've done. Carla's body is quite frail at this point—even aside from the cancer, her heart is failing—and when it dies I don't plan on surviving it."

"Why?" Jerre asked.

"I've lived an extremely long time," said the symbiont, "and seen and done a great many things I would rather not remember." A green circle appeared on the screen, began to blink. "One thing. No matter what happens, if you can, please see to it that Asha is taken care of."

"Why does that concern you?"

Something ragged showed in the symbiont's borrowed voice for the first time. "I had a daughter once."

The green circle stopped blinking, and suddenly enlarged. "Brace yourselves," said the symbiont, and placed one of Carla's hands on Asha's shoulder; the girl smiled up at the symbiont and placed one of her own hands atop it. An instant later the murmurs from below changed to a strident howl, the lifter fields cut in, and sudden acceleration slammed all three of them back hard into their seats. Jerre let himself sink back into the chair, watched the screen in front of him as the lander soared upward. The high clouds came closer and closer still, and then the lander shot past them and plunged into blue emptiness beyond.

Minutes passed. The lander's trajectory bent to the south-east, curving toward orbit, and Jerre's breath caught: the horizon appeared at the bottom of the screen, and it was an arc, not a straight line. Above, blue slowly faded to black as Eridan's atmosphere fell away behind them. Below, the eastern coast of the continent slipped past. The first of the islands of Eridan's far side, unseen by human eyes since Shalsha fell, came into sight.

He made himself look at the others. Asha was watching the screen, wide-eyed but with no trace of fear. The symbiont glanced his way with Carla's eyes, then faced the screen again. Jerre considered saying something, but the howl of the lifter fields was still too loud.

More minutes passed, and then the lifter fields shut off. The pressure of acceleration shut off just as quickly, to be replaced by Jerre's first taste of freefall. By then the sky was black except for a blue band curving along the arc of the horizon, and the blurred edge of twilight cut across blue seas and scattered islands far ahead. "Low Eridan orbit," the symbiont said. "If I've gauged the volume of the radar correctly, the starship should still be at least several days out from Eridan, so we don't have to use a brute-force trajectory to get to *Journey Star*." Then, with a wry little smile that was nothing like Carla's: "Besides, one never forgets one's first space flight. I'm vain enough to want yours and Asha's to be a pleasant memory."

"You've gone out of your way to let me know that you used to be human," said Jerre. "I'm curious why."

"Good. You already had more than enough information to figure that out—in fact, you probably have enough to guess who I was." Carla's shoulders shrugged. "I'm gambling, of course, that our present situation will keep you from shooting me."

Asha gave her a worried look, directed another at Jerre. "The judgment circle that tried my case," said Jerre, "barred me permanently from taking part in the work of the Halka. If you're involved in a primary case—a violation of one of the Six Laws—all I can do is report that to the next sen Halka I meet."

"You seemed ready to shoot me half an hour ago," said the symbiont.

"If I'd pulled the trigger I'd have been shot within a week," Jerre replied. "But you didn't know that, or didn't understand it."

"I don't pretend to understand your laws," the symbiont said.

"I know. I don't think anyone in the Directorate understood the concept of law at all."

"We did what we thought we had to do." Something ragged showed in the voice again.

Jerre regarded Carla's borrowed body again. "You're right," he said. "You've given me more than enough information to figure out who you were. A plant scientist who knew very high-level Colonial override codes, could quote the text of a secret Directorate paper on the dwimmerroot—and had a daughter. The one person who fits all those details is Carl Emmer, the last Planetary Director. The one difficulty is that he was in Shalsha when it was destroyed."

"No, he was not," said the symbiont.

A silence passed, broken only by the dim murmur of machinery.

"I had—certain sources of information," Carla's voice went on. "I didn't know exactly what would happen, but I knew enough to realize that staying in Shalsha wasn't an option. So six hours before the atomic weapon went off, an unmarked military aircraft took off for Facility Eight in the far north—you know it well, it was the place where you were born. I'd placed several projects there, to keep them entirely out of reach of the Halka. I knew what had happened long before I got there—the mushroom cloud over Shalsha was visible enough even though we were almost a hundred kilometers away. So once I arrived and confirmed by radio that the Directorate had fallen, one of those projects went to work. My brain was extracted, processed, and turned into eight symbiotic organisms. Those were placed in eight members of my personal staff, who scattered to hiding places across the far north."

Jerre took that in. "Why?"

"The atmospheric reengineering protocol," said Carl Emmer. "The hope of the redemption of Earth. I had no way of guessing that anyone else would take steps to preserve it. That Melissa would be able to create a secret network to guard it and pass it on—" An eloquent shrug punctuated the words. "I wouldn't have believed that such a thing could work, and keep working for two hundred years. So each member of my staff who had a symbiont found a band of refugees in the northern forests, impressed them with their knowledge of native medicinal and edible plants, and arranged for the symbiont to be passed on once old age required that. Then, of course, the refugees became the People, cannibalism stopped being a shameful necessity and turned into the heart of their culture, they very quickly figured out that we could advise them but we could not control them, and we became their servants—or more accurately, their slaves."

"Keep in mind," Jerre said, "that I can tell when you're lying."

That earned him a little bleak laugh. "And you can also tell that I told you a half-truth. Very well. We manipulated them and they exploited us. We helped create the Way that trapped us, and they did the rest and completed our prison. Of course we didn't intend it to be a prison. We intended it to be a weapon."

"And its target?" Jerre asked.

"The Shelter folk, of course. We hoped that if we could keep constant pressure on them, they would decide eventually that industrialization and advanced weaponry were the only things that could put a stop to the outrunners. We left the battle-drones in full operational mode for the same purpose. It might have worked, too."

"Except for the Halka."

"Exactly. And by the time we knew for certain that we had failed, when the Halka started moving north in force after the War, there was no time to prepare a new strategy, and no good reason to think that we could have found one even if we had the time. I can't speak for the other symbionts, but

I realized within a year or so what the Halka command had in mind—bottling up the outrunners in the far north, where they couldn't get access to Shelter folk, so that they would have no choice but to kill and eat one another."

"And the redemption of Earth," said Jerre. "The atmospheric reengineering protocol."

"By that time," said Emmer, "I was certain that the protocol would never be used. I didn't know about the Bredin Shelter network—none of us did—and I wasn't able to identify the group that seized Facility Eight and started manufacturing drones until I came south with Asha. The Shelter folk had settled into technological stasis, and as far as I could tell, that meant we'd failed and Eridan would never have the kind of industrial base that would be needed to build ships for the voyage back to Earth. So I stopped offering guidance to the band of the People that carried me with them, and left them to their fate."

Between them, Asha closed her eyes and huddled down into the chair. There was no surprise in the motion, only grief and resignation.

7

The lander sped on. Ahead, the edge of twilight came closer. "You knew about the dwimmerroot," Jerre said then. "*Mnemophora oswaldia*. You took it with Loren Frederic."

That got him a startled glance. "I had no idea anyone else knew that."

"It's one of the things your daughter passed on to the Bredin Shelter network. I was taught that the two of you did things with it the Halka and Halvedna have never even tried."

"One thing in particular," said Carl Emmer. "When I got access to Carla's memories I was astonished to learn that the Halka use only the refined extract we called mnemophorin, the Halvedna use only the raw root, and no one anywhere on

Eridan does the obvious thing, which is to use one and then the other. That was Loren Frederic's great discovery. Start with mild doses of the root, gradually increase the dose, build up the necessary psychological resilience, and then use mnemophorin to finish the process and open up access to what you call the innermind. That way you gain the same abilities the Halka have without the high death toll, and you also get certain other abilities very few of either order ever achieve."

"Polyphase vision," Jerre said at once. "Seeing multiple futures at once and testing actions against them."

That earned him another startled look. "Did you know that, or guess it?"

"A little of both. Tamar thought that the reason Stefan broke through into polyphase vision during the War is that he'd had much of the Halvedna training before he took baya."

"She was right. If the legal barriers between the orders didn't prevent her, she could have made polyphase vision a normal thing on Eridan." With a humorless smile: "You spoke of law earlier. It has its limitations."

Jerre gave Emmer's borrowed face a silent unwavering look.

"You hate me that much," Emmer said.

"Three quarters of a million people went to the factory camps in the six years you were Planetary Director," said Jerre, his voice level and hard "Hundreds of thousands died in the fighting during those six years—and then there was what happened to Shalsha. We don't even have to talk about all the people, Shelter folk and outrunners alike, that the outrunners killed for protein down through the years. If you had polyphase vision—if you could weigh your choices against the futures they brought about—why? You must have known you would fail. Why couldn't you have chosen some other path?"

Emmer met his gaze squarely. "Every other path led to a future that was worse."

"I don't believe you," said Jerre.

"It's true nonetheless. Most of them led to the extinction of humanity on Eridan."

A silence passed. "When I first used mnemophorin," Emmer said then, "and saw the trap the Directorate had made for itself, I was aghast. I seriously considered suicide. I realized that once Stark won the other Directors to her view, once the Directorate treated the first Andarre rising as a threat to crush rather than a warning to heed, we were certain to lose sooner or later. The only way to salvage anything was to force the war to its crisis as soon as possible, and hope that enough would survive—and it did. If certain other people had made different choices, I might have failed anyway. Then I went north and took another gamble, and it failed—again, because certain other people made their own choices."

The blurred line of twilight slipped beneath the lander. Jerre still regarded Emmer; Emmer regarded the screen. Numbers wrote themselves across the blackness of Eridan's nightside, cast pale light up into Carla Dubrenden's face. "As soon as we're hidden from the sun," Emmer said then, "I'll change the field of view so we can see directly behind. It's just possible that we'll get a glimpse of the starship."

"Do landers have radar?" Jerre asked.

"Not with the necessary range." To the screen: "Activate touch input." Five rows of colored dots appeared on the screen. The borrowed hands tapped intricate patterns on them.

A minute passed, two, and then all at once the screen looked back behind the lander, showed the horizon aflame with light from the just-hidden sun. Just above the line of light, a tiny uneven shape glittered.

Emmer's breath caught. Fingers jabbed at the dots on the screen, and suddenly the image seemed to leap closer, took on a form Jerre recognized at once: thin crescents of sunlight gilding the edges of spherical environment pods, and off beyond those, a greater and thinner crescent marking one end of the dust shield. Something bright blazed closer still: the engine pods, Jerre realized after an instant, braking as the ship slowed to orbital speeds.

"Something's the matter," Jerre said.

"Another miscalculation," said Emmer. "I tried to gauge how close the starship was from the intensity of the signal, and got the wrong result. It's much too close."

"Perhaps you'll tell me," Jerre said then in a measured voice, "why that matters to you."

Emmer shot him a hard glance. "The protocol," he said. "Haven't you grasped that yet? Now that there's a chance it can still be used, Eridan has to be kept—" He stopped. "Brace yourself. You too, Asha—this will be rough." To the screen: "Activate voice input."

"Acknowledged," said the unhuman voice.

"Recalculate trajectory for minimum flight time. Waive normal g-force limits. Use emergency parameters. Restore previous view orientation. Activate."

"Acknowledged," the voice repeated. The screen again showed Eridan's nightside and the space above it. The blinking green light appeared, stopped blinking, expanded. An instant later the lifter coils howled behind them and sudden acceleration thrust Jerre back into his seat, harder than before, hard enough to make him gasp. Halka disciplines let him release every tension he didn't need to hold and adjust his breathing and blood pressure, but even so the unrelenting acceleration bore down with brutal force.

Eridan's dim nightside sank down out of sight as the lander climbed. Time crept past: a quarter hour, maybe. Then the unhuman voice spoke again over the howl of the lifter coils: "Visual contact."

"Display," Emmer forced out.

The view through the screen changed. Off in the distance, against limitless blackness, sunlight gleamed on a shape Jerre knew in his bones. The great blunt cone of the dust shield in front; behind it, the spherical environment pods, arrayed in nine rings of three along the central mast, each sphere half walls pierced with windows and half transparent geodesic dome; further back, at the mast's far end, five kilometers from the dust shield, the great cylindrical power cores and the three angular engine pods just behind them—

Journey Star.

It was far off, a tiny shape against the blackness of space, but as the lander accelerated the starship grew noticeably closer.

"Radio contact," the voice said. "Life support systems are in standby mode. Activate?"

Emmer struggled to speak. "Yes." Then, with an effort: "Full boarding protocol."

"Acknowledged."

Minute by minute, *Journey Star* grew in the screen, until the engine pods slipped off the screens and the power cores followed them. Only then did the crushing acceleration cease as the lander matched *Journey Star*'s orbital speed. Jerre assessed his condition and flushed fatigue poisons out of his muscles— another Halka trick, that—as Emmer drew in a harsh ragged breath, another, a third.

Asha turned to Emmer. "Are you well?"

"No. It doesn't matter."

She ducked her head, said nothing more.

The lander drew closer, and closer still, until *Journey Star* blotted out the void. Jerre's hands tightened on the arms of the chair. He'd known in the abstract how huge the starship was, but that knowledge gave him surprisingly little help as he faced environment pods big enough to swallow a Shelter, a dust shield the size of a small mountain. Ahead, in the gap between the dust shield and the first ring of environment pods, he spotted the main command pod, an angular structure with the central mast passing through the middle of it. A row of four docking ports ran along the near side of it. Two of them had landers docked to them. The others were empty, and the lander they were on slowed, turned, closed in one one of those.

"Life support activated," said the unhuman voice. "Artifical gravity activated. Systems checks complete. Navigational data loading. Boarding protocol implemented." Then, in exactly the same expressionless tone: "Welcome to *Journey Star*."

A series of loud clanks and thumps shook the lander. The screen went black, dim lights came on, and freefall gave way to artificial gravity maybe half as strong as Eridan's. Jerre unfastened his straps, got to his feet, and turned to the others. Asha looked little the worse for wear and got herself unfastened promptly, but the body that had been Carla Dubrenden's looked waxen and bloodless, and breath came and went through its nostrils with an effort. Asha gave Jerre a pleading look, and he nodded, helped her with the straps, and then took hold of one frail arm and helped Carl Emmer to his borrowed feet.

8

"This way," Emmer said between ragged gasping breaths. "The bridge."

The lander hatch opened onto a bare room with uneven walls and low lights, where the air smelled of scorched metal. A heavy door on the far end hissed open, letting onto a stark white corridor, and closed behind them once they went through. Emmer led the way, though it took him a visible struggle to keep moving: down the corridor to the big circular room at its end, left to another door, and then through a narrow gap between heavy protective walls and yet another door to a room with chairs and consoles, where flat black screens waited for the commands that would waken them. The low hiss of air moving through ventilation ducts accompanied them the whole way.

"Let me—sit down," Emmer gasped. He settled his borrowed body into one of the chairs, slumped there for a while, then straightened and said in a loud unsteady voice, "Activate voice input. Override code eight, nine, six, eight, Kilimanjaro."

"Acknowledged." The voice from the ceiling speakers was different, but no more human than the one that had spoken on the lander.

"Master override code three, eight, one, two, Eridanus."

"Acknowledged."

"Set plenary system command." With an effort, he nodded at Asha, who managed an uneven smile and said aloud, "Asha Dubrenden." A nod to Jerre, a flicker of something that might have been clumsy innerspeech: it was enough. "Jerre Amadan," he said aloud.

"Activate," Emmer said then.

"Acknowledged."

"Suspend voice input."

The voice repeated its response one more time, and Emmer let out a long unsteady breath. "You and Asha now have complete control over *Journey Star*," he said to Jerre. "You can launch its landers, fire its navigational lasers, put it into a different orbit—anything. You know the correct syntax for voice input? Good. Get the visual observation systems working—not radar, we don't want to show our hand too soon, and—" A spasm passed through him. "Listen for messages from the starship. I'm not sure what else can be done at this point."

Jerre was watching him with narrowed eyes. Subtle awareness brought back warning signs from Carla's body. "You're not well."

"No."

"Would lying down help?"

A little fractional smile twisted the familiar mouth. "Yes, it might."

Jerre and Asha helped the frail figure out of the chair and onto the floor, face up. At Jerre's suggestion Asha tucked one of the packs underneath Emmer's feet, and the waxen look in the borrowed face eased somewhat. "If you can take care of them," Jerre said to Asha, "I'll try to get the ship to talk to me." She ducked her head in response, settled into *ten ielindat* next to Emmer, placed fingers on the borrowed wrist to gauge the pulse. Jerre turned away.

His mind was so full of thoughts that even the disciplines he'd learned from Stefan Jatanni twenty years back did little to clear them. The stark reality that he was aboard *Journey Star* at last, the uncertainties posed by the approaching starship, the immediate questions about what to do and how to do it, and pointless but inescapable worries about Amery, their children, and the rest of Eridan warred with one another as he walked a short distance away from Asha and Emmer, and said aloud, "Activate voice input."

It took maybe five minutes of interrogating the bodiless voice to find the console that controlled visual observation systems, figure out how to tell the ship what he wanted it to do, and wait while machineries hundreds of meters away did their work and reported back to the console. Finally an image from one of *Journey Star*'s three main telescopes appeared on the screen in front of him: a smaller sister to *Journey Star*, with three rings of environment pods instead of *Journey Star*'s nine. Its engine pods were turned away from the sun and not quite toward Eridan, the thrust coils glowing blue-white as it braked from interstellar speeds. Another request and a brief wait brought numbers to the screen: the starship was 67,848 kilometers away and would arrive in Eridan orbit in 15.44 hours.

He flung himself out of the chair and started toward Emmer, then stopped. Asha was huddled, arms wrapped around herself, shaking with silent sobs, and the face that had been Carla Dubrenden's had gone slack and pallid. Subtle awareness brought back indications he knew too well: nervous system activity gone, organ systems shutting down, cell death from anoxia spreading rapidly. After a moment he came over more slowly.

Asha looked up, tears streaking her face. "They're gone," she said. "Their heart stopped." Then: "I wish to sing the death-song for them."

Jerre nodded in silence, and Asha drew in a deep unsteady breath and began to sing the long mournful syllables:

"When we came to this world across the spaces of the sky,
Great was our sorrow, but greater was our need.
When we fled the places of dying and took refuge in the forest,
Strong was our dread, but stronger was our life.
When we became the People, when we embraced the Way,
We learned the lesson of the sharing of meat:
What comes from the People must return to the People,
For our need is great, but our life is strong."

The last syllable trickled away. Then Asha wiped her face on her sleeves and got up. "I wept for Carla when he told me she was gone," she said to Jerre, her face solemn. "I wept for the other before we came to Zara, too, because he said he would die here on *Journey Star*. So." She raised her head. "Tell me what I must do."

9

Tebbe splashed into two bowls. "Yes, I saw it," said Amery Lundra. "Call it luck if you want, but I was outdoors just then, sitting in one of the courtyards Jerre uses for astronomy classes at night, with a fine view of the southern sky. Something caught my eye, and I looked up and there it was." She handed one of the bowls to Tamar, kept the other. "A little pale dot rising straight up, and leaving a white vapor trail behind it. I wasn't the only one who spotted it, of course." She sipped tebbe. "I'll grant many good things about Jerre's students, and one of them is that they're quick. They had a big reflector telescope set up and trained on the thing faster than I'd have thought possible, and I was one of the people who got to look through it."

"And?" Tamar sipped at her own tebbe. Something Amery couldn't read at all moved behind the familiar placidity of the sen Halvedna's face. Late afternoon light spilled through the windows, bringing a troubling day toward its close.

"A Colonial lander," said Amery. "Exactly as the old books describe it: a big white cone with lifter coils in the base. And it took off from the place Jerre said he and the others were going, or close to it. So I have to assume that there was a lander in working order in the facility Carla told him about—and that Jerre and Carla and Asha are on their way to *Journey Star*." With a little helpless gesture: "What I don't know is why."

"Because they should have come back and called a judgment circle?"

"Exactly. Except in emergencies, old technology has to be cleared by a judgment circle before it can be used. Jerre and Carla know that perfectly well, and Jerre's been extremely careful about the legalities of this whole project."

"Is it possible that there's an emergency?" Tamar asked.

"Yes—and that's an even more troubling thought."

"Granted." She set her bowl down, and Amery refilled it.

They were both silent for a while, sipping tebbe. "But I don't think you came here to ask me about the lander," Amery said finally.

"No, though it's just possible that that's connected." Amery gave her a surprised glance, and Tamar went on: "I got something very strange this morning. One of the junior students at the College of Healing came to my room and said that Carla Dubrenden sen Halka asked him to bring some papers to me. I could see from his thoughts that he was telling me the truth, which made the papers in question all the stranger." She brought out a sheaf of folded papers from inside her robe, handed them to Amery. "Look at the handwriting. Do you recognize it?"

Amery nodded. "Carla's."

"I know. And yet I find it impossible to believe that Carla could have written it. There's another thing, too. I haven't seen her since she arrived, and that's not because I didn't try. She's been very careful to avoid me—not the behavior I'd have expected from my oldest friend. I'm fairly certain she had a way of knowing my whereabouts, at least some of the time."

"Asha's asked more than once where you were," Amery said.

"Yes, I thought that might be involved. Go ahead and read the papers."

Amery unfolded them, read the brief and impersonal note on the first sheet, set it aside and started into the next, then glanced up sharply at Tamar.

"I know," said the sen Halvedna. "A protocol for dwimmer-root and dwimmerwine use that cuts straight through the barriers raised by the Convention of Zara. A protocol she claims to have used, by the way—that's a little later on. There are other details that suggest that she also tested it on unwilling subjects."

Amery blanched. "Carla couldn't possibly have done that."

"I know. Yet we have her own written testimony." Tamar picked up her bowl, sipped at the tebbe. "And the oddest thing of all is that some of the material mentioned in the papers touches on some of the research I've been doing, and she had no way of knowing about that. I don't think I've ever been so baffled."

"I wonder—" Amery began, and stopped. Tamar, knowing her habits, smiled and sipped more tebbe in silence, sensing the quick play of thought behind the solemn brown eyes.

All at once footsteps came pounding down the corridor outside at a dead run, slowed. The door slid open, hard, revealing one of Jerre's students—the new one from Dammal Shelter, Amery remembered, Tallis Dumaren. "Sen Lundra," he gasped out, "it's sen Amadan. The radio room." Wide-eyed: "He says he's on *Journey Star*."

Amery scrambled to her feet. "Go," Tamar said. "This can wait." She rose more slowly and shook her head in amazement as two sets of footfalls headed up the corridor to Zara's main radio room.

CHAPTER 5

A WHEEL OF STARS

1

"All Shelters copy and relay. All Shelters copy and relay."
Twenty years had passed since Jerre had learned the message
codes from Stefan Jatanni, but they came to his mind at once,
framed in hard-edged memories. "This is Jerre Amadan of the
College of Space Sciences." Would anyone on the planet below
believe the news he had to pass on? There was only one way to
learn. "I'm aboard *Journey Star*. An unknown starship has been
detected approaching Eridan. It's of the same general design
as *Journey Star* so it probably has humans aboard, but I know
nothing about their intentions. I request the Halka to consider
invoking the Red Sky emergency code." He repeated the whole
thing word for word a second time, then said, "All Shelters
copy and relay" one last time and tapped a colored circle on
the screen.

"Transmission sent," the unhuman voice told him.

Now, for the message that mattered. Even with Asha's
help—and she had all Carl Emmer's knowledge about *Journey
Star* at her disposal—it had taken him most of an hour to get
the onboard computers to explain to him how to send a radio
message in one direction and not in others, and then he had
to send it at the right time, when *Journey Star* was well past

the northern continent and the signal would reach horizontally polarized antennas. He could imagine the view from Zara, the familiar glittering dot low in the eastern sky as the sun sank toward the western horizon.

His fingers jabbed at colored circles, narrowing the radio beam so that it reached only a narrow slice of the northern continent. One more tap, and he began to speak. "Zara Shelter, copy but do not relay. Zara Shelter, copy but do not relay. This is Jerre Amadan aboard *Journey Star*. I've just sent a lander down to you. It'll touch down on the north meadow launch pad in just over five hours. It will stay there for one hour, and then lift off and return to *Journey Star*. There are fifty seats on it. I'm asking for sen Halka and teachers and students from the College of Space Sciences to board it for the return flight—enough sen Halka to form a command circle, and as many trained people as possible who can help me run *Journey Star*. Everyone who boards must be in good health—it's a rough flight up here, and there's been one casualty already. Bring food and gear for a week. Don't relay or mention this on the radio net—we have no way to judge the intentions of our visitors, and they may be listening. Message ends."

He tapped the colored circle, waited for the voice to tell him the message had been sent, and then glanced at Asha. She was sitting on the floor of the bridge, in *ten ielindat* as always, eyes red but face composed. An hour or so back, they had carried Carla Dubrenden's body to the sick bay on the far side of the main command pod, left it on one of the beds there, walked back to the bridge without speaking. Only when they were back on the bridge and Jerre had gone to work with the communications interface did Asha huddle down into herself again and sob for a while: silently, as before.

"I'd like to eat something," she said, looking up at him.

"That's probably wise." Jerre got up from the chair, settled down near her with the two packs beside them. Metal containers from inside the packs opened to reveal travel food—green bread with yeast paste, soft white triangles made from edible fungoids—and two bottles of water. They busied themselves with those, said nothing.

After a while Jerre glanced up from his meal as Asha did, noted a change. "The light trace," he said, "the reflection in your eyes. It's almost gone."

"I had to take the herb every day." Her nose wrinkled. "I'm glad I can stop now. It tastes very bitter."

"Once it's completely gone, you could go to the outrunners if you wish."

She met his gaze then, and the look in her eyes wasn't that of a thirteen-year-old. Wary and tired, it sent a chill through him. "No. That door closed once he started teaching me. I know—" Her hands spread in a little helpless gesture. "Agronomy, botany, population ecology, enough astronautics to pilot this ship. I can't stop knowing any of those things, and there's no place in the New Way for someone who knows them."

"Do you know what you want to do?" asked Jerre.

"No." Her voice was toneless, low. "No."

"You'll always have a place with Amery and me if you want one."

She ducked her head. "Thank you."

"You're welcome. Carla, back when she was still Carla, wrote to Amery and asked us to become your hearth-parents once she died. Of course we agreed." With a little choked laugh: "Besides, Tami would stop speaking to me if we did anything else. I'm glad the two of you are friends, by the way."

That evoked a slight uncertain smile. "So am I. She's very kind to me."

They finished the food in the silence that followed. "I would ask a question," Asha said then, and when Jerre gestured to invite it: "He told me what he told you—that the Halka drove the People into the barren lands so that they would have to kill each other for meat. Did the Halka plan that, or did it just happen that way?"

Jerre considered her for a moment. "They planned it. There were bitter debates over it—it's not an easy thing to decide to exterminate a people, even after two hundred years of Shelter folk being killed and eaten by them. The debates always circled back to the same decision, though. The Halka made sure that any of the outrunners who were willing to leave the Way could do that and live, and the rest—those who insisted on living according to the Way—were left to die according to the Way."

Asha ducked her head. "When I was young," she said, "the hunters of my band came back often with meat. They ones they shot were of the People sometimes, I think, though they always said they were—Shelter folk. Once they brought back one of the Halka, and we celebrated. But later on, they would go out and come back with nothing, over and over again, and finally bring back one of our band, saying that the Silent had shot him but they had driven them off and brought back the meat. I believed them, but I think now that they lied. They shot members of our band because they couldn't get meat any other way."

Jerre winced, closed his eyes.

"That should hurt more than it does," said Asha then, her voice quiet. "I think he did things to me, so that it would hurt less. But I also know that the hunters in my band could find no better choice, and I know the Halka could find no better choice, and I think Carl Emmer spoke the truth when he said he could find no better choice, and I wonder if anyone has been able to find a better choice since we first came to this world across the sky."

Jerre said nothing. Asha gathered up the containers from their meal and tucked them back into the packs. "Is there anything I should do?"

Jerre considered her, sensed readily enough the strain she was under, burdens of half-processed grief, echoes of the grueling flight to *Journey Star*. "I think you should rest," he told her. "It'll be eleven hours before the lander arrives, and there'll be plenty to do then."

She ducked her head. "Please wake me if you need to know anything."

"Of course." He got to his feet, and she curled up with her pack for a pillow and closed her eyes. He glanced at her, then went to the communications console, settled in one of the chairs there, and started tapping on buttons. The screen in front of him soon displayed Eridan's nightside, and numbers told him how soon *Journey Star* would circle around to the dayside and come within sight of the other starship. With that in mind, he turned his attention to the radio systems again, set them to listen for incoming messages.

After that was done he went to the engineering console. There he was able to call up, one at a time, status reports on all of *Journey Star*'s systems. That was comforting in some ways, daunting in others. The power cores were still at seventy-two per cent of their original output, the carefully chosen blend of radioisotopes inside still following their predicted decay sequences and pumping out energy. Two of the three engine pods were in deep standby, requiring weeks for activation, but one had rotated onto shallow standby and could be generating thrust in minutes. All but one of the environment pods, which wouldn't be needed until the time came to head back to Earth, were in deep standby and used next to no power, while the one that was active yielded ample oxygen for the main command pod. The telescopes, radars, communication systems, and navigational lasers were all operational, and so were the secondary thrusters that ringed the dust shield and the last circle of environment pods.

He thought then about the twenty years of hard work he'd put into teaching his students astronautics, all in preparation for a day that had come far sooner than he'd ever imagined. If he and *Journey Star* and Eridan could get through the next few days and weeks intact—

The thought broke apart in his mind before he could finish it. He pulled himself out of the chair and glanced at Asha—still curled up, her nervous system signaling sound sleep to subtle awareness—and then went to his pack, the one she hadn't used for a pillow. That disgorged a notebook and a pen, familiar companions of his since childhood. He paused, then, sat down at one of the consoles, turned the chair to face her, and began to draw.

2

"Visual contact," said the unhuman voice.

"Display," Jerre replied at once. The view through the screen in front of him changed abruptly, showed the curve of Eridan, blue ocean and purple-brown land against a bright arc of atmosphere and the blackness of space. Closer, a tiny shape he knew at once blotted out a little of the ocean: the lander he'd sent to Zara, closing in on *Journey Star*. He let out a breath he hadn't been conscious of holding.

Asha, sitting next to him, got to her feet. "Should I go wait for them?"

"Please."

She ducked her head, left the bridge. He glanced after her, turned back to the console and brought up the view from one of the main telescopes. Minutes passed. *Journey Star* was about to pass into the shadow of Eridan's nightside again, but the other starship was still visible above the limb of the planet, the blue incandescence of its thrust coils blazing as it slowed to orbital speeds, the thin arcs of sunlight on its dust shield and environment pods glittering like polished gold. A glance at the numbers below gave the interval of space and time he had left: the starship was 8042 kilometers out from Eridan and would enter orbit in 3.93 hours unless it changed its trajectory. Its crew had made no attempt to communicate with *Journey Star* or Eridan, or none that he could detect.

"The lander has docked," the voice of the ship's computers said then. "Passengers are disembarking. Do you wish to speak to them?"

"No," said Jerre, grinning with relief. "I've sent a crew member to brief them."

"Acknowledged," said the voice.

More minutes passed and the starship passed out of sight behind the curve of Eridan. Finally footfalls sounded in the corridor outside the bridge, whisper-soft at first and then louder. Jerre stood up and turned to face the door as familiar figures came through it: Asha first of all, a small quick figure in gray and blue; behind her, fourteen Halka in close-fitting black barkcloth, guns at their sides, Amery in the midst of them; behind them, thirty-six teachers and senior students from the College of Space Sciences, staring around themselves in astonished delight.

Innerspeech linked him and Amery for a moment, said everything that needed saying between them. "Jerre," she said aloud, "I've been chosen as Speaker for the command circle. Are we in immediate danger?"

A quick shake of his head answered her. "Eridan's shielding us from the other ship for the next—" He glanced down at the console. "Seventy-nine minutes. It's made no hostile moves so far."

"That's something. As soon as you can spare the time we need a thorough briefing."

"Give me a few minutes to get the crew to their stations," Jerre said. She nodded, and the Halka went to a bare section of floor out of the way of the consoles and settled into *ten ielindat* in a circle, leaving a gap. The minutes that followed were busy ones: "Asha, can you take Dafed and Sherel to the engineering console and show them how it works? Thank you. Barra, I want you and Irina at the visual observation console over here. Jon, just a moment—" Finally, though, every console had people seated at it and Asha was trotting from one console to another, answering questions and tapping on buttons. Jerre glanced from one side of the bridge to the other, and went to join the command circle.

As soon as he settled into *ten ielindat* with the others, he could feel the presence of the groupmind, but he still took the time to enter into trance and descend two levels, deep enough that he could communicate complex images and ideas easily to the groupmind and the members of the circle. He entered rapport, and a moment later the groupmind brought him Amery's thoughts: *Please inform the circle of everything that happened since you left Zara.*

I'll need to start a little before then, he sent back. He paused to sort through memories, then described the conversation with Carla when she'd told him about the spaceship, the unloaded gun the next morning, the journey into the ecological reserve south of Zara, the deeds and words that followed. He could sense easily enough the sudden shock when he gave the Indweller's name, and another, quieter reaction when he described Emmer's death. A quick summary of his actions afterwards rounded off the account. *I'm well aware that some of my actions may not have been appropriate*, he sent finally. *I will of course accept whatever judgment the circle reaches.*

We can leave the legalities to a judgment circle later on, sent one of the other sen Halka, a legalist named Janis Palsam whom Jerre knew slightly. *You are sure the symbiont is dead?*

As sure as I can be without dissection, Jerre replied. *I sensed no nervous activity at all, and all the symptoms of anoxia and cell death.*

At this moment, Amery reminded them all, *we need to decide on a course of action. You know this ship better than any of us, Jerre. What can it do?*

More than you would think from a ship that wasn't built with combat in mind. How many of you know about the dust shield and the navigational lasers? The groupmind brought him positive responses from Amery and one of the others, negative responses from the rest. *Both were meant to deal with one of the big problems of starflight, which is that space isn't empty.* He built up an image of dust clouds in deep space, with a scattering of comets and rocks. *Go fast enough and grains of dust strike like bullets; anything larger could destroy an unprotected craft. Go faster still, and the dust would go right through any possible shield. So the designers of the evacuation ships put heavy conical shields on the bow to protect the ships from dust, designed the engines to keep the ships at speeds that would allow the shields to protect them, and equipped the ships with radars and lasers to identify and clear away larger objects.* Another image: a laser beam striking a space rock, vaporizing part of its surface so that the jet of vapor sent the rock tumbling out of a starship's path. *But the shield and the lasers can also be used in combat. The shield is heavy enough to screen us from laser fire and the lasers are fully operable. Of course the other starship has the same advantages.*

As we orbit over the dayside, Amery asked, *can you turn the ship to keep the dust shield between us and the other ship?*

Easily. The secondary thrusters are designed for maneuvers like that.

Is there a way of communicating with the other ship? one of the other sen Halka asked, and another: *Do we have any reason to think they even know our language?*

Yes and yes, Jerre said. *I've had the ship computers monitoring radio frequencies in case the crew of the other ship tries to speak to us, and we can also send a message the same way. As for language, everything I've read claims that the people aboard all the colony ships used the same artificial language our ancestors on* Journey Star *did, in place of Earth languages. Whether they still speak it, they should know it.*

After a brief pause, Amery sent: *Are there any other questions?* There were none. *The circle will make its decision. Thank you, Jerre.* He nodded, broke rapport, rose out of *ten ielindat* and went to the engineering console.

3

"One minute," said Tallis Dumaren, the young man who'd approached Jerre in the helicopter hangar of Dammal Shelter.

The mood on the bridge was tense and hushed as *Journey Star* sped toward the dayside of Eridan. Jerre was seated in what Asha had told him was the captain's chair, set back from the consoles with a clear view of all of them. Each console had people seated at it, images of various kinds on the screens, touch input activated, rows of small colored circles waiting to be tapped at the proper moment. Amery stood by the communications console. Other sen Halka stood elsewhere, forming an innerspeech net that could relay messages more quickly and precisely than the human voice. Asha sat in *ten ielindat* next to his chair, ready to pass on what she knew if he needed it. At that moment, *Journey Star* and everything aboard it was under Jerre's command: the old dream of his childhood suddenly made real.

"Thirty seconds," said Tallis.

They'd spent the nightside transit figuring out how to get the radar and the secondary thrusters to work together, so *Journey Star* could keep its dust shield pointed toward the approaching starship. A few other necessary preparations had filled what little time was left after that. The first of two critical moments was about to arrive.

"Now," said Tallis.

At that moment, on two of the screens Jerre could see, the dust shield of the other starship rose up, tiny and distant, above the curved horizon of Eridan. Fingers tapped quickly on screens. The bridge remained silent, tensed.

Half a kilometer ahead, Jerre knew, just behind the blunt point of *Journey Star*'s dust shield, the main radar had begun to sweep back and forth, searching for space debris and letting the crew of the other starship know that *Journey Star* was crewed and functioning. The maneuvers that had turned the dust shield and the laser turret at its forward point toward the other starship, and would keep it so turned all through the dayside passage, would communicate that message in a second way. Another, more direct way of sending the same message would begin as soon as—

A gray-haired man seated at the communications console turned to Amery, and signaled wordlessly: go.

"Unknown starship, this is *Journey Star*." Amery's voice, clear and precise, broke the silence on the bridge, streamed out over hailing frequencies toward the glittering shape ahead. "Unknown starship, this is *Journey Star*. Please respond."

Silence returned. What were they thinking, Jerre wondered, aboard the other starship? They could hardly have missed the radar signal or the change in *Journey Star*'s orientation in orbit, and every scrap of information he'd been able to gather together suggested that they would likely be monitoring the hailing frequencies as well. He could easily think up a dozen different ways they might respond, but had no way to tell which one to expect.

"Unknown starship, this is *Journey Star*." Amery repeated the words. "Unknown starship, this is *Journey Star*. Please respond."

Silence returned again. Jerre glanced around the bridge. Subtle awareness brought back fifty different shades of wary tension.

Amery drew in a breath to repeat the words. At that moment a different voice came through the speakers in the ceiling. It was not unhuman, far from it, and it spoke recognizable words, but even through the static, Jerre could hear details of accent and stress that set it apart from every other voice he had heard. Past the unfamiliarities, he could sense the presence of a person: a middle-aged woman as tense and wary as anyone on *Journey Star*'s bridge, leaning forward slightly—he could sense the slight compression of her chest in the tones of her voice—as she stared at a screen and the image of a starship. "*Journey Star*, this is starship *Bright Circle*. We request permission to orbit your world. Our mission is one of peace. We intend no harm to you or your world. Please respond."

A moment of shock, and then Amery turned toward Jerre. In a burst of innerspeech: *Can their ship avoid orbiting Eridan at this point?*

Yes, he sent back at once. *If they stop braking, their ship will be deflected by Eridan's gravity and head off into some other part of space.* An image followed: the starship curving around the outer edge of Eridan's gravity well and then hurtling away on a new bearing.

Quick glances around the room gathered the response of the command circle. "*Bright Circle*, you are permitted to orbit," Amery said aloud.

Jerre caught the evasion in the words at once, stifled a wry smile. Under Halka law and tradition, neither Amery nor anyone else had the right to forbid the starship from orbiting. Two centuries of Halka legal opinion agreed that the Six Laws and the authority of the Halka applied only to the planet's surface: "on Eridan," as each of the Six Laws phrased it.

"Be thanked," the response came.

Through the screens, Jerre could see *Bright Circle* rising higher and higher above the blue arc of Eridan's dayside, the dust shield still turned toward the sun and the engines still braking in a glare of blue-white incandescence. The events of the next few moments, he knew, sent possibilities raying out in more directions than he could gauge.

"Please state your ship's origin and its mission," Amery said then.

A pause, and then another voice spoke: male, and with a different accent, full of broad vowels and hard consonants. The personality that came through the voice was at least as different: a confidence almost amounting to brashness over the top of harshly disciplined insecurities. Less methodical than the first voice and more volatile, Jerre thought. More dangerous? Surely.

"This is a complex matter," the second voice said. "I give you a simplified version. *Bright Circle* was built in orbit above the colony world Delta Pavonis V. For reasons I describe at length if you wish, that world is not habitable indefinitely, and must be evacuated. This and other ships were built to search for other habitable worlds. *Bright Circle* went first to Epsilon Indi, the nearest system settled from Earth, and found the colony failed, no survivors, only ruins and an abandoned starship in orbit. Its crew sent word back home at once, for Epsilon Indi II is most certainly habitable, and then there was a decision to go beyond.

"The next settled system after Epsilon Indi is Tau Ceti, and there *Bright Circle* found two colonies, Tau Ceti II and Tau Ceti III, both thriving. There *Bright Circle* remained for some while, a matter of a few of your years. Landers came and went, people descended and returned, gifts were exchanged. Finally there was again a decision to go beyond. The next settled system from Tau Ceti is Epsilon Eridani. So we set out, and we are here."

"And your mission?" Amery asked, when nothing further followed.

The first voice spoke again. "I have read that in my grandparents' time, when *Bright Circle* left the Epsilon Indi system, their one thought was to find out if Delta Pavonis V was the only surviving colony of Earth. When *Bright Circle*'s crew and passengers voted to leave the Tau Ceti system and go on—I was a child then—we hoped to do as we had done in the Tau Ceti system: learn what we could about another colony, exchange gifts, replenish certain stores, and then go on."

Amery took that in. "Where will you go?"

The second voice spoke. "Sirius! That is the next settled system as we proceed. Our records say there are two colony worlds there, Sirius VI and the second moon of Sirius VII. Does either of them survive? We do not know. What happened there after the ships arrived? We do not know that either. If all goes according to hope, we will find out—and then *Bright Circle* will go on to the Procyon system."

"Our plan," said the first voice, "is to visit every one of the worlds colonized from Earth. Of course none of us will see the whole journey. No one who left Delta Pavonis V is still alive, and it will be the children and grandchildren of those on board now who will see Procyon IV. It will take six hundred of your years for *Bright Circle* to justify its name and circle past Delta Pavonis V on its way to the new colony in the Epsilon Indi system. But that is our plan."

"What do you want from us?" Amery asked after a moment.

"That depends a great deal," the first voice went on, "on what you and the authorities on your world—does it have a name besides Epsilon Eridani II?"

"Eridan," said Amery.

"Thank you. On what you and the authorities on Eridan will permit. Please understand that we know that we are guests here. We have no right to demand." When Amery said nothing in response: "If it is permissible, we wish to send a few of us to speak to you directly aboard *Journey Star*. Later we wish to send parties down to Eridan to see your world and your ways. We wish to gather as much knowledge as we can. We wish to replenish our supplies of water and take aboard new food cultures. Since yours is a world with its own biology, we wish to explore the possibility of taking life forms from your world aboard one or more of our environment pods. If it is permissible, and only if it is permissible, some of those aboard *Bright Circle* may wish to stay on Eridan, and some of your people may wish to join us when we resume our journey, as happened in the Tau Ceti system. Then, in a few years, we wish to leave for the Sirius system. That is all."

A silence followed. Amery glanced back toward Jerre. *I sense no dishonesty*, she sent. *If they are telling the truth—*

If, Jerre sent back. She nodded, acknowledging.

4

"I know it's unusual for sen Halka and Shelter folk to sit side by side in judgment," Amery said. "But this is a very unusual situation."

"We fought side by side," said Dafed Serrema, a big gray-haired man who was probably the best rocket engineer on Eridan. It took Jerre a moment to recall that Dafed meant that in no abstract sense. He'd fought alongside sen Halka, defending Talin Shelter from battle-drones during the War. "This isn't much more unusual than that was."

"True," Amery acknowledged. "You know spacecraft and astronautics. We know strategy and law. It'll take all of those to figure out what we're going to have to do."

Most of those aboard *Journey Star* sat in a rough circle in the round room near the bridge, leaving Asha, two sen Halka, and half a dozen people from the College to stand watch. The screens in front of them showed space and a darkened world: *Journey Star* was making another darkside crossing, with Eridan's mass between her and *Bright Circle*.

Maybe it was Dafed's comment that caused it, but all at once the scene reminded Jerre forcefully of the days before the battle of Mirien, when he'd watched thousands of Shelter folk gathering to help the Halka fight off the last great force of battle-drones on Eridan. The memory cheered him, though the price he'd paid to end the War was never far from his thoughts.

"So," said Amery then. "The Halka here have discussed the message from *Bright Circle*. None of us detected signs of dishonesty in either voice, but that's not conclusive. A voice over radio communicates only so much, especially when the speaker comes from a culture we know nothing about—and they may have forms of mindtraining we've never encountered. So there's no way we can be certain whether it's safe to trust them."

"True," said Dafed, after waiting a moment for others to speak. "And there's this. When we came around Eridan with dust shield and lasers turned at them, it's like you stepped out from behind a tree with your gun pointed at me and mine was still in its holster. Even if they had something bad planned for us, you can be sure they'll find something nice to say until they can get us to lower the gun."

"How fast could they have turned their ship?" another sen Halka asked.

"Not fast enough," Dafed said. "And they'd have had to stop braking and go—" His gesture swept *Bright Star* off into deep space. "Far enough that it would take them a good long time to circle back to Eridan."

"So their behavior doesn't answer us one way or the other," said Amery. That got nods from the students and teachers. "What will answer us?"

"What we see when we come around to the dayside again," said Jerre. Amery and the others looked at him. "As Dafed said, we took them by surprise earlier. If they have hostile intentions, the one chance they have now is to move into a defensive position while we're crossing the darkside and open fire the moment we come into view. They could use lasers, or they could have something else—even atomic weapons. If they're still braking, still side on to us and vulnerable, then we can probably trust them. If not—" he shrugged.

One of the teachers of astronomy spoke, suggesting what their next steps might be, but Jerre suddenly found that he couldn't make himself pay attention. Carl Emmer's words whispered in his mind—"if they have technology more advanced than ours and no scruples about using it, they could quite conceivably do to us what we did to the outrunners"—and then Asha's bleak summary of the whole human experience on Eridan: "I wonder if anyone has been able to find a better choice since we first came to this world across the sky."

And here we sit, Jerre thought, trying to decide if we can find a better choice, or if the only option we have is a battle to the death between two starships, which could very well end in the destruction of both. He could see clearly enough how to fight it—a sudden burst of laser fire against one edge of the other ship's dust shield, turning enough of it into a gust of hot vapor to send the ship yawing to one side and opening the way for a direct shot at the engine pods and the power cores—but the captain and crew of *Bright Circle* would doubtless be aware of that possibility, would have their own lasers trained on *Journey Star*'s dust shield and their thrusters ready to counter the yaw.

He forced his way back to clarity as Tallis Dumaren spoke. "I know it's foolish of me," the young man said, "but I want to believe them."

"So do I," said Dafed. "I'm sure all of us do. If we're wrong, though, all of Eridan gets to pay for our mistake."

Tallis nodded glumly. "We'll find out soon enough," said Amery. "We should be in sight of *Bright Circle* again in a little over twenty minutes. We've settled what I'll say if they do turn out to be telling the truth. Does anyone else wish to speak?"

No one did, and Amery got to her feet. The others followed. "One thing more," she said then. "Jerre's had effective combat command since he got here. I'd like to suggest that we give him that role formally."

He gave her a sharp look. "You know I'm barred from that."

"We're not on Eridan," Amery said, "and the General Code of Halka Regulations doesn't apply in orbit. For all practical purposes you're the captain of *Journey Star*, the first one it's had since colonization. Since we're the crew, I propose we make that rank official."

A chorus of nods and murmurs of agreement answered her. He stood there for a moment of utter silence, then made himself nod.

"Well, Captain Amadan," Dafed said, grinning, and motioned to the corridor that led to the bridge. He nodded again, and headed that way.

The bridge was quiet as he settled into the captain's chair. Screens on the consoles near him showed Eridan's darkside slipping away below, a growing edge of light on the curved horizon ahead. Asha trotted over and settled in *ten ielindat* next to him. There had been an officer who assisted the captain on *Journey Star* when it crossed the abyss from Earth to Eridan, an irrelevant memory reminded him—captain's yeoman? Was that the title? He pushed the question aside, turned to the things that had to be done.

The main radar was still active, sweeping space in front of *Journey Star*, and he'd had the crew at the radar console activate the secondary radars that kept track of potential threats from all sides. One step remained. "Dafed," he said, "I want you and Jesi to go forward to the laser turret. There's a control station there. If they manage to hit the main command pod with a missile or a mine you'll still be able to operate the lasers from there." He turned in his seat. "Asha, can you show them how to get there? Thank you." Asha sprang up, went to the two teachers and led them out of the bridge.

Amery turned to face him. "How long will it take them to get there?"

"About five minutes. There's a high-speed shuttle that runs the length of the mast." He gestured, indicating the tubular vehicle moving from the laser turret to the engine pods and back. "It's waiting less than fifty meters from here. Asha should be back before we see *Bright Circle*." She nodded, turned back to the screen nearest her.

Minutes slipped by. Through the screens, the edge of Eridan ahead grew brighter, and then the sun detached itself from the brightness and rose slowly up, its radiance filtered by the screen but still dazzling. Irina Dassil at the engineering console turned to face Jerre and said, "Dafed and Jesi are in the turret—they've just sent word." Jerre thanked her, watched the screens. Soon, he thought. Just a few more minutes, and we'll know whether Eridan's history will plunge into another cycle of blood and useless death, or—

He couldn't make himself think of an alternative. Ahead, the brightside of the planet came closer.

Whisper of soft quick footsteps announced Asha's return. "They're at the control station," she said, and settled down again next to Jerre's chair. He nodded, turned back to the screens that showed the view forward.

An instant later something small and bright glittered in the distance past the upper edge of Eridan's atmosphere. Jerre stared at it. Little by little it rose up, until he could see it clearly: the dust shield of *Bright Circle*. It was still turned toward the sun. Minutes passed and the rest of the starship came into view, broadside to *Journey Star*, every part of her from the main command pod to the engine pods exposed to laser fire, and her own laser turret pointed away from Eridan and *Journey Star*.

"Radar—" he managed to say.

"Nothing," said Jon Farrey at the radar console. "No missiles, no mines, nothing bigger than dust grains."

Jerre let out a long ragged breath, turned to Amery and nodded. She turned to the crew of the communication console, waited for them to signal their readiness. A moment passed, and then she spoke the words they had settled on already: "*Bright Circle*, this is *Journey Star*. You spoke of sending a few of your people over to us. We are ready to send one of our landers to bring them here. Please respond."

5

"It is a long story, as Olev said." The woman, Casi darh Sheri, had a shaved head and, like the others, wore a curious blue garment, close-fitting but with large pockets, that covered all of her except hands and head. Her voice, half-familiar already—it was the first voice that had spoken over the radio—had its own oddities, roughening consonants and bending vowels in unexpected ways. "It begins on Pawo, the world you know as Delta Pavonis V, the world where my grandparents were born."

Like the other two visitors, the big gray-bearded man and the small woman with white hair, she sat on a chair. That was another oddity: the people from *Bright Circle* didn't sit on the floor as the people of Eridan did, and Asha had to remember where chairs were kept aboard *Journey Star* so the visitors could sit at their ease. The three of them and half of *Journey Star*'s improvised crew sat in a rough circle near one side of the one environment pod that wasn't on deep standby: one last caution, keeping the visitors far from the bridge in case they had weapons or explosives hidden on or in their bodies.

Nearby, the closest of the pod's huge tanks of blue-green algae gathered sunlight, and more marched away into distance beyond it. The great geodesic dome of the pod bent over all. Outside the dome was the blackness of space, the great blue arc of Eridan low on one side, the sun blazing low on the other, and just visible past the edge of the dust shield ahead, a hundred kilometers away in a matching orbit around Eridan, the glittering shape of *Bright Circle*.

Getting to that moment had been more complex than Jerre had anticipated. Three of the crew had gone to the sick bay and had some of their blood drawn by a machine there, to be compared with data from *Bright Circle*—the colonists who left Earth had been cleared of pathogens, but the risk that some once-harmless organism might have mutated had to be taken into account. Details of *Bright Circle*'s docking ports had to be sent over and examined, to be sure *Journey Star*'s lander could dock there.

Then there was the intricate dance with thrusters needed to get both ships into matching orbits: Jerre knew all about that in theory but the practice was another matter, and even with the ship's computers to help the crew, hard work had been needed to accomplish it. Finally, though, the lander went and returned, and three sen Halka and Asha went to the docking port to wait for the visitors while those who could be spared from the bridge took the shuttle to the environment pod to be ready to meet them.

"The evacuation authorities on Earth believed that Delta Pavonis would remain stable for another hundred thousand years before it began to grow to red giant status," said Casi. "They were wrong, and the colonists on Pawo discovered within a short time of settlement that they had less than a thousand years to find another home. Fortunately for them, Pawo is a world very rich in metals and radioisotopes, and once the colony was established and could spare the resources, the colonial government began building starships to search nearby systems and find a place where the colonists could go. *Bright Circle*—it did not have that name yet—was the fourth such ship, and its mission was to go to the Epsilon Indi system, make contact with the colony, and see whether some of the people of Pawo might be welcome there.

"What they found was that the colony on Epsilon Indi II had failed. The world was hospitable enough. It was lifeless when the colonists from Earth arrived, but they had followed the usual protocol. The planet had algae and lichens thriving on its surface and a breathable atmosphere by the time the starship arrived from Pawo. No, it was the human factor that caused failure. As far as the searchers could determine, a power struggle between leaders of the colonial government ended in war. By the time the fighting ended, too much technology had been destroyed and too few people survived to keep the colony viable. The last survivor died perhaps seventy of your years before the ship from Pawo came.

"The starship that had brought the colonists was still in orbit. It was damaged, but not severely. The crew of the ship from Pawo had a decision to make, and made it. A third of them chose to board the starship from Earth, perform the necessary repairs, restock a few of the environment pods, and return to

Pawo, where the ship could be restored fully and used to ferry people from Pawo to Epsilon Indi II. The others decided to go on to the next system colonized from Earth, the Tau Ceti system. So they parted, and the ship from Pawo took a new name, *Bright Circle*, to commemorate its new mission.

"Many years later we reached Tau Ceti. I was a small child then, but I still recall how everyone aboard *Bright Circle* talked about what we might or might not find, how we hoped that Pawo was not the only surviving colony. I recall also how delighted everyone was to find two thriving colonies in that system—Tau Ceti II, which its people call Turquoise, and Tau Ceti III, which its people call Umber."

The white-haired woman, who'd given her name as Lat Sireen, spoke next. "I was young when *Bright Circle* came to Turquoise, where I was born. I will tell you something about Turquoise, so you will know what that arrival meant to us. Its name is well earned. It is an ocean planet, with many hundreds of islands but no continents like the ones you have here, and it had no life when we arrived but was stocked thereafter with plants and animals we brought from Earth. Most of its people live in floating towns that drift with the currents, so the islands can be used to grow crops and timber. I grew up knowing that winds and currents might take two towns that had been close together for a long time and send one of them far away from the other, or bring two distant towns close. That was what it was like when *Bright Circle* came: as though a part of Pawo had drifted close to us for a time. We welcomed the people from Pawo and celebrated with them, and when it came time to go, I was one of two hundred eighteen young people from Turquoise who went with them."

"All this while," said the gray-bearded man, "I am an infant." His was the second voice on the radio, and his name was Olev Ifais. "Of course we heard on Umber what happened. There is radio, and there is also an asteroid hollowed out and turned into a ship, in an orbit that brings it close to Umber and Turquoise alternately, and the two worlds send cargoes and passengers each to the other that way, so we are not strangers. So everyone on Umber heard, and when the people aboard *Bright Circle* wished to come to our world, the Council of Fifteen debated and then gave permission. I speak briefly. Umber is as dry and cold as Turquoise is wet and warm. It is a harsh world and it teaches its people to take risks. So another few hundred, I do not recall the exact number, asked and got permission to go with *Bright Circle* when it left. My parents were among them, and they brought me."

"There were people from Pawo who left the ship," said Casi. "Old people, mostly, some to stay on Turquiose and some to stay on Umber. We left behind copies of books and other things that came from Pawo, and took on books and other things from Turquoise and Umber. So prepared, we set out for the next system colonized from Earth, which is yours, and after the necessary span of years we have arrived."

"May I speak?" Olev said then, and before anyone could answer: "When we came into this system we listened and watched your planet, and nothing showed us the colony survived. This is when we are far off, that I grant, but we found no trace of cities, no pollutants in the air, a little longwave radiation that could have been from some natural source. We listened for radio signals and heard nothing, and this ship, *Journey Star*, did not respond to our data transmissions. We judged it had been abandoned and wondered if anyone survived on your world. Then with no warning, after we have rounded your sun and have begun braking into orbit, *Journey Star* comes around Eridan and its radars are active, its dust shield and laser turret are pointed toward us, and a voice comes over hailing frequencies calling us to respond immediately. I will not say I was frightened." Then, with a rumbling subterranean laugh: "Who do I deceive? Of course I was frightened. All of us were."

"So were we," said Amery. "All we knew was that an unknown starship was coming toward Eridan from the direction of the Sun, as though you didn't want to be seen."

"That was not our intention!" said Olev. "We used Epsilon Eridani's gravity well to brake from interstellar speeds, and then came here by the quickest route. Since we heard no radio signals from your world we saw no need for any other course." He tilted his head. "But perhaps you will tell me this. You knew we were coming. How?"

A flicker of subtle awareness from Jerre to Amery and back again asked and got permission to speak. "Our radio net picked up your radar signal," said Jerre. "Yes, we have one. Our technology's not advanced by Earth standards and the net uses very modest amounts of power, but the receivers picked up the navigational radar as static. Once we knew what it meant we used one of *Journey Star*'s landers to come here."

The visitors processed that. After a moment Casi made a motion of her head, like a nod but with the upward motion emphasized. "So the story ends. I hope that misunderstandings have now been settled and you can convey our greetings and wishes to your government."

"We don't have one of those," said Amery.

Casi gave her a puzzled look. "I may not be using the correct word."

"No, it's the right word. We had a government here until the year 84 after planetfall. It killed millions of people, so we destroyed it. We haven't had one since."

That earned her baffled looks from all three of the visitors. "But who makes your laws?" Casi asked, obviously perplexed.

"Those were established at the Convention of Zara just after the Insurgency," Amery said, "a little over two hundred years ago."

The visitors looked at each other. "You have had the same laws for more than two centuries," said Casi in a wondering tone. When Amery nodded: "I will want to learn about them when that is convenient."

"I can repeat the Six Laws to you now if you like," Amery replied. "Any of us could."

"You have only six laws?" Olev said in evident disbelief, and when Amery nodded, blinked as though trying to clear his vision.

"Please," Casi said after a moment. "I would like to hear them. I think all of us would."

6

"First, no hierarchy of superiors demanding obedience from inferiors," said Amery then, "nor any organization claiming the right to interfere in the affairs of communities except in defense of the six laws here established, shall exist on Eridan. Deliberate violation of this law shall be punished by death."

Watching the puzzled and attentive faces of the visitors, Jerre felt a sudden sense of kinship with them. Of all the people from Eridan aboard *Journey Star* just then, he and Asha alone had encountered the Six Laws when they were old enough to know that there were alternatives. All the others heard the Laws in infancy and learned them by heart in early childhood. What will they think, Jerre thought then, down on Eridan, when they meet so many people for whom the Six Laws are not the self-evident principles that govern human life, but a set of strange rules kept by the people of an alien world?

"Second, no permanent community of more than ten thousand persons, nor any community located less than ten kilometers from any other community, shall exist on Eridan. Deliberate violation of this law shall be punished by death."

Following his thought, he glanced toward where Asha had been sitting, only to find that the girl had gotten up silently and gone over to the nearest edge of the pod, where the geodesic dome slanted down to the floor. Off past her, Eridan shone in sunlight. She was still listening, subtle awareness told him that, but most of her attention was turned toward the vast blue curve of the planet and the abyss of space beyond it.

"Third, no act or threat of violence by members of one community against members or property of any other community, except in defense of the six laws here established, shall occur on Eridan. Deliberate violation of this law shall be punished by death."

Jerre turned his attention back to the three visitors. Casi listened with a puzzled look, not quite a frown. Olev nodded slowly, as though he was piecing each phrase of the Laws together and trying to grasp the shape they made. Sireen—that was her personal name, she had explained—kept her face perfectly blank. The different reactions were partly culture and partly personality, Jerre could sense that at once, but what mattered more was an unexpected uniformity behind those differences: none had the smallest trace of mindtraining. Their reactions were so completely unscreened they might as well have been shouting them out loud.

"Fourth, no weapon of mass destruction, nor any armed or armored vehicle, nor any weapon having an effective range of more than one kilometer, shall exist on Eridan. Deliberate violation of this law shall be punished by death."

Jerre glanced next at his makeshift crew, Halka and Shelter folk alike, and wondered what the visitors saw when they looked at them. The people from the College had only such rudiments of mindtraining as the Halvedna passed on to anyone who could and would learn them, but even that might seem uncanny through eyes used to the folk of Pawo or Turquoise or Umber, eyes that knew nothing of dwimmerroot or dwimmerwine—and it sank in just then how vast of a difference those things had made on Eridan, how wide a gap a simple native plant with unexpected effects on the human mind had opened between the people of Epsilon Eridani II and the people of every other planet where humans lived. As for the Halka, what would people who knew nothing of the innermind or its powers think of the Halka way or the people who embodied it? How could they understand?

"Fifth, no contact with machines or remains of machines made by or under the former Planetary Directorate, beyond that required to repel or destroy them, shall occur on Eridan. Deliberate violation of this law shall be punished by death."

It took no particular effort of subtle awareness to sense what moved through the minds in the room as Amery finished reciting the Fifth Law. To the Shelter folk, the Directorate was the shadow of a past never to be forgotten; to the Halka, the Directorate was the enemy their order had been born to fight and whose last creation, all unknowing, they had just defeated. And the visitors? Their minds were untrained but not incapable, and all three of them caught the echoes of a terrible history in the words of the Law.

"Sixth, no action that causes significant damage to planetary or regional ecologies shall occur on Eridan. Deliberate violation of this law shall be punished by death."

As Amery spoke, all three of the visitors, not quite at the same moment, thought of the same image—a desolate sweep of gray plain dotted with rocks and, here and there, patches of lichen, and in the midst of it all, the weathered shape of a human skeleton. It took Jerre a moment to read their thoughts a little more closely and recognize it as an image all three had seen aboard *Bright Circle*: the remains of the last human colonist on Epsilon Indi II. The image chilled him, woke a memory of one of the things Carl Emmer had said. We came close to that, Jerre thought. More than once, maybe many times more than once.

"Those are our laws," said Amery then. "They apply to everyone on Eridan. If you or anyone else from *Bright Circle* land on our world, you'll be subject to those laws while you're there. Please understand that those laws are very strictly enforced. If you break one of them, there'll be no hope of a reprieve. You'll be tried by a judgment circle and shot."

"In that case, we may not be able to land at all," said Casi. "All of us on *Bright Circle* are members of—what was your phrase? A hierarchy of superiors demanding obedience from inferiors. *Bright Circle* has a captain and officers, and we obey them."

"That won't be a problem," Amery said at once. "Our legalists worked out what to do in that case a long time ago. Anyone from your ship who lands on Eridan must first be released from the authority of the captain and crew, and the proof of that release is that they cannot be forced to return to the ship if they don't choose to go."

Olev's shaggy eyebrows went up. "You expected to be visited, then?"

"We knew it was a possibility, but that wasn't the reason it was worked out. Our legalists work with hypotheticals—cases that haven't happened, but can be used to understand some detail of one of the Laws."

Sireen broke into a sudden smile. "I will hazard a guess," she said. "Your legalists—they debate these hypotheticals, and also famous cases of the past? They write commentaries, summaries, collections of case law?" When Amery nodded: "On Turquoise they do the same with certain old texts from Earth. I think I understand you a little better."

"These six laws," Olev said then. "They say nothing about a thousand and one kinds of trouble people get into. What about crimes within a community?"

"Communities have the right to establish whatever rules they wish," said Amery, "and choose whatever ways they wish to make decisions. As long as they do nothing that violates one of the Six Laws, no one else has the right to intervene."

Jerre could read his reaction instantly—*that could permit a great deal of mischief*—and knew an instant before Amery spoke exactly what she would do.

"Of course it could," she said, as though Olev had spoken the words aloud. "We think that it permits less mischief than handing over power to a government."

A moment of perfect silence followed, and then Olev said, "You heard my thought."

"That's correct."

His face turned bright red. "That is unsettling. Do all of you do that?"

"No. Only those who've been through certain training and experiences."

"Those in black."

"And a few others."

Olev swallowed, obviously uncomfortable. Before he could say anything, Amery went on. "The positive side of that is that we now know that when you said your ship came here on a mission of peace, you were telling us the exact truth. The members of the command circle here have already conferred through what we call innerspeech, and I'll send a message down to Eridan shortly, recommending that your people be welcomed when you land on our world. Provided, of course, that the requirements of our laws are followed."

"Thank you," said Casi, visibly shaken.

Amery rose, glanced at each of the other sen Halka, and then turned to the visitors. "I'll send that message now. The command circle has dissolved itself since there's no danger we have to face." She gave each of them a bright smile, nodded, turned and left for the bridge.

Another silence followed. Dafed Serrema broke it with his big rumbling laugh. "Well," he said. To the visitors: "Amery Lundra has a reputation as a strategist, and it's well earned."

"Tell me this," said Olev, with the first stirrings of a smile. "On Eridan, do you play games with cards?"

"Of course," said Dafed. "Interested?"

"Not against her," said Olev.

That got a more general laugh. Dafed turned to Jerre. "Captain Amadan, what now?"

"That's up to our visitors," Jerre said.

"If there are no obstacles," said Casi, "we wish to descend to Eridan as soon as that is convenient. The three of us are what we call a contact team. We have trained for years now to make contact with you and your world, and—" She made a little angular shrug. "I am anxious to begin as soon as we may."

"*Bright Circle*'s captain will have to release you from his authority," Jerre said, "but we can see to that by radio. Once that's taken care of, we can board a lander together. Some of us are interested in getting back down to Eridan too."

"Sen Amadan," Tallis Dumaren said then, tentatively. "I think some of us would like to stay here longer."

Jerre nodded. "Of course. We've got a lot of work to do, and now we can get started on it much sooner than we expected. For now, though, we should go back to the bridge." He motioned to the visitors. "If you'll come with us."

Barkcloth garments rustled as Halka and Shelter folk stood, and the visitors rose from their chairs, their coveralls making a subtly different sound. In a ragged line, all but two of those in the pod went toward the ramp that led down to the elevators and the shuttle to the command pod. Jerre turned, saw Asha still standing by the dome, staring out at the blue arc of Eridan and the blackness beyond it. After a moment she seemed to notice his gaze, turned away from the view into limitless space, and came to join him at the line's end.

7

The lander's hatch clanked, hissed, and opened. Asha hung back, waited politely for the others to leave the craft, and then followed two sen Halka whose names she hadn't learned. A few more moments and she stepped out into sunlight and fresh air, with Zara's wind turbines looming up in the near distance and the hills to the south a mass of blue further off. The sky was clear, the sun well over toward the western horizon. A crowd had gathered on the meadowmoss surrounding the concrete launch pad, students and teachers from the colleges, Shelter folk from communities nearby, drawn by simple curiosity or by the knowledge that the opening of the hatch would change Eridan forever.

She could see the visitors in their odd blue garments half a dozen meters away, Jerre introducing them to the deans of the other colleges at Zara. Amery stood among a little group of senior Halka legalists close by, engaged in what looked like a busy conversation in which no one spoke a single word aloud. All around, faces watched, voices spoke in low excited tones, the presence of the crowd pressed in on her. Being surrounded so many people made Asha uncomfortable as always, but she forced herself to wait until her new hearth-mother and hearth-father could take her home to the college and the room that was now hers alone.

That thought sent grief for Carla surging up in her again, and she had to struggle not to shame herself by weeping there in sight of Sun and of strangers. She fought back by calling to mind a day on the walk south from Dammal Shelter, one of the three times she and Carla had slept under the stars, awakened as sunlight glowed on new summer leaves high above, washed and laughed and eaten and then walked for hours through the forest. That stung but it also cheered her, reminded her of how she'd found happiness again after another time of bitter grief. She drew in a deep unsteady breath, let it out again.

Movement in the crowd nearby resolved as a familiar figure pushed through and climbed up onto the concrete launch pad: Tami Lundra. She went to stand by her mother for a few moments without saying a word, then looked around, saw Asha, and hurried over. Seizing both of her hands: "You're well? I was so worried when sen Tamar told me what happened. I knew Tati and sen Carla could take care of themselves—sen Carla used to hunt battle-drones, you know—but I wasn't sure if you'd be safe."

"I'm well," Asha reassured her, and braced herself for a painful duty.

Tami forestalled her. "I heard about sen Carla. I cried, of course, but at least I got to see her again before it happened. That must be very hard for you, though."

Asha ducked her head. "I cried also, but I knew it would happen soon."

In response Tami gave Asha a hug, which embarrassed her but also pleased her. To cover her embarrassment, Asha asked, "Is Stefan here?"

"Out in the crowd somewhere. He's patient. I'm not. I wish we could go home and talk. I want to hear all about *Journey Star* and the visitors and everything that happened."

That spurred a sudden hope in Asha. "I would like that," she said. "I don't like being near so many people."

Tami tipped her head to one side, considering. "Let's do it. I'll go let Noni know where we're going, and then we can head back home."

"I hope she doesn't mind being interrupted," Asha said, looking at the legalists.

"I won't interrupt her. I'll stand near her and think about what we're going to do, and she'll read that and know." She trotted back over to the circle of legalists and stood there, close to Amery, as though attending to the silent conversation. After a moment, Asha followed and stood a little further off. If some signal passed between mother and daughter, Asha didn't perceive it, but after a moment Tami turned, beamed at her, and motioned with her head toward a place where the crowd was thin.

Making her way out through the crowd in Tami's wake was difficult, not least because so many people turned to stare at her, but soon enough the two of them were walking across open meadowmoss toward Zara with the crowd behind them. "What do you want to hear about first?" Asha asked, knowing her friend's habits.

"*Journey Star*. Tell me what it's like on board."

Asha ducked her head. Fumbling with words at first, she tried to describe the bare corridors and rooms, the bridge with its screens and chairs, the shuttle that ran up and down the central mast as quick as thought, and then the luminous glory of Eridan and the vast soaring blackness of space as she'd seen it from the environment pod. She was most of the way through the description when Tami suddenly looked off to the east and her breath caught.

Asha looked also. The blue of the eastern sky was deepening as afternoon turned toward evening. There, rising above distant trees and the geometries of a Shelter's wind turbines ten kilometers away, a glittering point of light appeared. It was only after a moment that Asha realized it was too small to be *Journey Star*, and by then a second point, brighter, had emerged behind it. High overhead, in their matching equatorial orbits, the two starships circled.

8

A different afternoon deepened as eight people crossed meadowmoss toward the soaring white shape. Seven of them wore blue coveralls, the eighth a short robe and trousers of green barkcloth. For reasons Jerre had never learned, all four of the great monuments to the dead faced south, and so the word carved high up on this one—KELTESSAT—was legible long before they reached it. The sculpture group on the pedestal in front of it could not be made out clearly until they were much closer. Well before they reached the monument, however, Jerre sensed the sudden shock that went through one visitor after another as they recognized it. Only Olev Ifais, the one member of the contact team to accompany them, said anything aloud, and all he said was a single sharp monosyllable Jerre did not recognize. A word borrowed from one of the languages of Earth, or a scrap of slang from Umber? Jerre set the question aside. Other things demanded his attention just then.

Presently they reached the foot of the monument, stood there gazing at the sculpture group: the sprawled and contorted dead, and a child, thin and haggard, dressed in rags, walking out from amidst them. It was not an allegorical image. When Keltessat was liberated, a year before the mushroom cloud rose over Shalsha, the insurgents who seized it found heaped corpses, and here and there survivors, dazed and starving, who picked their way out from hiding places among the dead once they realized they were free. Knowing that the attack would come soon, the Directorate had ordered everyone interned there to be shot, and Security Command personnel were busy following those orders when the insurgents struck.

Did you tell them to do that, Carl Emmer? Jerre flung the question up toward space. Was that another thing your vision showed you, another thing you thought you had to do to save the knowledge that could bring Earth back to life? There could never be an answer, of course. Carla Dubrenden's body and the dead symbiont inside it had been incinerated by devices aboard *Journey Star*, compressed into a solid mass, and expelled from the ship to fall into the atmosphere and vaporize on reentry, a tiny streak of white flame crossing Eridan's night sky.

"Sen Amadan," said one of the visitors—Ammi Kaath, a middle-aged woman who looked as though one of her parents had come from Umber and the other had ancestors on Pawo. A historian, Jerre remembered. "May I ask a question?"

"Of course."

"This was made entirely with hand tools?"

"Yes. It's what we had."

Olev repeated the same monosyllable, and Jerre glanced at him before going on. "I wanted you to see this before I spoke any further," he said, "about the secret I mentioned a few days ago. Thank you for being willing to come with me. I don't know if it will matter, but—" A shrug dismissed the question.

"You've all realized by now that this is the site of one of the factory camps you've been told about. It was the first one built and the last to be liberated, and many of the prisoners here were forced to handle radioactive materials without protective gear, so it had the highest death toll of all, a little under two million people. I want you to keep that in mind as I go on, because the secret I'm about to discuss is the reason why that happened.

"What I was told when I was a child is that Eridan was a rare discovery among the colony worlds, the only one with a biosphere close enough to Earth's that the atmosphere's breathable and human beings can live comfortably on the surface. Because of that, I was told, the passengers aboard *Journey Star* included some of the best ecologists and biologists on Earth. The evacuation authorities wanted to be sure that what happened to Earth never happened here. As far as anyone knows, they didn't expect the scientists on *Journey Star* to set out to find a way to reverse the runaway greenhouse effect that doomed the homeworld, and they certainly didn't expect them to work out all the details of an atmospheric reengineering protocol to accomplish that. Still, that's what happened."

Jerre watched them as he finished, wondering what their reaction would be. To his astonishment and dismay, they nodded as though what he'd said was perfectly obvious.

He made himself go on. "But that was why the people who founded the Directorate seized power and used it so ruthlessly. They wanted to develop an industrial society here as quickly as possible, build new starships, and send them back to Earth with everything that was needed for the atmospheric reengineering protocol. That was why the factory camps were built, why four and a half million people died in them, why there was so much hunger and poverty and misery here until the Directorate was overthrown. Even after that, Eridan's entire history was twisted out of shape more than once by people who thought the dream of Earth's redemption was enough to justify whatever atrocities they thought they had to carry out in its name."

Ammi, the historian, was nodding slowly by this point. The others watched Jerre, calm, interested, unmoved. Subtle awareness brought him their emotions, but that only emphasized the vastness of the gap he began to realize he would not bridge.

Saying more seemed futile, but he kept going anyway. "The secret I mentioned, as I'm sure you've guessed by now, is the atmospheric reengineering protocol. We have it. More to the point, I have it. I inherited it. Yes, that means my ancestors were among those who committed the atrocities I just mentioned. I want you to take the protocol with you when you leave this planet—but I want you to know what a dangerous thing you're taking with you. That protocol has been Eridan's curse for three hundred years. I can only hope it won't be a curse for you, or for any of the other colony worlds that learn about it from you."

He fell silent, certain that he had failed. In the silence that followed, he could sense with utter clarity how little of Eridan's long ordeal he could communicate to the visitors, and found himself wondering how much of the histories of their home-worlds the people of Eridan would never be able to grasp.

"So," said Olev then, breaking the silence. "I think I understand you a little better, you and this world of yours both. When we came aboard *Journey Star* and I first saw Halka, I wondered: who are these people, wary, disciplined, dressed without ornament, armed and poised as though they expect to fight and die this very day? Then we landed on Eridan and saw the way you live here, dwelling in guarded Shelters, sitting and sleeping on bare floors, having few possessions and fewer luxuries, and I wondered again: what do these people fear and what do they guard? Now you have answered all these questions."

"The Halka don't guard the protocol," said Jerre, perplexed. "Neither do the Shelter folk. Until twenty years ago it was secret from nearly everyone on Eridan."

"Oh, I do not speak of the protocol. What they fear is this." A gesture jabbed at the bronze images of the dead, the stark

white shape of the monument rising behind it. "The Directorate, it was called? Yes. That or anything like it, the fist that
closes tight until life is impossible in its grip." His fist clenched,
illustrating, and then opened to embrace empty air. "What they
guard is a space, the gap left open by the curved hand, where
human beings have room to live their lives. When I heard your
six laws I found them a puzzle, but I think I understand them
now, and I think also that I understand this concern of yours.
You mean to say: here is a danger, here is a seed that could give
birth to a new Directorate wherever it is planted. It is generous
of you to warn us of that, and I thank you for it."

Jerre nodded. Maybe, he thought, just maybe some scrap
of what he'd hoped to communicate would go with them to
Sirius and beyond.

"But there is another thing you do not know." Olev turned
to another of the visitors, a thin brown man with a shaved
head. "Aron, you know what I have in mind, and you know it
better than I do. Speak."

"I believe I do," said Aron sunh Jorj. "Sen Amadan, I am
very pleased to learn that you have a complete atmospheric
reengineering protocol for Earth. I am eager to study it, and
eager to see to it that it reaches other worlds, because the three
worlds I know of had not proceeded so far when *Bright Circle*
left them."

Jerre was still processing that when Aron went on. "It does
not surprise me to hear that so many biologists and ecologists
went from Earth to Epsilon Eridani. What you may not know
is that none of the starships lacked specialists in those fields.
The plan of the evacuation authorities was that each world
that had no native life forms would be seeded with Earth
life—chemosynthetic bacteria first, then blue-green algae and
lichens, and then others. On Turquoise that proceeded very
quickly, for it is a hospitable world, and when *Bright Circle*
arrived, there were already whales swimming in its oceans
and orchards on its islands. On Umber the work goes more

slowly, since it is so cold and dry a world, but when we came there, grasslands ringed the equatorial belt and groves of pine and birch had been planted in sheltered areas. On Pawo—" He shrugged expressively. "Once they realized that they would have to leave, they saved their stores of Earth life for other worlds. By now some of those will have gone to Epsilon Indi II.

"But these are details we can discuss later. The matter of importance is that on all three of those worlds, there are those who have thought of someday taking those same skills and using them to heal Earth. On Pawo the discussion had not proceeded far, as they had a much more urgent problem to face first. On Turquoise and Umber things had gone much further, and doubtless have gone further still since *Bright Circle* left. Of course we do not know what the other colonies have done, but it would surprise me if none of their inhabitants thought the same thoughts and dreamed the same dream as Eridan's people did."

"Tell me this," Jerre said. "On Pawo, Turquoise, Umber— did anyone try to seize power in the name of that dream?"

"No," said Ammi. "Each of those worlds has had conflicts, political struggles, killings, but for other reasons. If you're interested in knowing more, the books we brought down to Zara a few days ago give all the details."

"So," said Olev. "Now you know. When we leave Eridan, we will gladly take the protocol with us, and communicate it to scientists on each world that *Bright Circle* visits. We will also pass on your words of caution. Maybe some of them will have the resources to send a starship to Earth and put the protocol to work. Maybe by the time *Bright Circle* comes back around to Pawo more than one world will be able to spare such a ship."

"They'll be latecomers, then," said Jerre, with a slow unwilling smile. "I've spent the last twenty years getting ready to refit *Journey Star* for the voyage back to Earth, with everything that's needed for the protocol. We still have a great deal to do and it'll be another twenty years at least before the mission leaves, but by the time *Bright Circle* reaches Sirius, *Journey Star* will be well on its way to Earth."

"But this is splendid!" Olev said, beaming. "When we come to the Sirius colonies, if they have survived, we will say, here is the protocol, here are its dangers, and here is what we know of the people from Eridan who are already on their way to use it. Perhaps, if they have the resources, they will send a ship to assist you. Perhaps someone further along will do the same. How much time will the protocol require?"

"Almost two hundred years before people can land on Earth's surface," Jerre said. "And then the same kind of work that's happened on Umber, a great deal of it over many years, before Earth has a self-sustaining ecosystem again."

"We will tell them that," said Olev. "We will tell them that, in each colony we reach, and some of them will send ships to help you. I am sure of it."

After a moment, Jerre began to nod. Though he'd never experienced any trace of the visionary states he'd glimpsed now and again in Stefan Jatanni's eyes and mind, all at once he could see the future Olev spoke of, a pattern of possibility luminous before him: the colony worlds coming into occasional contact as a handful of starships picked their way across the immense distances that separated star from star, tracing a complex pattern of arcs around Earth; then, one by one, ships heading inward, spokes of a wheel rimmed with stars, each with its own contributions to the grand design; Earth slowly struggling back to life, a colony of its own colonies; and Eridan, with all the burdens and triumphs of its history, no longer the sole bearer of the secret, caught up in that larger pattern, moving toward futures neither he nor anyone else could possibly imagine yet.

"Yes," he said. "Yes, I think you may be right."

CHAPTER 6

A FAREWELL TO ERIDAN

1

Two days later, just south of Zara, Asha led two more of the visitors across the meadowmoss plain to the edge of the ecological reserve, where daulas soared skyward. She had done the same thing five times before with other groups of visitors who wished to see Eridan's forests. As she'd done each of those times, she matched her pace to the slowest of the others, an old woman with a shaved head named Sera dhar An, who had one bright green eye and one scarred and empty eye socket. The other was a boy named Paul: fifteen years old, Asha guessed, and then caught herself. Eridan's years weren't the same as those of Umber, where Paul's parents had been born, or those of Pawo, which the crew of *Bright Circle* used to keep track of their own cycles of time and travel.

"Tell me this," said Sera in her sharp thin voice. She'd been asking Asha questions since they left the college, and Asha was irritated that none of them had been about Eridan's botany, which was what she had been told the old woman would want to know. She pushed aside her reaction, kept a neutral expression fixed on her face.

"Tell me this," Sera repeated. "On this entire world is there such a thing as a bed?"

"I don't know that word," Asha admitted.

The old woman let out a sudden snort, perhaps a laugh, perhaps not. "And so you answer my question. A bed, child, is a place for sleeping above the floor, a place that's soft."

Asha gave her a startled look. "I've never heard of such a thing."

"You've spent your whole life sleeping on mats on the floor, then?"

"No, when I lived in the north country we slept on the ground."

The only reaction those words earned her was another snort from the old woman, and a faint choked sound from Paul. Asha glanced at him, saw the muffled laughter in his eyes, had to struggle for a moment to keep her own expression properly polite. She didn't mind the effort. There were many reasons why Asha offered to take visitors to see the daula forests, but their reactions were high among them: no one from *Bright Circle* stared at her or shunned her as an outrunner girl. To them she was strange, but only as the rest of Eridan was strange.

"Tell me about the plant life here," Sera said then in a weary tone. "Might as well get that out of the way."

Asha's irritation surged again, but she stifled it. "What do you wish to know about it?"

"Start with the colors of the leaves, if you know anything about that."

Asha smiled. "Of course. There are two families of photo-synthetic pigments here, the cyanophylls and the rhodophylls. Windflowers have only cyanophylls, but most sporophyte plants have both. The combination's supposed to be about three per cent more efficient at converting sunlight into sugars than Earth chlorophyll."

That earned her a long assessing look. "Sugars," the old woman said. "Edible?"

"Not very. Some ferment into alcohol."

The old woman snorted again. "Trust humans to figure that out wherever they land." Paul choked back another laugh. Asha glanced at him, tried and failed to suppress a smile. He answered with one of his own, hid it quickly before Sera could see it.

They walked further. "This is odd," Sera said then, half to herself. Then, to Asha: "How far is the forest? I thought we were nearly there."

Asha puzzled at that, then realized that with one eye missing she couldn't gauge distances. "Most of a kilometer still."

Sera turned suddenly to face her. "How tall are those trees?"

"Almost two hundred meters."

The old woman stared at her, then turned and started walking toward the trees without another word. Asha and Paul caught up to her promptly, walked with her in silence, as the great blue-leaved trees rose, and rose, and rose before them. Finally they reached the thickets at the forest's edge, found a gap between shrubs, and walked further, into the indigo shadows and leaf-dappled sunlight of the daula grove.

"Soul of my power," the old woman breathed, looking up at the leaf-canopy high above. She stood there staring for what seemed like a long while, then suddenly let out a harsh laugh. "Do you know," she said, "when I was your age, Paul, and *Bright Circle* was in orbit around Umber, I went to see one of their forests. Paul, raise your hand as far as you can. Yes. That was how tall the tallest trees were. Sturdy little shore pines—" She turned to face Asha. "Like the one beside your college. I thought your forests were like that. But these—"

She clenched her eyes shut, opened them again, and to Asha's astonishment, tears trickled down one of the old woman's cheeks. "There were forests like this on Earth before it died. I've seen images of them. I never thought to stand in one."

A long silence passed as Sera stared up at the forest canopy high above. A jewelfly darted past, suddenly brilliant as it flew through a stray beam of sunlight. "These trees," the old woman said then. "Evergreen or deciduous?"

"Neither," Asha said. "These are summer leaves. They fall in autumn when the winter leaves come out, and those fall when the summer leaves come in spring. All the trees on this continent are like that. They belong to the Bifoliaceae."

The old woman glanced at her, nodded slowly. Another silence passed, and then the old woman turned to Paul. "You'll want to expedite your training," she told him. "It's possible that I'll be staying here when *Bright Circle* leaves." Paul took that in, then made the quick upward equivalent of a nod the visitors used.

Sera turned to Asha again. "I trust there's no shortage of trained botanists here."

"I think there are many."

"Good. I'm going to advise the crew to give at least one environment pod to Eridan's life, and we'll need a locally trained botanist to come with us and tend them. For all we know there may be planets better suited to these than to Earth plants. Animal life?"

It took Asha a moment to realize what the old woman was asking. "Jewelflies, ground-scuttlers, groundworms. Fourteen species on this continent. Eridan's much younger than Earth was and life hasn't been on land very long here."

"Easy to transplant the whole ecosystem, then." She started walking, and Asha and Paul went with her. "If only it wasn't so cold here."

Asha gave her an astonished look. "This is cold to you?"

That earned her another snort, and a glance of bleak amusement. "I suppose to you it isn't a bit cold."

"When I lived in the north country," said Asha, "and it was this warm, we would go unclothed all day."

Paul looked away suddenly and turned bright red. Asha noticed and said, perplexed, "I'm sorry if that was a wrong thing to say."

"It was nothing of the kind," said Sera. Paul made an indistinct noise.

Asha ducked her head. "I don't understand."

"No?" The old woman's eye regarded her, amused. "You will."

2

That same afternoon, in one of the cool high-ceilinged rooms of the College of Law in Zara, Amery Lundra settled into *ten ielindat* and tried to still the turmoil of her thoughts. She'd donned the formal black robes that were hers by right as a qualified legalist, trained by no less an expert than the famous and much-mourned Benamin Haller, her knowledge honed and tested in ceremonial debates in the College and then honed and tested again in fourteen years as legal adviser to the College of Space Sciences. The robes and the mental disciplines that went with them gave her little help, though. One of the pillars of her world had just shifted incalculably.

The pillar in question, Tamar Alhaden, sat comfortably on a cushion not far from her, glancing through a sheaf of papers in her hands, reminding herself of the contents. She wore a plain practical robe of blue-gray barkcloth, not the rainbow-colored robe of a sen Halvedna. Across from the two of them, five senior Halka legalists in black sat in silence, communing with one another through innerspeech from which Amery was politely but definitely excluded.

One of them finally cleared his throat: a gaunt white-haired old man with dark eyes. Mical Kesseth was one of the most respected legalists on Eridan, and Amery had discussed with him the intricate legal issues surrounding Jerre's rocket program more than once. Just then, that offered her no comfort at all.

"As far as we know," he said, "your request is quite unprecedented."

"I understand that, sen Halka," said Tamar. "To the best of my knowledge, though, it's not forbidden by Halka regulations, nor by any interpretation of the Six Laws. If I'm mistaken, of course, I'll accept correction."

"You are not mistaken," the old man admitted. After a moment's pause and a quick burst of innerspeech with the other legalists: "Sen Lundra has told us the reasons for your request in brief outline. Perhaps you would be willing to explain further."

"Of course. You're aware that Stefan Jatanni and I were close." Kesseth nodded, and she went on. "For obvious reasons, we were both interested in his visionary experiences before and during the War. Our theory all along was that he was more than usually susceptible to visions because he had been in Halvedna training and had tasted dwimmerroot repeatedly before he took baya. The sen Halvedna who spoke with him just after the War agreed with that guess, and we did such explorations as we could together, probing the edges of the visionary condition, but the legal barriers between the orders made it impossible for them or anyone else to take the matter further. So I let it rest until Stefan's death earlier this year. After that—" She shrugged. "I decided to pursue it in the time I have left.

"My plan originally was to come here and look for records of the Halka of Judith Mariel's time, before the Convention of Zara established the barrier between the orders. That turned up quite a bit of information—much more than I expected. The most important source that came to me, though, had another origin."

"We were informed," said the old man. "The symbiont."

"The symbiont who had been Carl Emmer. I didn't know that when I received the papers, of course, but once I learned his identity, the conclusion was obvious. The procedure his papers describe was close enough to the one hinted at in the other records that I'm sure they had a common source.

That could only have been Loren Frederic, who taught both Carl Emmer and Judith Mariel, who created the *Book of Circles* and the Sequence deck, and who originally discovered the effects of the dwimmerrroot.

"With that in mind, I spent weeks in the archives reading all of Frederic's papers that survived, and finally found a note jotted at the bottom of a botanical manuscript of his. It gave a sequence of numbers—the same sequence that Emmer's protocol gives for the doses of the raw root—followed by 'mnem,' for mnemophorin, the term Emmer used for the dwimmerwine. So I had the protocol. The only thing remaining was to test it, and I could do that quite readily up to the final step, where the barrier between the orders intervened. Under the circumstances, my decision was the obvious one."

One of the other legalists glanced at Mical Kesseth. Innerspeech passed between them, and then she spoke. "I am surprised your order—your former order, I should say—would permit you to act on that decision."

"The Halvedna order has renounced using coercion on any person for any reason," Tamar replied. "Its own members are included in that. Any sen Halvedna can leave the order at any time. It's very rare after the Outer Circle training, but it does happen from time to time." With a wry smile: "You'll doubtless be interested to know that the senior sen Halvedna who received my resignation were all just as troubled as you are."

"Understandably," Kesseth said tartly. "You have explained how you reached your decision but not why. Perhaps you will favor us with that detail."

"Of course. You've read Stefan's supplementary judgment on the Convention of Zara?"

A corner of the old man's mouth bent upward fractionally. "We have discussed little else since it arrived here."

"He and I talked about it a great deal in his last months. The Halka order stands at a parting of the ways that will shape the history of Eridan for hundreds of years. *Bright Circle* is orbiting through our skies. The books and knowledge we've received already from its crew will have effects on this world none of us can even guess at. With all these things in mind, do you really wonder why I'm willing to take certain risks for the sake of polyphase vision?"

Kesseth nodded, closed his eyes. Amery, sitting in enforced stillness, watched him, felt innerspeech dart from one legalist to another.

The old man opened his eyes. "Your reasons have been noted," he said, "and will be included in our judgment. The central fact remains, as you have pointed out, that no law or regulation forbids you to drink the dwimmerwine if you desire, while quite a substantial body of law and regulation forbids us to deny you that right if you choose to exercise it. I assume you know the fatality rate among those who do so without preparation."

"Stefan said it was ninety-eight per cent."

"Slightly over that."

"Understood. I'm not unprepared, however."

The old man's gaze considered that, offered no response. "It will take just over an hour to prepare a standard dose for you. Where should it be brought?"

"My room," Tamar said. "First level, room 113, in the College of Space Sciences wing."

"Eat nothing and drink only water until afterward." He rose to his feet, sent a quick burst of innerspeech to Amery. The others rose also, and the five of them left the room in silence.

3

Amery waited until they were gone, and then turned to Tamar. In the calmest voice she could manage: "Sen Kesseth asked me to stay with you and report on what happens."

"I'm glad," said Tamar, smiling. "I was about to ask the same thing."

They got to their feet, Amery in a single smooth movement, Tamar more slowly. Not until they had left the room and started along the corridor outside it did either of them speak again. "Amery," Tamar said. "I know you're worried. Don't be."

"I've watched people die in dwimmertrance," said Amery in a measured tone. "Shrieking and flailing in mindless terror until their hearts stopped. Those aren't pleasant memories."

"Of course not." They turned a corner, onto a wider corridor that stretched straight into the distance. Others moved past them or along with them—legalists in black robes, sen Halka with guns at their hips, a scattering of Shelter folk come to consult with the College of Law over some detail of Shelter regulations or trade network policy—and the two of them fell silent again until they crossed the broad domed space where the radial corridors came together, angled across it, started up the corridor that went past the rooms given to the College of Geology to those at the far end of that arm, where the College of Space Sciences had its home. A plain concrete stair led up one floor to the surface level, and two more corridors brought them to Tamar's room.

Once they were inside and the door slid shut, Tamar started for the kitchen unit. "Only water," Amery reminded her, and the old woman stopped, allowed a rueful laugh, and then settled onto a cushion. The room had none of Tamar's usual clutter in it, and when Amery gave her a questioning glance, the old woman laughed again. "I put everything in the closet," she said. "It'll be a frightful mess to sort out once this is over, but it seemed sensible."

"It was," Amery replied, started to go on and then stopped.

"Amery," said Tamar, gently chiding. "We've been friends for twenty-four years. Nothing you can possibly say to me will upset me."

Amery met her gaze, then closed her eyes and nodded. "As I told you earlier," she said, "I'm horrified by this entire project of yours."

"Of course you are. You don't know the preparations I've made over these last weeks."

"Can you speak of those?"

"Of course. I'm not a member of the Halvedna order now." Amery nodded, and Tamar went on: "I followed Loren Frederic's protocol exactly, starting with small doses of the root and working up to the kind of doses only the sen davannat normally use. The day before yesterday I spent more than seventeen hours in a ninth-level trance, remembering every detail of my life from earliest childhood."

Amery opened her mouth to speak, then stopped. Tamar chuckled and said, "Yes, I know that's part of the experience of baya. Stefan and I discussed in quite some detail what he went through when he took baya. I don't believe that conversation was forbidden by Halka law."

"No," said Amery. "It's just not something most sen Halka like to talk about."

"Of course not. Since human beings are what they are, so much of what's remembered inevitably has to do with pain, anger, shame, and the like. That's never easy. The only reason I wasn't shattered by the work I did the day before yesterday is that I've done the same thing in a less intensive way as part of my Halvedna work, and then relived much of it again with the lower doses of the root."

Amery nodded again, and for a while neither of them spoke. Finally Amery broke the silence. "It occurs to me that in a certain sense, we're about to trade places. Twenty-four years ago you sat beside me after you gave me a dose of catamnetic and waited to see if I would come out the other side with my mind intact. Now—" She left the sentence unfinished.

"True. But I watched you forget, and you'll watch me remember." The old woman considered Amery for a time. "I recall very well what it was I made you forget, too, and what I had to help you remember afterwards. I've been wondering for months now about your feelings now that the outrunners are gone."

Amery glanced up, met her gaze, looked away again. "My feelings? A hopeless tangle, of course. Relieved, because no one else will have to go through what I did when they killed Tam. Appalled, because the only way we could stop the killing once and for all was to force the outrunners to do to one another what they did for so long to the Shelter folk. Troubled, because Stefan was right: now that the battle-drones and the outrunners are gone, the reasons why Shelter folk have supported the Halka for all these years have gone too. Jerre and I will live out our lives before that finishes working itself out, I imagine, and maybe so will Tami and Stefi and Asha—but eventually the Halka will no longer be able to defend the Six Laws, and Eridan risks having the same kind of ugly history Earth had before it died." She glanced at Tamar. "No doubt you'll tell me that's another reason why you should risk your life with the dwimmerwine."

Tamar smiled, said nothing.

Time passed. Finally Amery sensed the stirrings in the inner-mind that told her another sen Halka was approaching the door, told her also what he carried. She braced herself. Another glance at Tamar told her that the old woman had sensed the same thing in her own way. The discreet tap on the door came almost as a relief.

"Please come in," said Tamar.

The door opened and admitted an apprentice legalist in plain Halka black, carrying a cylinder of metal and black plastic with a combination lock on the lid. "Sen Alhaden."

"Yes."

"The dwimmerwine." He handed her the cylinder. "The combination is four, two, three, nine." He paused a moment, waiting for questions, and then nodded a farewell and left the room, pulling the door shut behind him.

"Four, two, three, nine," Tamar repeated. "How do I open this?"

"Set the wheels, then pull up on the cover and turn it to the left." Then: "It's traditional to take off your clothing. You may vomit or foul it in dwimmertrance."

A little choked laugh broke some of the tension between them. "I'll take that chance. I'm a little old to be sitting around stark naked."

She turned the wheels, pulled on the cover; it rose with a sudden loud click. Amery had to stifle a sudden desperate urge to shout at her, plead with her, anything that might make her stop. A quick glance of Tamar's told her that the old woman had sensed the urge; a little smile a moment later thanked her for checking it.

Then Tamar raised the cylinder to her lips. Without haste, she drank the contents, and then set the cylinder aside, settled her hands in her lap, and closed her eyes.

To Amery, the minutes that followed were an ordeal. Each one crept past, marked by Tamar's slow almost-silent breathing. The first stage of the dwimmerwine's effects drowned memory, thought, self for a time, leaving only a silence and a darkness that subtle awareness could not read. Once that ended, the perilous part of dwimmertrance began, and how soon that first stage would end was a detail no one had ever learned to predict.

Time passed. The silence and the darkness wavered, as though wind blew low over a night ocean: the metaphor came instantly to Amery's mind, and not just because Halka training manuals described that stage using those same words. The first fragmentary stirrings of mind and memory always seemed to ripple in just that way. Soon enough those ripples would begin to coalesce, and when they did so, the crisis would come. That, too, the manuals explained.

The fragments began to coalesce. Amery drew her awareness back as courtesy required—it was not her place to wander through a mind laid bare by dwimmerwine—but she could still sense the shift as Tamar's memories began to surface. Well-worn images from Amery's own baya rose up in her mind, edged with terror and triumph: repressed memories flooding into her mind with overwhelming force, full of pain, anger, shame, a hundred other bitter feelings; the desperate struggle to face them and not flee from them, until finally they overwhelmed her and sent her plunging into her own depths; the slow ascent to the surface of consciousness that followed. She braced herself, waited for Tamar's crisis.

It never came.

More minutes slipped by. Amery watched, and finally let herself believe that Tamar had been right and Loren Frederic's protocol made as much difference as Carl Emmer had claimed. What subtle awareness brought reminded her of the opening of a windflower, the uncoiling of the spiral bud that spread the featherlike blossom before the wind, except that this uncoiling went on and on, opening ever more of itself, rising up to inscrutable heights to catch winds of the innermind that neither the Halka nor the Halvedna knew and that Amery could only dimly sense.

"Oh," Tamar said, then, her voice less than a whisper.

Amery waited, silent and attentive.

"Oh." She paused, then went on as though to herself: "So it really was that simple."

"Tamar," said Amery. "Are you well?"

Tamar blinked, tried to focus her gaze. "I—" She stopped, tried again. "Yes."

Do you understand what I'm saying? Amery sent.

Yes—yes, I do.

That called up a wry smile. *I have no idea what to do now. Normally if someone survived dwimmertrance it would be my task to welcome them to the Halka order.* Then, more tentatively: *But I think you've just entered another order, one that's only just started.*

Yes. Tamar's innerspeech was unsteady, but knowledge trembled in it. *Yes, I've seen it beginning to take shape.*

Amery considered her. *Polyphase vision.*

Yes. I'll need some time to sort through what I've seen—what I'm still seeing—but in a few days I'll want to talk to the Halka and Halvedna both. Then: *In the meantime, do you think it's too soon for me to drink a bowl of tebbe?*

Not at all, Amery sent, laughing. *But you shouldn't try to make it yourself, not until your nervous system settles down. Your coordination won't be up to it. May I?* Then, with a hint of her own feelings: *I know I would welcome a bowl myself just now.*

"Please," Tamar said aloud, and Amery went to the kitchen-unit in the corner.

4

Two weeks later, Asha told her hearth-mother and hearth-father that she would be going to the forest that day, and left early, when the rising sun still cast long cool shadows westward from the towers and turning blades of Zara's wind turbines. The meadowmoss stretched gray and smooth to the south; beyond it, daulas rose to catch morning sunlight. Winds high up drove a few shreds of cloud off to the east, where two bright dots—*Bright Circle* and *Journey Star*—sank slowly toward the horizon. Asha set herself a comfortable pace. There was no cause for hurry. The choice she needed to make would wait for her.

A half hour or so brought her to the forest. She gauged the hills ahead of her, set off at an angle that took her across a long uneven slope and then down into a narrow valley deep in leaf-shade. Rush and murmur of water splashing over stones told her that she'd remembered correctly, and after a few more minutes she stood by the bank of a brisk busy stream, the one she and Jerre and the Indweller in Carla's body had followed on their way to the lander and *Journey Star*. This time she had no need to go further into the hills, though. Instead, she walked alongside the stream until she found a shallow pool with a rocky bottom and a flat area strewn with fallen winter-leaves on the far side of it. There she began taking off her clothes.

The People had a method of seeking answers to a question when no ordinary means could find them out. Asha had learned it along with hands and hands of other customs that belonged to the Way, and though she'd made use of the knowledge only once, she could still sing the song that told of it without a moment's hesitation. All it required was a place that people did not go, a state of purity to be attained through strict rules, and a great deal of patience. The Halvedna had another way to do the same thing, a method that used a pack of cards they called the Sequence deck, but those were a puzzle to Asha. This was not.

She took off the last of her clothes, folded them neatly, left them on dry leaves a meter or so from the edge of the pool, and waded in. Every part of her body had to be washed with cold flowing water before she could cross to the other side of the stream: that was one of the rules. She picked her way out to the middle of the pond where she was almost neck-deep, ducked down to submerge herself completely, ran fingers through her hair to rinse it, made sure that no scrap of fallen leaf clung to the soles of her feet or any other part of her. That task completed, she crossed to the far side of the pool, climbed up on the bank on the far side, found a place where she could sit comfortably, and settled into *ten ielindat* to wait for a sign.

The waiting was surrounded with rules as strict as those for the washing. They demanded perfect silence, perfect stillness, the attentive focus of a hunter waiting for prey. The sign might come quickly or it might take hours, but she could not move until it appeared or until Sun sank to the western horizon and took the hope of an answer away with it. Those were the rules, and though the People were gone, the Way was gone, and the landscape around her was nearly as far from the northern plains where she'd learned those customs as she could go without crossing the ocean, she followed them precisely.

As she waited, the part of her mind that was not caught up watching for the sign slipped back across years and kilometers to the one time she'd done the same thing before, when she was one of the People, when she lived according to the Way, and decided to look for some scrap of hope when one of her hearth-mothers lay dying of an illness no one could name. The stream where she'd washed had been bitterly cold, the trees around her little scrubby thildas huddled against the wind from the barrens further north, and hours passed before the sign finally came: a dry winter-leaf fluttering by on the wind, gray and tattered, warning her of what she'd find when she returned to the camp. From that recollection, other memories unfolded, bright bittersweet glimpses of people long dead and a life that was no more, everything that had fallen away from her when Carla had taken her by the arm and lifted her from the place where she'd huddled among roots, the place where Shrey died.

And to say more farewells now, to more people and another life—

She stilled her thoughts with an effort, waited.

Even so, she almost missed the first stirrings of the sign, the little restless movements of fallen leaves on the ground maybe a meter from her. Her breath caught as she saw those, realized what they meant: an egg laid among the leaves was about to hatch. Maybe a ground-scuttler, maybe a jewelfly, she knew, and realized that she would have her answer in moments.

The leaves stirred again and settled into an uneasy stillness. Then a little clump of them flopped awkwardly over. Beneath was the angular black eggshell, gaping open—the force when it split had flung the leaves aside—and a spindly dark shape with many legs pulled itself slowly out of the shell. For a moment Asha could not tell what it was, but then the abdomen unfolded long and slender behind it, and gossamer wings unfolded, too, from the middle of its back. It fanned them dry, made a few tentative flutters with them, and then suddenly rose up into the air in a flurry of wingbeats, hovered there for a moment, and darted away into the forest.

Asha did not move until the jewelfly had vanished from sight beyond the trunk of a nearby daula. Then, with a little ragged sigh, she rose and waded back across the pool. She gave the warmth of the day and the fitful breeze a little while to dry her, then pulled her clothes back on and started back toward Zara. Sun shone down bright and hot once she was out from under the trees. She wondered how she would feel when she looked at it from far away, a tiny yellow dot only slightly larger than the pinpoint stars that would surround it.

5

Though only a few months had passed since she'd come to Zara with the Indweller, the way to the room Amery and Jerre shared seemed freighted with memories. She paused at the familiar door, heard unexpected voices: Tami's, Jerre's. There were no classes that day, she knew, but it was rare for any of her hearth-family to be in their rooms near midday. She tapped tentatively on the door, as Carla had taught her to do.

"Please come in, Asha," Amery called out.

Asha pulled the door open a short way, saw Amery and Jerre sitting close together on one side of the room, Tami facing them with tears streaking her face, young Stefan sitting some distance away, his thoughts elsewhere. She needed no Halka training to sense the strained emotions that filled the room. "I can go away," she said.

"No, you should be here," said Jerre, and gestured, inviting her in. Once she'd come through the door and closed it behind her: "Tami has just told us that when *Bright Circle* leaves, she wants to go with it."

Startled, Asha still found the presence of mind to cross the floor and sit near her friend. "Then I should be here," she said. "Because I've come to say the same thing."

That got her an incredulous look from Tami and then a luminous smile. Jerre and Amery simply looked at her, their feelings hidden. "Will you tell us why?" Amery asked.

"You both have been very kind to me," said Asha, guessing at one misunderstanding she wanted above all else to avoid. "It's nothing you've done or not done." Then, pausing to put her thoughts in order: "They want people who are young, and I'm young. They want a botanist who knows Eridan's plants, and I know them. And—" It took her an effort to go on. "Here, with you, I'm Asha, but when I meet Shelter folk, I'm always only the outrunner girl. I know why they feel what they do, but it hurts. To the people from *Bright Circle* I'm Asha, nothing more."

She tried not to notice their reaction, went on in a different tone. "And when I was on *Journey Star* and we went to the environment pod and I could see past Eridan into space, it reminded me of when we lived on the edge of the northern plains, and our camp was a little circle of warmth and talk, and all around it—" She gestured, fingers splaying. "Wind and a far horizon and the sky going on forever. That's still a bright memory to me. You're very good to me and Zara is pleasant and the daula forests are beautiful, but there are so many people here, and the horizon is so close. So I want to go with *Bright Circle* when it goes."

Amery and Jerre glanced at each other, and Asha could all but sense the Halka not-speech as it passed between them. "I'll say to you the same thing I said to Tami a few minutes ago," said Jerre then. "For the time being we won't say yes or no. If you still feel the same way a year from now, then we'll give you our permission to go."

Asha ducked her head, acknowledging, then shifted out of *ten ielindat* and went to them. She took Jerre's right hand in both of hers and pressed it to her forehead, then did the same thing with Amery. "Thank you."

"You're welcome," said Amery. Asha went back to sit beside Tami, then glanced at Stefan. "You aren't going."

"No." The boy turned to face her. "I want to help get *Journey Star* ready for her voyage back to Earth but I won't be going when she leaves. I want to make sure the protocol survives and that people understand it. Someday another ship will come to Eridan—that's what sen Alhaden says—and I want to make sure that the ship can take it to other worlds too. I decided that a few days ago, after Tami and I talked."

Asha considered that, ducked her head in response, acknowledging.

6

The big cool high-ceilinged room in the College of Law filled with a crowd more diverse than usually came there: sen Halka, sen Halvedna, students and teachers from the other colleges, a scattering of visitors from other Shelters, a scattering of visitors from *Bright Circle*. Amery and Jerre waited with others, filed into the room. Heads turned as they passed, murmurs of speech followed them. That was nothing new, though something sharp-edged tinged the minds that noticed Jerre's presence, something that reminded Amery of the year or so after the War. *He's the one who saved us*, the thoughts whispered, or maybe it was *He's the one who made this world so different*. Was there really a difference between the two?

They found places in the midst of the crowd. Amery settled into *ten ielindat*, arranged her legalist's robes into a black geometrical shape from which only her hands and head emerged, sent a reassuring flicker of innerspeech to Jerre. He met her gaze, nodded, turned to face the figure seated on the cushion. She regarded him a moment longer, then glanced around the room as the last voices quieted. As she'd expected, every sen Halka at Zara was there. Though they made up fewer than half the crowd, she knew they were the ones that mattered most just then.

"Mical Kesseth sen Halka, the speaker for the judgment circle called to assess my vision, asked me to speak about what

I've seen," said Tamar Alhaden then. "So did the Halvedna elders who had the same task. I'll try to be as clear as I can."

The gray Shelter robes she wore still looked out of place, contrasting in memory with the rainbow-colored robes of the Halvedna she'd worn for so long. Even so, that was far from the strangest thing about her. White hair pulled back in a long braid, round contours and fine wrinkles of her face, little mannerisms of movement that spoke volumes to subtle awareness about her personality and her thoughts: all these were familiar. The strangeness was within that, something crystalline and vast that subtle awareness could only brush against. Understanding came after a moment: Tamar had gone as far beyond the Halka and Halvedna into the deeps of the innermind as they had gone beyond the Shelter folk.

"I've foreseen a great many things, some personal, some less so. One of the personal things is that when *Bright Circle* starts toward Sirius, I won't be alive to watch it go. One of the less personal things is that another starship is already headed this way from another colony world—I think, though I'm not sure, one of the colonies in the Alpha Centauri system. It'll arrive in a little over a hundred years."

A murmur spread through the listeners, fell silent.

"The most important thing that I've seen, though, has to do with the future of the Halka order. That matters to the Halka, but it also matters to everyone on Eridan. For more than two centuries the Halka have defended us all from battle-drones and outrunners, and enforced the Six Laws that allow us to live in peace with each other and the planet. Now battle-drones are a fading memory and the outrunners are dead or have taken up the New Way, as most of you have heard. Only the Six Laws remain.

"Before he died, Stefan Jatanni wrote a supplementary judgment to the Convention of Zara. That's been discussed at great length by the College of Law here. It's also been discussed more quietly in Shelters all over Eridan. His judgment raised two points, and my vision shows me that they're just as important as he thought. First, now that the battle-drones and outrunners are gone, it's only a matter of time—a generation or two—before Shelter folk will balk at supporting the Halka order as generously as they've done for all these years. Second, now that the battle-drones and outrunners are gone, there won't be anything like as many people willing to take baya and place themselves under the discipline of the Halka. Stefan's judgment raised those two points, and then proposed that nothing should be done about them.

"He was quite correct. That's what my vision tells me. This is what I've seen.

"If nothing is done, if the Halka order keeps its traditions and customs intact and makes no attempt to change its ways to fit changing times, the number of sen Halka on Eridan will decline steeply for the next fifty years and more slowly after that. Most Shelters will convert their Halka rooms to other uses, and simply find a spare room on those rare occasions when a sen Halka visits them. The burden the order places on the Shelter folk will shrink as Halka numbers do. Meanwhile Shelter councils will take over much of the work of watching for violations of the Six Laws, calling in sen Halka to enforce the Laws rather than waiting for the Halka to investigate primary cases themselves.

"In a little over a hundred years, when the next starship arrives, there will be fewer than five hundred sen Halka on Eridan, and most of them will be legalists, here at Zara and at a Shelter further north which will become another center of scholarship—I'm not yet sure which Shelter that is. By then the Shelters themselves will have changed. It was only because of battle-drones and outrunners that we had to live close together, guarded by concrete walls, drone traps, and Halka guns. Over the next century more people will settle outside Shelter walls than live within them, and in the country beyond Wind Gap there will be areas where no Shelters will be built, where people live in smaller communities above ground.

"What will happen after that? My vision doesn't tell me. There will be other visionaries, though. Both the Halka judgment circle and the Halvedna elders I've consulted have suggested that I should make Loren Frederic's protocol available to qualified students, and begin the process of founding a third order to stand alongside the Halka and Halvedna orders. I've agreed to that, not least because my vision has shown me glimpses of that order.

"That is what will happen if the Halka do nothing to address the challenges Stefan set out in his judgment. Are there other options? Only if the Halka abandon their traditions, their regulations, everything that has guided them all these years. The First Law forbids them from interfering in the affairs of communites on Eridan except to enforce the Six Laws. To make Shelters continue to pay for the upkeep of the Halka at anything like current levels would be the kind of interference that judgment circles have always condemned. Anything they might do to induce people to take baya would be an even greater violation of that law.

"I wish I could say that any such steps are unthinkable, but that isn't what my vision shows. The Halka could still choose to do those things, in the name of preserving their order and defending the Six Laws. What this means is that the Halka have always had three great enemies, not two. With the help of the Shelter folk, they defeated the battle-drones, and then went on to defeat the outrunners. Now they have to defeat their third enemy, which is themselves. That last struggle can't be won with bullets and grenades. It can only be won if the Halka accept the future that their own victories have made for them, and for all of us."

Beneath the outward silence, Amery could sense the Halka in the room react. It was the same reaction, varying only in details, and Amery felt it in herself as well. Of course we are our ultimate enemy: that was it, or as close to it as could be put in words. She had learned that, all of the Halka had learned that, in the depths of baya, when they'd faced themselves. For two hundred twenty years, every sen Halka had known that, and all the details of their harsh discipline were meant to keep that enemy at bay. And since that was true—

"When I was a child," Tamar went on, "growing up at Istal Shelter, one of the sen Halvedna who taught there used to say that Eridan's history sorted out neatly into three periods. The first was the time of settlement, and that ended when the Directorate seized power in 16. The second was the time of the Directorate, and it ended when the atomic weapon destroyed Shalsha in 84. The third period, she said, didn't have a name, and wouldn't get one until it was over. Now it's over, and I know its name. It was the time of the Halka, and it ended this year when the Halka defeated the last of the outrunners. Whatever they choose to do now, we've entered a new time, and none of us can know what its name will be."

Silence followed, watchful: a Halka silence, differing from combat mode only because there was no need for anyone to reach for a gun. After a moment, Mical Kesseth glanced at Tamar. Innerspeech passed between them, Amery could tell that instantly, though what they said stayed hidden from her.

"The judgment circle," he said to the listeners then, "has already discussed sen Alhaden's vision in detail, and prepared two judgments. The fine details are only relevant to legalists, though I am of course prepared to discuss them with anyone who has the patience." A faint dry smile bent the ends of his mouth. "I'll summarize. The first is a primary judgment declaring sen Alhaden's vision undecidable, but offering tentative support for its conclusions. The second is a supplementary judgment in support of Stefan Jatanni's proposal. Unless a significant body of Halka legal opinion opposes both judgments, which appears unlikely to me, the order will do as sen Alhaden has suggested. Our laws and traditions permit no other choice."

Even before he had finished, the watchful tension in the silence trickled away. Once again, Amery could sense the same response moving through all the sen Halka in the room: the knowledge of victory. Words she had flung at her own thoughts in a bitter moment twenty years back returned to her then: we kept ourselves from becoming tyrants at the point of our own guns. The bitterness had left the words. What remained was clarity—*tessat-ni-Halka shol ielindat*, the first great lesson of the Halka path—and in that clarity, the certain knowledge that the long struggle, all of it, really was over at last.

"I'm glad to hear that," said Tamar. She turned back to the gathering. "If anyone has questions I'll answer them if I can."

Amery glanced at Jerre, sensed the tremendous ambivalence in him, and sent, *We can leave now if you wish.*

Please. He stood, waited for her, and wove his way through the crowd to the door.

The corridor outside was quieter than Zara usually got. A few other people left the gathering at the same time, but none of them spoke, and they scattered this way and that. By the time Jerre and Amery reached the College of Space Sciences no one else was in sight. Not until they were back inside their room, though, did Jerre finally say, "The time of the Halka."

Amery heard everything his words hadn't said, and took his hands in hers. "I know. Did you feel how the sen Halka reacted?"

"Of course." With a choked laugh: "As though Tamar had to tell them who their true enemy always was."

"She can't know. She's tasted dwimmerwine, but with Loren Frederic's protocol it isn't the same. It can't be."

He nodded, managed a little bleak smile. "How does it feel to be an anachronism?"

Amery burst out laughing. "Good," she said. "I can imagine Stefan saying exactly those words, you know." Then, serious again: "But it's not just the Halka. The Eridan I grew up in, the Eridan in which we both took baya and put on Halka black—it's gone, or going. Eridan is a very different place now.

Of all the ways our Eridan could have ended, though, can you think of one you would have preferred?"

"No," Jerre admitted. "But it's still a shock."

"Of course it is." Then, smiling: "Maybe the time that's just begun will be called the time of the starships."

He drew her close. "Maybe it will," he said, just before their lips met.

7

Quick movements of an oddly shaped trowel opened a deep narrow hole in the soil next to the trunk of a two-year-old daula sapling. Asha glanced at the knobby gray root in the bucket next to her, put a little of the soil back into the hole, then got the root settled in place and began filling in soil around it. Once it was entirely covered—the buds wouldn't sprout unless they had a few centimeters of soil over them, one of *Oswaldia mnemophora*'s many oddities—she stood, fetched the end of the water hose, and aimed a slow steady stream of water all around the daula sapling until the place where she'd planted the root was thoroughly soaked.

She glanced around, made sure her work was done, gathered up her tools. Only then did she reward herself by looking upwards.

Above her, the transparent arc of the geodesic dome curved protectively. She could see one of the ship's robots picking its way along the outside, a tiny shape high up, inspecting the great triangular panes. Beyond the dome and its attendant robot, Eridan's northern continent glowed blue and violet in full sunlight. She gazed up at the rumpled landforms, suddenly recognized the broken shape of the mountain she'd grown up calling Pillar-of-Sky, the hills reaching westward from it toward other mountains she knew just as well. Even from orbit, she thought she could tell the hill where she'd received the Indweller, where Shrey had died, where Carla had taken her arm and drawn her into an unexpected new life. Those memories still burnt like ice. She turned away from the vision, toward the little world she'd helped to make.

It had taken two years of hard work to fill the environment pod with Eridan's life forms, and a good share of that work had been Asha's. To be sure, she'd had no part in the agreement that sent three pods full of Earth plants and animals to *Journey Star* and brought three empty pods to *Bright Circle*. The labor that filled lander after lander after lander with cargoes of crushed rock, then subsoil, and finally topsoil, and unloaded them in those three pods, had been left to other hands as well. Once that was finished, however, she'd begun to spend long hours aboard *Bright Circle*, partly to get used to the ship that would be her home for the rest of her life, partly to learn the other tasks that would be hers once the starship left Eridan, but mostly to help plant saplings, scatter spores, encourage trees and meadowmoss and arrowgrass to grow in the places given over to them. Only one pod had been filled with trees and moss and arrowgrass before the voyage began. She would spread those things to the other two, one seed or sprout or sapling at a time, as *Bright Circle* crossed the void to the Sirius system.

More than once during those two years she'd fretted over delays, waited impatiently for ground-scuttler and jewelfly eggs, spent hours searching the memories Carl Emmer had given her to try to figure out why carbon dioxide levels stayed too low or why Calley's windflowers wouldn't grow in a particular spot even when the soil had plenty of calcium—they needed manganese too, it turned out, and days passed before enough manganese-rich rocks could be found and brought up to *Bright Circle*. The dwimmerroots were the last thing she'd had to fret over. It was not until ten days before departure that she was sure she would have enough of them to fill their proper roles in the little ecosystem within the environment pod, and not until the day of departure that she'd been able to get the last of them planted.

Their presence in the little forest she'd helped to make wasn't simply a matter of ecology, of course. Sen Halka and sen Halvedna had flown up to *Bright Circle* to discuss the matter with the captain and the ship's officers, and a few of the sen Halvedna had stayed, to travel with *Bright Circle* toward Sirius and to teach anyone who wished to learn about the dwimmerroot and its uses. The ship had taken aboard new and strange things from Turquoise and Umber, Asha knew now, and would doubtless take on new and strange things from every other world it visited in turn. Would the people from Pawo whose ancestors were settling Epsilon Indi II recognize anything aboard the ship when it returned to them after completing its voyage? And would anything *Bright Circle* brought them be stranger than the dwimmerroot? It pleased Asha just then to realize that she would never know.

A quick glance around, and she picked her way through the newborn forest, careful not to disturb the shoulder-high saplings she'd spent so many months planting and tending. Beyond those, a ramp slanted down into the lower half of the environment pod, the metal walls to either side incongruous amid pale young arrowgrass leaves. Bucket and tools went into a storage locker set in one wall. Asha herself slipped through the fine netting that kept jewelflies where they belonged, veered sharply to the left at the ramp's foot, and went down a long corridor lined with metal doors to the identical door at its end.

She had asked for a cabin with a window, not expecting to be given one, and was startled to learn that they weren't in high demand and *Bright Circle* had more cabins in its environment pods than it had crew and passengers to fill them. The space on the far side of the door was hers: no smaller than a room in a Shelter on Eridan, and almost as pleasant, with a little dial on the wall that let her make it as warm as she liked; the setting she'd chosen was apparently cold by everyone else's standards, a detail that still amused her. They'd taken out bed and chair and lowered the desk so she could sleep and sit comfortably, another courtesy she hadn't expected, and the window in the far wall was a circle a full meter across, a delight to her. Through it she could see part of the nearest environment pod, the alien green of trees from Earth visible through its dome. Beyond it was Eridan again, the northern continent slipping past as *Bright Circle* swept around the planet.

Just at the moment she had no time for the view. She skinned out of the blue coverall she wore—its knees and soles were gray with Eridan's mud—and dropped it in the laundry chute, then donned another from her closet. The mirror and sink in the corner beckoned. She went to them, washed face and hands, found a comb, extracted two leaves and a twig in the process of getting her hair to behave, and stopped, remembering the first mirror she'd ever seen, the yellow gleam of the light trace in her eyes. That was gone forever, but the memories were not.

I am Asha, she told herself again, with a little quiet smile. I bear what I bear.

Before her thoughts could go further, a quick tapping came at the door. "Please come in," she called out, then remembered that doors on *Bright Circle* let through much less sound than doors on Eridan and went to push the button that opened it. As she'd guessed, Paul and Tami—Tamar, she reminded herself, she's Tamar now—were standing outside.

"There you are!" said Tamar. She'd grown in the three years since Asha had met her, and stood head and shoulders taller than her friend. "We went looking up under the dome and didn't find you. We've only got a little while to get to the command pod before the voyage starts, and I don't want you to get in trouble with the captain."

"I won't," said Asha. "He knows I had planting to finish. I told Paul about that."

Paul made an indistinct noise. He'd made those fairly often over the year just past when dealing with the two of them, and Asha knew why: he was in love with both of them and couldn't decide what to do about it. Neither of them had told him yet about the long talk they'd had with an old woman from Turquoise, who'd told them how sometimes on that world two women married the same man and raised their children by him as brothers and sisters. The same thing happened now and then among the People, and once Tamar had time to think it over, they had agreed to it. Once the voyage was under way and life on *Bright Circle* settled down to its normal routine, they'd decided, it would be time to explain it to him.

"I'm ready to go now," Asha said then.

"Before we do that—" Tamar said, and turned to Paul. He handed her a small flat package wrapped in barkcloth, which she handed to Asha. "Open it. It's from Tati. He had it sent up with the last lander but one."

Deft fingers untied the cord that held the package shut, and the barkcloth fell away. Inside, in a simple black frame, was a drawing Asha recognized at once: herself, curled up asleep with her head cushioned on a pack, abstract angular lines to one side evoking the harsh metallic shapes of the bridge of *Journey Star*.

Tears welled in Asha's eyes. Though she'd said so many farewells already in her life, it still hurt to think of her last hearth-father Jerre and her last hearth-mother Amery, and know that she would never see them again. "I—I'll have the radio crew send him my thanks," she managed to say. "I've loved this since he first showed it to me." She blinked back the tears, glanced at Tamar. "Did he send you one?"

She nodded. "One that I've adored since I was little. I cried and cried when I saw it."

"When we get to the Sirius system," said Asha, "we can show them to the people there. Maybe they'll understand."

"Maybe they will," said Tamar, her face lighting up.

Paul made another indistinct noise. "Oh, I know," said Tamar. "We have to go."

Asha put the drawing on her desk, went out into the corridor with them, and tapped the button that closed the door.

As she turned to them, Tamar glanced past Paul at her, smiled, and took one of Paul's hands. Asha smiled back at her, and took the other.

Paul made another noise, no less indistinct, and gave each of them a look in which hope and panic were equally mixed. They smiled at him. Beneath their feet, a faint vibration trembled through the floor as the secondary thrusters did their work and *Bright Circle* began moving into position for its flight out of Eridan orbit.

"I'll tell the captain you both helped me with the roots," Asha said then. "And we can hurry." They started down the corridor to the elevator.

8

"The problem all along was that we thought we were alone," said Jerre. "The only colony that had the knowledge that could restore Earth to life. That was a frightful burden."

Olev Ifais' sharp upward nod seemed almost normal now. "It was the same on Pawo, or so I have heard. Maybe it still is, unless they sent a ship to the Tau Ceti system, or found some way to send a radio signal over such distances."

"Is that even possible?" Jerre asked.

"In theory, yes. In practice? The energy cost is prohibitive."

The two of them sat in one of the courtyards atop the College of Space Sciences at Zara, Jerre seated comfortably on the ground, Olev perched less comfortably on a low chair. Some distance away, Amery stood facing south, gazing up into the sky, saying nothing. Further off, a group of Jerre's students huddled around a reflector telescope taller than any of them, aimed it at the same portion of the southern sky, where two bright dots moved slowly from west to east. Elsewhere, alone or in groups, others sat or stood, looking the same direction.

"And now?" Olev asked.

"I have no idea. I don't think anybody on Eridan does."

Olev's rumbling laugh answered him. "When *Bright Circle* came into the Tau Ceti system, both worlds had spacecraft, satellites, the asteroid I spoke of circling from Turquoise to Umber and back with passengers and cargo. Those on each world knew the other's history, the other's ways of living. Even so it was a shock, or so I have heard, to learn about Pawo and Epsilon Indi II, to hear histories so different and find ways of living so strange. Now you have had the same shock—and so have I. When I first began training as a contact team member I tried to think of what might be waiting on Epsilon Eridani II. I laugh to remember how wrong I was, how little I departed from what I knew when I thought I was chasing wild fancies."

"I hope you don't regret staying," Jerre said.

"I? No. I was born on Umber, I spent most of my years aboard *Bright Circle*, I will grow old and die on Eridan. A very sober and sensible life." He laughed again.

Just then one of the students by the telescope straightened up from the eyepiece, turned. "Sen Amadan, *Bright Circle*'s changing angle."

Jerre got to his feet and glanced at Olev, who motioned for him to go. A moment later he was beside Amery, his arm circling her shoulders.

She glanced at him then, with a little uncertain smile. Behind it he could read grief, pride, the hard but necessary acceptance of the inevitable that Eridan had taught all its children: feelings mirrored with equal strength in his own mind. He met her gaze, but the flicker of innerspeech he sent had no words in it, just an attempt at comfort. All the words either of them could think of had long since been said.

All over Eridan, he knew, people were watching the two bright points in Eridan's sky, knowing one of them was about to leave its orbit and begin the next stage of its long journey. Some of them watched in simple curiosity or awe, while others had more personal reasons. Three hundred eleven people from Eridan, most of them less than twenty years old, were aboard *Bright Circle*, waiting to begin the journey to Sirius. Two hundred ninety-eight people who had come with the starship, most of them more than sixty years old, had chosen to stay on Eridan. All three members of the contact team were among those who stayed. And among the others—

Memory brought up bright vivid images of the two of them, daughter and hearth-daughter. He'd fathered one and helped raise her from infancy; he'd met the other by seeming chance at Miriem Shelter, shared with her the desperate flight to *Journey Star* and the events that followed, made her part of his life for a few short years thereafter. It ached to know that they belonged to *Bright Circle* now and he would never see either of them again, but it was a familiar ache. He thought then of all the others who had felt the same way since the first starship from Earth set out for the Alpha Centauri system, leaving behind a world already too far gone to save, and then in a sudden rush, those who would watch when *Journey Star* left to begin its long-delayed voyage, carrying with it the hope of the redemption of Earth.

A glance to one side showed him the students, intent at the telescope. Another showed the roofs of Zara, the people who stood or sat there in silence, watching: Halka, Halvedna, Shelter folk, visitors from *Bright Circle* who'd chosen to stay behind, and a little cluster of people in plain gray robes whose minds blazed, even at a distance, with a crystalline clarity Jerre recognized at once. That reminded him of another loss, almost as recent and just as bitter.

One of Tamar Alhaden's predictions had already proved exact. Jerre and Amery had paid their final respects to her a few weeks before, standing by her body in a room many levels down, stooping to cast long tasseled windflowers onto her. Both of them had thought of the outrunner death-song, but Asha was already aboard *Bright Circle* by then, along with Tami and the others. Another ending, that: the resettled outrunners who followed the New Way had a different song for their dead, or so the teachers at the College of History said. That Carl Emmer had been the last person ever to be honored with the ancient haunting song Asha had sung for him was appropriate, Jerre thought: a good end to the Eridan that Emmer had helped to create, a good beginning for an age that had finally laid his legacy to rest forever.

High in the south, the two points of light circled eastward through Eridan's blue skies. Jerre gazed up at them and waited for one to move.

GLOSSARY

Affirmation, the: fundamental Halvedna statement of principles

Andarre: region in the southern foothills of the northern continent's one mountain range, famous for its hermits and mystics

Annan River: principal river of the north country and the Kaya Hills region

Annum Tal: site of a Directorate factory camp

battle-drone: computer-guided armored fighting vehicle of the Directorate

baya: first drinking of dwimmerwine by a Halka candidate, the initiation into the Halka order

Book of Circles: work of mystical philosophy partly written and partly compiled by Loren Frederic in the first decades of the Eridan colony; contains forty-eight glyphs expressing basic categories of human thought, which form the Sequence deck

Bredin Shelter: in hill country legend, a Shelter inhabited by survivors of the Directorate; code name for a network of Directorate survivors who preserved the atmospheric reengineering protocol for Earth

catamnetic: a drug that erases memories temporarily or permanently, used by sen Halvedna to heal certain severe mental illnesses

Colonial government: original democratic government on Eridan, set up aboard *Journey Star* and overthrown by a coup in 16

command circle: Halka structure for planning and conducting combat operations

command language: artificial language created under the Directorate to control battle-drones and other advanced technologies

Convention of Zara: agreement establishing the Six Laws and setting out the responsibilities and limitations of the Halka and Halvedna orders, signed at Zara in 87

daula: sporophyte forest tree, *Daula altiora*, found on both of Eridan's continents, growing up to 200 meters tall

Directorate: see Planetary Directorate

drone: see battle-drone

drone trap: a mechanical device using a lifter field detector and a powerful spring to drive an iron spike into a battle-drone's lifter field lattices

dwimmerroot: rhizome of a shrub, *Mnemophora oswaldia*, found on Eridan's northern continent, with powerful psychoactive effects on human beings; dwimerroot intoxication weakens barriers between the conscious and unconscious minds

dwimmerwine: distilled preparation made from dwimmerroot; dwimmerwine intoxication erases barriers between conscious and unconscious minds with sometimes fatal results

Emmer, Carl: 26-84, agronomist and politician; Director of Settlement 63-72, Assistant Planetary Director 72-78, and Planetary Director 78-84; believed to have been killed at the fall of Shalsha

Eridan: common name of the colony world Epsilon Eridani II

factory camps: slave labor camps established by the Directorate, in which some 4.5 million people died from malnutrition, disease, and overwork fireflower: a windflower that flourishes in soil tainted by atomic fallout

Frederic, Loren: –34-53, chief botanist in the Department of Settlement 21-38, discoverer of the dwimmerroot

fungoids: native Eridan saprophytes, edible by humans, which crawl over the ground looking for material to digest

ground-scuttler: native Eridan decapod, slightly resembling Earth crabs

Halka: warrior mystic order derived from guerrilla soldiers of the Insurgency, charged with preserving the Six Laws by force

hallow room: Shelter space for meditation and ceremony

Halvedna: pacifist mystic order derived from the hermits of the Andarre region in Insurgency times, committed to improvement of Eridan society but forbidden to use coercion or violence in any form

Indweller: outrunner name for the neural symbiont that guided outrunner bands

induction probe: Halvedna neuroelectrical device that stimulates activity in specific portions of the brain; used for neurological and psychological testing

innermind: common Eridan idiom for the unconscious mind, understood as a mental continuum uniting individuals

innerspeech: Halka method of communication through subtle awareness

Insurgency, the: twenty-year guerrilla war that brought down the Directorate

jewelfly: native Eridan flying decapod, resembling Earth dragonflies

Journey Star: the colony starship that brought human beings to Eridan, still in equatorial orbit

judgment circle: Halka structure for assessing violations of the Six Laws or Halka tradition

Keltessat: site of a Directorate factory camp

lifter fields: levitation device used by battle-drones and other Directorate equipment, an offshoot of reactionless drives developed for starflight

meadowmoss: lichenoid ground cover found throughout Eridan's land surface

meria: sporophyte forest tree on Eridan's northern continent, found mostly in the northern regions; its outer bark is a source of fiber and paper and a widely traded commodity

mnemophorin: Directorate term for dwimmerwine

Morne River: principal watercourse on Eridan's northern continent; its broad valley forms the core of the human settlement

Noni: Eridan slang term, "mommy"

north country: Eridan idiom for the country north of the Morne's headwaters and the Kaya Hills

outrunners: bands of nomadic brigands living on the edges of settled territory and obtaining protein through cannibalism

Pawo: Delta Pavonis IV, one of the original fourteen colony worlds settled from Earth

polyphase vision: a visionary state in which the visionary can see multiple futures radiating from specific choices, and choose actions based on their future consequences

Planetary Directorate: totalitarian government of Eridan's human colony, established in a coup in 16 and destroyed by nuclear attack in 84 after two decades of guerrilla war

Red Sky: Halka emergency code declaring a potential threat on a planetary scale

samahane: outdoor space for music and dancing

sea-scuttler: native Eridan seashore decapod, slightly resembling Earth crabs

sen davannat: Member of the Halvedna order who uses high doses of the dwimmerroot to seek union with the innermind

Sequence deck: divinatory tool used by Halvedna and others, based on the Book of Circles

Shalsha: capital of the Planetary Directorate beginning in 28, destroyed and abandoned after atomic attack in 84

Shelter: standard Eridan community form, concrete structure housing 5000 to 8000 people, generating electrical power with wind turbines and growing food in hydroponic vats

Shelter council: coordinating body for Shelter governance

Shelter folk: Halka idiom for members of the general population of Eridan

Shelter work: labor expected of each person living at a Shelter toward community needs

subtle awareness: Halka idiom for extended powers of perception made possible by the long term effects of dwimmerwine use

Tati: Eridan slang term, "daddy"

technician: semi-hereditary class of technologically skilled people, the object of old prejudices among Shelter folk

tessat-ni-Halka shol ielindat: "the way of the Halka is clarity of awareness," one of the fundamental Halka maxims

ten ielindat: "posture of awareness," Halka seated meditation position

thilda: sporophyte forest tree common on Eridan's northern continent

Turquoise: Tau Ceti II, one of the fourteen original colony worlds settled from Earth, named for its color when seen from orbit

Umber: Tau Ceti III, one of the fourteen original colony worlds settled from Earth, named for its color when seen from orbit

Wind Gap: principal pass through the mountain range on Eridan's northern continent, located just north of the headwaters of the Morne and south of the north country

windflowers: primitive wind-pollinated vascular plants of Eridan

Zara: Shelter and former city in the southern Morne valley, site of the Convention of Zara 84-87 and center of historical, legal, and scholarly activities on Eridan

Printed in the USA
CPSIA information can be obtained
at www.ICGtesting.com
JSHW031040231024
72178JS00007BA/63

9 781915 952134